THE DEVIL

RAISES HIS OWN

Books by Scott Phillips

The Ice Harvest
The Walkaway
Cottonwood
The Adjustment
Rake
Hop Alley
That Left Turn at Albuquerque
The Devil Raises His Own

THE DEVIL
RAISES HIS OWN

Scott Phillips

Published by
Soho Press, Inc.
227 W 17th Street
New York, NY 10011

Portions of this book appeared in very different form in the first
issues of *Vautrin* magazine.

Library of Congress Cataloging-in-Publication Data

Names: Phillips, Scott, 1961- author.
Title: The devil raises his own / Scott Phillips.
Description: New York, NY : Soho Crime, 2024.
Identifiers: LCCN 2024007594

ISBN 978-1-64129-493-5
eISBN 978-1-64129-494-2

Subjects: LCGFT: Noir fiction. | Thrillers (Fiction) | Novels.
Classification: LCC PS3566.H515 D49 2024 | DDC 813/.54—dc23/
eng/20240304
LC record available at https://lccn.loc.gov/2024007594

Interior design by Janine Agro

Printed in the United States of America

10 9 8 7 6 5 4 3 2 1

To Willie and the Girls

THE DEVIL

RAISES HIS OWN

PROLOGUE

1915

Shortly past eight in the evening on the Wednesday before Christmas, Flavia Purcell, *née* Ogden, sat next to the radiator reading the current number of *Popular Mechanics* magazine, half-listening to the piano music accompanying the motion picture playing downstairs on the first floor. She had eaten her evening meal—a pork cutlet and some stewed turnips—a couple of hours previous, alone, after which she had chucked her husband's uneaten portion into the trash, though they could scarcely afford the waste. Their apartment was entered from the rear of the building and was not directly accessible from the motion picture house, and when she heard him tramping arrhythmically up the back staircase, she affected her best look of frosty indifference, knowing he'd want a fight.

On first opening the door he leaned in too far and nearly fell, saving himself and a sliver of his dignity by holding on to the frame. "Home," he called out.

She kept her eyes on the page.

"Dinner in the ice box?"

She deigned now to look up at him. His fine, thin features had once struck her as noble; now they looked churlish and petty. "What dinner?"

"You know goddamn well what dinner."

"Yours is in the bin. You can dig it out if you want, I don't care."

He backhanded her across the face. He stumbled as he did so, and the blow was glancing, but it infuriated her and she stood up and brushed past him into the bedroom. He followed her and sat down on the sagging old bed. The springs jangled. "I'm sorry, sweetpea. I don't know what gets into me sometimes. Forgive me?" He made little smooching sounds.

"Booze is what gets into you. You don't come home after work and when you do get in you're stiff as a plank and you smell like a still. And I work hard all day too, and yet I manage to do the shopping and fix you a nice meal and you can't even be bothered to show up, and it's the third time this week and I've had enough."

He waved her off. "Go to Hades, you fishwife." He slid off the mattress and onto the floor, and she had to suppress a laugh. "I don't have to take this shit off of you, I know my marital rights."

"Watch your language, this isn't the saloon." She went back into the living room with the intention of getting her coat and leaving. She might be able to use the telephone in the motion picture theater's office to call her parents and have her father come fetch her for a day or two.

"Go fuck yourself," he called from the bedroom.

"I won't have talk like that in this house," she said.

"You are not head of this household, missy. Soon as I get up off this floor I'm going to show you who's the boss. And you know how I mean to do it."

"You ought to know, Albert, I've been looking into hiring an attorney." She hadn't intended to tell him yet.

"The hell you have."

Flavia had her coat on when she passed in front of the

bedroom door and saw he'd arisen, pulled his revolver out of the chiffonier and was fumbling with a bullet. She went back to the coat closet and got out the baseball bat. She'd had it since the age of eight, a tomboy's gift from a doting father, and had kept it all this time for sentimental reasons. She was still athletic at twenty-five, and when Albert came grimacing out of the bedroom holding the gun with both hands she bounded forth and in three steps was upon him, bat cocked behind her head. She swung it with her whole body, twisting at the waist as her father had taught her, and connected with his temple. There was a crunching sound that made her think she'd cracked the bat, and as he went down to the floor the gun went off, sending a bullet into the wall.

SOMETHING STICKY AND warm dripped onto Ernie Kassler's bald head. He was sitting between the machines in the projection room of the Marple Theater, cuing up the second reel of *A Woman's Past*, a pretty good Nance O'Neil picture about adultery, set in a leper colony. It had been twenty minutes since the ruckus upstairs, nothing out of the ordinary for the two troublemakers, except for what sounded like a gunshot.

He put his finger to the substance and, examining it in the dim glow of the fifteen-watt bulb dangling naked from the booth's ceiling, determined that it was blood. He jumped out of his chair and screeched—he was squeamish—loud enough that the pianist stopped playing, and he became aware of the auditorium full of people turning their attention from Nance's romantic troubles and toward the projection booth. Looking up at the ceiling he saw that a goodly amount was dripping from upstairs onto the nice clean linoleum.

LATIN TEACHER BLUDGEONS HER HUSBAND

He Assaulted Her on Returning Home
CITY ATT'Y WILL NOT PRESS CHARGES
She Was Unhappy that He Frequented Saloons

Mrs. Edith Purcell, of 417 East Douglas Ave., last night struck her husband Albert in the head with a blunt object, possibly a fire-place poker, causing his death. The victim had, per Assistant City Attorney Sidney Foulston, returned home from the saloon in the Eaton hotel, where several patrons affirmed that the decedent had become belligerent and had fallen down taking a drunken swing at a companion, then become enraged at the laughter of those assembled. Mr. Foulston is satisfied with the widow's account of the incident and believes that Purcell assaulted his wife upon his return to the domicile and that she reacted in self-defense.

Albert Purcell, of the above address, was by all accounts a well-liked and successful certified public accountant employed by G. W. Gertz and Co. and was expected to advance there quickly. Mrs. Purcell is employed as a teacher of Latin and Greek at Wichita High School and is on break for the holidays. Mr. J. Calhoun Runcie, Assistant Superintendent of Schools, reports that her employment will be terminated regardless of whether she is charged.

◆ ◆ ◆

AND THUS FLAVIA learned, from an article in the Wichita *Morning Eagle* that didn't even print her right name, that she would be unemployed as well as widowed at the New Year. She had emptied the apartment of her belongings Christmas Eve morning, leaving Albert's behind for whomever might find them tempting, except for a prized silver pocket watch that had belonged to his grandfather and which she planned to sell. The sight of her late husband's black, coagulated blood on the throw rug next to the bedroom door excited in her neither grief nor remorse. She wasn't proud of the deed, but she didn't regret it, either, and she knew she would never miss him for a second. It would have been better if she'd retained a lawyer months earlier, but she hadn't and that was that. She decided there, just before leaving the apartment for the last time, that she would not consider herself widowed, nor even divorced, but as a woman who had never married. She would have to leave town; some things could be forgotten in such a place, but the Christmas week bludgeoning of a successful and well-liked certified public accountant was not among them.

Her own grandfather lived, after decades of flitting about the country, in Los Angeles, California. He had long ago taught her the rudiments of photography, and in his letters often suggested that she should come out there and live in the healthy sunshine and assist him in his studio. She had always considered the idea as a childish fantasy, but now it seemed not only a valid solution to her troubles but something of an adventure as well.

Dear Gramps,

I don't know if you have heard but I recently collapsed Albert's cranial vault and though I am in no danger of legal jeopardy I will face considerable prejudice in Wichita regarding employment, matrimony et ca., and I believe it is time for me to leave the old hometown for fairer climes. I am hoping you were serious when you suggested I relocate to Sunny Southern California because I am heading there anon and will be counting on you for employment and lodging at least temporarily. Maybe I can find work in the pictures!

    I will wire you details when I know them.

Love,
Flavey

1

1916

M rs. Chen had taken to her bed with the ague. Bill's breakfast consisted of coffee, two eggs, sunny side up, and flapjacks with butter and marmalade, consumed at leisure while seated on an upholstered stool at the horse-shoe-shaped lunch counter of the local Pig and Whistle. The red-nosed, sallow-complexioned counterman had opinions about the war in Europe and about the role Freemasonry played in the United States' potential entry therein, and though Bill let his attention drift back to the city section of the *Examiner*, with its lively accounts of stabbings and burglaries and boarding house sneaks, there came a point in his soliloquy where he seemed to want acknowledgment of something he'd just said.

"Is that right," Bill said.

"You can bet your life on it, friend. They won't rest until the whole world's under their thumb."

He gave the man a thoughtful frown and nodded, uncertain whether he was still het up about the Freemasons or if his fancy had meandered over to world Jewry, the papacy or the Bolsheviks or some combination thereof.

He returned his attention to the California state section. A man in the hamlet of Three Rivers had murdered his wife's brother, embedding an iron spade in the left side of the man's head, and at trial neither he nor his spouse would give a motivation for the crime; near Bakersfield a farmhand aged thirteen years had taken an axe to the sleeping foreman of the chicken ranch to which he was on hire from a local orphanage, after which crime he turned himself in to the county sheriff; before the eyes of a shop full of customers, a San Francisco jeweler had shot and killed a fleeing thief after the latter smashed a display case, emptied it and sprinted for the door.

A loud klaxon sounded outside, followed by the ringing of a bell, and he looked up from the paper to see a man prone on the streetcar tracks, stirring with apparent difficulty. "Looky there at that," the counterman said. "Trolley knocked that smart son of a bitch right over on his ass."

A crowd formed and the conductor came down off the trolley to examine the stricken man, a beefy fellow dressed sportily in an ascot and a sleeveless sweater with a carnation in its breast pocket. At his side was a petite young woman with peroxided hair done up in a permanent wave, wailing with more excitement than the matter seemed to call for. Among the crowd were a couple of newspapermen, one of whom carried a handheld rangefinder camera. The other took notes, addressing the trolley's victim, who had risen to his feet uninjured. The conductor started berating the fellow, pointing variously at him and the train and the tracks, yelling something vehement Bill rather wished he could hear.

Approached by a policeman, the dandy held out his hand to shake, which the copper ignored. He then indicated, via the exaggerated gestures of a pantomime artist, that he was physically undamaged, upon which the patrolman gestured to the conductor to be on his way. The assemblage dispersed and the young fop and his bottle-blond companion, accompanied by the two newspapermen, crossed the street and came into the Pig and Whistle, where they took seats at the counter a few down from Bill. They were in a jolly mood, the four of them, and once they'd ordered, the first pressman got up to use the telephone booth. Bill nodded at the one with the camera.

"That a Speed Graphic?"

"It sure is," he said.

"Wonderful piece of machinery. When I started out the cameras were portable but you needed a mule to get them from one place to the next."

The man who'd been knocked over looked at him with a vacuous lack of expression. "Are you all in one piece?" Bill asked him. He was a handsome fellow, better dressed than Bill suspected was his habit.

"I'm all right," he said. "Takes more than a streetcar to get the best of Jack Strong." His accent was distinctly Southern, from Tennessee or Arkansas. He extracted a business card from his inside pocket and handed it to Bill.

"Bill Ogden." He produced his own carte de visite and flung it spinning across to the young man's side of the counter. The actor caught it with a studied insouciance that might have looked good in a picture show.

The girl's eyes widened and she gave Bill a big, closed-mouth smile. "I'm Purity Dove. Pleased to meet you." She sounded just like her beau did; he guessed they'd come west together to be in the pictures, and Bill couldn't see such a story ending up happily.

"You in the pictures?" he asked.

Young Jack Strong fairly beamed. "You've seen me, then."

"No, I don't see too many of them. But your names sound made-up, like Bessie Love, and when you had your mishap there just happened to be a couple of newspapermen present, one of them with a camera."

The two of them looked nonplused, and so did the photographer, but after a moment they laughed. "It's all part of the business. Jack here gets some free publicity, we get an exclusive," the lensman said.

"Which paper?"

"The *Examiner*."

He held his copy up, tapped it and nodded. "It's a good newspaper, but I don't see how you manage to fill a whole section out of motion picture news."

"Photoplays are more popular than anything in the show world any more," the actor said, as though that were a good thing.

"I suppose they are. It can be a hard life. My second wife was an actress."

The first reporter came back from the phone booth. "We're in the evening edition, but they may run it in the city section instead of the motion picture pages."

The girl was crestfallen. "That's awful luck. Jack could've gotten himself killed with that stunt, and we don't even make the pictures section."

"Think of it this way," Bill said. "All sorts of nobodies get mentioned in the motion picture pages. But if you're in the city section it means he's important enough to rate a mention as real news. If you see my meaning."

She nodded and exchanged an enlightened look with

the actor. "I see. If some plumber got knocked down by a trolley, it wouldn't make the papers at all, would it?"

"There you go." He didn't believe it himself, but was glad to make her feel a bit better.

He picked up the evening edition after he'd finished his darkroom work for the day, just to see if Jack had made it in. The incident had been deemed worthy of the front page of the city section, accompanied by a photograph of a grinning Jack Strong that must have cost the photo editor a couple of hours' worth of retouching.

PICTURE STAR SHAKEN BUT UNINJURED IN STREETCAR MISHAP

A streetcar accident this morning at Spring and Third Streets upended one of the Film Colony's brightest up and coming lights, Mr. Jack Strong, whom readers will recall as the stalwart younger brother in last year's Foxfilm production of *A Tale of the Bowery.* The wheaten-haired thespian was not wounded, but a patrolman at the scene warned the train's conductor to pay closer attention to pedestrian traffic before letting him proceed with only a mild rebuke and no fine or order to appear. Our photographer at the scene snapped a candid pose of Mr. Strong, who will shortly appear on screen in the Cowper comedy production entitled *The Jiltin' Fool.*

There wasn't any mention of the girl who'd accompanied him, which made Bill a little sad.

♦ ♦ ♦

IT SEEMED TO Grady that the trouble with Trudy was she looked like a streetwalker. Which, to be fair, she was, but this was a girl-and-girl picture, and those worked better if it seemed to be two virgin innocents succumbing to the temptations of Sappho, and not a couple of hard-worn veterans of the sidewalk groping one another for the benefit of a movie camera. Not that either of them was particularly old, or looked it, but there was a hardness to Trudy's features, and she turned resentful when told the next shot called for her to place her index finger between the other girl's labia.

"Play like it's fun, Trudy," he said.

"Go fuck yourself, Grady, you can pay me to do this dyke business but you can't make me like it." The afternoon had grown hotter than anyone had expected, even under the mildewed rooftop canvas. The sun was at a low angle and the white reflectors shone straight at the performers, shiny with sweat.

"I like it fine," the other one said. Victoria was her name. She was hopped up and game for anything, not really pretty but passably attractive, and happy enough that she did exude a sort of innocence.

"Never mind which it's about two hundred goddamn degrees on this fucking roof."

"Can't be helped. Anyway you're in your birthday suit."

"I like the rooftop," Victoria said. "Reminds me of getting a tan at the beach."

"Roll," Grady called again, without much optimism.

This wasn't a goddamned Lasky production, he had to make use of just about every frame of raw stock just to break even, and he was just about to call it a day in order to hire a new girl tomorrow. The sun was getting low, anyway.

"Whoops," the cameraman said.

"Sweet Jesus, what now?"

"I ain't got enough film in here to run but about ten, fifteen more seconds. You want me to change or shall we burn through it?"

"Why not," Grady said. Fifteen seconds of finger-fucking was all he needed, if it came out all right, even if he had to replace Trudy tomorrow. What did a bunch of punters at an Elks smoker in Fort Wayne care if the girl changed faces in the middle of a scene, anyway? "All right gals, make it look like it's true love. Roll."

Trudy bared her upper teeth and stared at the ceiling as she bore down on Victoria's clitoris with her right fore-finger. Though her intent seemed malign, the latter made a face of such ecstasy that Grady knew he had a take. He'd never before thought of using any fancy, Griffith-style business on a flicker like this, but now he had an idea that next afternoon he'd get Trudy's replacement to do that same thing with her finger and get a close-up on Victoria's face as her eyes rolled back in her head. Maybe insert an intertitle, something he'd never bothered with before. Something like:

"OH! OH!! OH!!! Edna Dear! Your Finger's Found its Way to my Naughty Pleasure Button!"

As the camera ran empty Victoria let loose with an

ecstatic wail, her co-star's finger pressing spitefully hard, and Grady wondered if replacing Trudy was really the solution. There was something between these two, something that might work on the screen. He considered how many fraternal organizations there were in the country, and how many of them held the sorts of stag parties where blue movies were shown, even—especially—in the more conservative, blue-nosed precincts. Obviously Grady, a man with studio experience, could make a better product than your average moron off the street. Though he'd never considered these stag pictures to be art, maybe there was enough craft in the making of them that a real artisan could make a product that would stand out amongst the run-of-the-mill filth others were putting out. Maybe there was money to be made in a better dirty flicker.

"You want me to reload, boss?" the cameraman asked. His name was Milton, and he was a pretty good operator. He'd lost jobs at any number of studios for showing up pickled, and Grady suspected he was in his cups now, but his work for Grady was always acceptable, and it spared him having to shoot the pictures himself.

"Let's shut it down for the day. Want to talk to you about something."

"COUPLE THINGS WE could be doing to improve the product," Milton said over a pint of Falstaff. Grady had broached the subject of improving the pictures artistically, and they'd wandered down Gower to a saloon called Kirby's. There was a bowl of peanuts in front of them and he crushed the shell of one between thumb and forefinger, then popped the meat into his mouth with a flick. "Shoot indoors with arc lights."

"With the camera we're using? That lens? We'd need a dozen lights."

"Not if you bought a camera with a faster lens. One we've got must be fifteen years old."

"Just like the camera. Can't afford a new one of those either."

"Still. Imagine converting the third floor to a filming stage."

"I don't see the problem shooting on the rooftop."

"That rooftop's lower than the buildings across the street. What if someone sees the operation and calls the coppers?"

Grady took a swig and waited a moment before answering. He was still hot and the cold beer was a relief. "Just warehouses. Some fellow pushing a hand truck gets a thrill looking at some naked girls."

"What about aeroplanes?"

"First of all, the canvas blocks most of the view from above. Second, when has an aeroplane ever flown over that building?"

Milton was petulant. "It could happen."

Grady had thought in the past about moving out to Ventura County or El Segundo where a barn might be converted via skylight into a proper studio, but that would involve bringing performers from LA, putting them up overnight and feeding them, or wading out into the demimonde of those locales and recruiting performers, the sort of thing that could draw the interest of the police or, worse, the local pimps. Maybe the purchase of a new camera and some lights would allow him to continue the lease on the Gower property, a former paper warehouse he'd rented for a pittance. The first order of business would be a bank loan, and he pondered what his approach would be. A former director of one-reel comedies for White Star Studios wanting to reintroduce himself in the film world? Why not? He took a swig of his beer and reached for a peanut. "Milton, let's do this thing."

IT WAS GETTING dark already as Trudy strutted down the concrete, Victoria lagging behind. "Slow down, Trude. What's your hurry?"

"Go fuck yourself, Victoria."

"What's the matter with you, anyhow?"

"Can't you take a goddamn hint? Quit following me. The fingerbanging's over with for the night."

Victoria laughed at that. "I wasn't expecting any more of that, hell, it was just for the camera, wasn't it?"

Trudy wheeled around to face her. "Listen here, we're not friends and I don't want you following me."

Victoria seemed incapable of offense. She gave Trudy a cheerful wave. "All righty, you're feeling cranky. See you tomorrow at noon."

SHE STEAMED ALL the way home. Tonight's crossing of the city felt significantly longer than the usual. Even with the sun down, the trolley was hot and her fellow passengers ripe, and the city around it appeared hostile and sinister. Arriving at her third-floor apartment she opened the front door as quietly as she could, but when she entered the dark room she heard a small voice. "Mama? The light burnt out."

"Pearlie. What are you doing up so late?"

"I can't see the clock." She stood there in the light from the hallway in her little raggedy nightdress. Trudy shut the door.

"Did you eat your supper?"

"Uh-huh."

"Don't say 'uh-huh.' Say 'Yes ma'am.'"

"Yes ma'am."

"And you fed Ezra?"

"Yes ma'am."

"He's asleep?"

"Yes ma'am."

"All right. You've got school in the morning."

The little girl got into bed. Trudy got some of her medicine then sat down in the dark at the window next to the table, poured herself out a dose and took it. The tiny kitchen looked out onto the rooftops of the one-story buildings behind it, and as she started feeling warm and happy she watched the night sky, and the stars started forming eddies and pools and before long she'd forgotten about the sound of Pearlie's voice in the unlit room.

2

"Cocksucker."

The speaker was a woman to Bill's right, aged about sixty. He didn't believe she was addressing him directly because she hadn't opened her purplish eyelids since his arrival, though her posture was fully erect. Every few seconds she licked her lower lip as if to remove an excess of mucilage she'd accidentally painted onto it; her upper lip was delicately covered with fine white and black hairs and divided by fine vertical lines, and every couple of minutes she'd mutter another toothless, spittle-soaked "cocksucker" and take a sip of her beer.

His intention in stopping into this pit had been to convince the owner that he might profit from a handsome photograph of the interior of his saloon. A handsome wooden sign affixed to the exterior of the building featured a six-masted galleon and the name THE FLYING SCOTSMAN, of a quality quite at odds with what turned out to be its squalid interior, and he deduced that many years of neglect and mismanagement had reduced it to its current hellish state. This derelict contrast excited him for reasons more artistic than commercial—surely the landlord lacked the funds for a promotional photograph—and as he sipped his lager he was blocking his views in his mind's eye.

To his left stood a small, poorly shaven man telling a

story, a battered derby resting on the damp zinc beside him. He might have been telling it to Bill or the bartender or an invisible hobgoblin, but he looked straight down at the bar as he told it. A long-ago romance spoiled by the death of the beloved in a fall from a horse, filled out with a number of asides regarding poor dead Betsy's brothers (Alf, a no-account, and one-armed, industrious Mickey) and sisters (pretty Jane, homely Gloria and wall-eyed Edna) and pets (a dog, Blue, and a kitten, Puff, tragically run down by a wagon before attaining cathood) and, finally, her appearance when naked. Betsy did sound splendid in his telling; if she was anywhere near as enchanting as his description Bill could understand his descent into alcoholic despondence at her loss.

The sweaty young fellow behind the bar moved very slowly and kept his eyelids at half-mast in the time-honored manner of the hop fiend dreaming his way through a tedious workday. The more Bill watched the place, the more he thought he might like to have a picture of it and its resident sots for his own edification and amusement, and so he initiated a conversation with the intoxicant.

"You the owner?"

He shook his head with some difficulty, as if struggling to remember the mechanics of the operation. "He's dead."

"Would you mind if I came around with a camera tomorrow and took a picture or two?" He had appointments to photograph a funeral parlor and a bakery down the street.

For the first time the barkeep looked him in the eyes and squinted. "Of this place?"

"I am making a photographic study of the leading

saloons of the west coast of the United States and Canada," he said, which was only half a lie, as he had made a habit of making such pictures in the course of his meanderings. Few of the barrooms he'd photographed were anything but wine dumps and dives, dismal places where men and a few women drank their way to the bone orchard. Something about the Flying Scotsman appealed to him, though, maybe the light, or maybe it reminded him of a certain saloon in Crider City, Idaho.

He cocked his head to one side. "Suppose you might as well," he said, enunciating very carefully in an effort to disguise his condition. "For sale, you know. Owner just bought the place to get out of the house, is what I think. Widow never approved of this place. Might be you could get a bargain."

Bill's ears perked up for a moment at the sound of the word "widow," but just for a moment; this one sounded like a scold and prohibitionist to boot. "I'll be in tomorrow afternoon, then," he said. His appointment to photograph the bakery, its wares and personnel, was at nine in the morning, the undertaker's parlor at eleven.

But the barman seemed not to have heard, having returned to whatever reverie his noggin and his dope had conspired to dream up for him. Bill looked around the room and allowed himself a moment's rumination. Long ago he had quite enjoyed the experience of running a saloon in a small Kansas town, and the running of it had led him to a peripatetic way of life that seemed now to have settled. Maybe it would be nice to have a spot like this to repair to on occasion.

"Cocksucker," said the woman to his right.

◆ ◆ ◆

THE NEXT AFTERNOON, after fulfilling his professional obligations to the baker and undertaker (or, as the latter had corrected him with a touch of horror, the *mortician*), Bill returned to the saloon and found the same bartender on duty, standing upright and describing with his head a series of little circles with his feet as fulcrum. It was a remarkable feat of balance for one so clearly opiated as he, and when asked if he remembered Bill and his permission from the day before he said nothing, but smiled sweetly. Betsy's mourner was nowhere to be seen, but his lady friend from the day before was parked in the same spot, still letting out a "cocksucker" every few minutes, at one point yelling it and adding the modifier "lousy."

He had experienced some difficulty in adjusting to semi-retirement. His granddaughter had come to Los Angeles after some unpleasantness in her hometown of Wichita and, after a few months of preparation, had taken over the day-to-day operations of the portrait studio he had been running, in different places across the west, for forty-five years. Inactivity disagreed with him, though, and so he'd taken to wandering the city and photographing this business and that, for advertising or commemorative purposes. For the first time in a long time he'd begun photographing places and things that appealed to him visually, just to amuse himself.

Now he set up his Calumet 8 x 10 with a three-and-a-half-inch Wollensak lens, and placed three pans of flash powder at strategic locations throughout the saloon. When he had focused and readied the first plate, he prepared to snap the shutter and activate the powder.

But just then the front door opened and a young man stepped inside. Bill waited for him to close the door again before tripping the shutter, and as he set about activating the flash powder caught a look of horror in the fellow's face at the sight of Bill or the camera or both, and before he had a chance to close the shutter the door was open again, flooding the room with light and ruining that exposure. The interloper, unnerved, fled.

Muttering a curse he replaced the plate holder and the flash powder and took three more negatives of the room that had so intrigued him the previous afternoon and which now looked to him even more a misbegotten hellhole. Before packing his gear away, as a courtesy, he ordered a draught of beer.

It was at this juncture that a deathly figure entered the saloon, dressed in widow's weeds and a velvet hat adorned with a black veil thick enough to lead the observer to imagine a death's head beneath it. She might as well have carried a scythe. To Bill's horror, though he was not a particularly superstitious man, she raised a bony *digitus secundus* and pointed it at him. He nearly voided his bladder when she rasped, "You."

Thinking he might be sharing a hallucination with the hophead bartender, Bill looked back in his direction to see him nodding. "Here's the fellow," said the hophead to the apparition, and she responded by pointing at one of the tables.

"Here," she said. "I will not approach the bar of a doss-house."

At this point he understood, or hoped he did, that he was dealing not with a malevolent spectre but with the proprietress. With no interest in buying the place, but fascinated by her cadaverous aspect, he pulled up a rickety chair and, following her lead, sat down.

"I am told you wish to make an offer on this foul place."

"No, ma'am," he said. "I only wanted to take some pictures."

"The price is three thousand dollars, as a going concern. Lease, fixtures and stock, all licenses transferred."

That was not an unfair offer, and he acknowledged as much, but reiterated that he was not an interested buyer.

"You haggle in the manner of a Jew. One thousand, five hundred dollars. That is my final offer."

He still couldn't see her face through the veil, and probably couldn't have in broad daylight, but her voice sounded as though her lips were pinched tighter than a cat's asshole. Her skin covered her hands so thinly that every bone and sinew and artery was as clearly delineated as in an anatomy textbook. One thousand five hundred would indeed have been a fine offer had he been in the market for such a business.

"I will ask around and see if I can't find you a taker, madam," he said. He held out his hand to shake, and she recoiled with such visceral revulsion that it wasn't necessary to see her face to sense it.

3

They'd been riding together all day on the roof of a boxcar without saying anything, except for monosyllabic greetings exchanged when the other fellow had first climbed on top of the car. It was about four in the afternoon and he was wondering whether the man had anything to eat. It would be a couple of hours at least before they hit Bakersfield. Now, he decided, was the time to decide whether he was friend or foe, and he made his way to the rear end of the car where the man reclined, up on one elbow.

"I'm Ezra," he said to his fellow traveler, lowering himself carefully into a similar posture.

"Henry." He didn't stick his hand out, but his expression was friendly enough. He wasn't too old but had the polite wariness of a veteran freight rider.

"Heading for Los Angeles, figure on hopping another in the next yard," Ezra said.

"Likewise."

"Got a wife and three babes waiting for me there. Oldest is six now. Youngest about two."

"Been gone long?"

"Long enough. Went off to make some scratch." The other fellow's expression didn't change, but he knew he shouldn't have mentioned money. "I ain't got it on me, if that's what you're thinking," he said.

"Figure you'd be riding a passenger train if you had it on you."

"That's right. Wired it to the bank out in LA, you ever hear of that? Wiring money by telegraph?"

"Sure, I heard of it." He looked at him with his head tilted to the left, and Ezra fought back a flash of irrational resentment at the notion that this Henry didn't believe him.

The younger man had on a patched-up wool jacket and trousers but a pretty new-looking pair of boots. They were several sizes smaller than what Ezra could have worn, so he set aside the thought of stealing them.

"I got some hardtack my aunt made me," Henry said, and he reached inside his jacket. He held out a rectangle the consistency of a pine shingle. "My granddaddy used to talk about how shitty it was during the war, marching and eating hardtack and pemmican. Thought I might get some money for the road from my old auntie in Des Moines and she thought what I needed was some hardtack instead. Anyhow it's better than an empty belly, if you want you a piece."

"Well, sure," Ezra said, and he knew his instinct not to kill the interloper had been a good one. Here was a new friend, a rare enough thing.

WHEN THEY GOT down off the car in the Bakersfield yard, wished one another luck and made their separate ways in the dark through the labyrinthine tracks, Henry was relieved to be done with Ezra. One side of the big man's mouth was fixed open ever so slightly to expose a jagged eyetooth, which gave him a look like he thought something was funny, especially when he squinted, which was pretty near always, and it gave Henry the fantods, a man smiling over nothing.

He was creeping around a boxcar, checking for bulls, when he felt a sharp jab at the small of his back.

"Give me the rucksack," someone said. It was a low-pitched voice, slurred and indifferent.

"The hell I will," Henry said without turning around.

A blade cut a slice into the back of his neck and he gave a yell.

"Jesus!"

"Turn around."

He turned to face the man, who held in his right hand a big buck knife ready to slice him again. He was six feet or taller and thick, lurching side to side.

Henry had a knife of his own in his ankle sheath, but dropping to one knee to get it would leave him awfully vulnerable, and he weighed the option of running. Besides being drunk his nemesis looked old.

And then there was a wet sound, and the hobo went straight down onto his knees and onto the ground. He dropped his knife and pitched forward, and standing behind him was Ezra, holding a hammer with its claw end bloodied, and that wry expression still on his face.

"Looks like I saved your ass," he said.

Henry looked at the supine hobo, blood darkening his dirty shirt in a quickly spreading stain. "Reckon we ought to get him some help."

"Help that son of a bitch?" He kicked at the man's hip with the side of his boot. "He was ready to take your rucksack. Probably would have fucked you too."

"Were you following me?"

"I wasn't going to, then I saw you heading this way and I told myself 'Ezra, boy, you got no idea where to grab an LA-bound freight, maybe the kid does know.' So I started this way and that's when I seen this bindle stiff here trying to get smart with you." He gestured to the fallen man with his chin, that glib look still on his face. "You might could thank me."

"Thanks," Henry said.

Ezra reached down and picked up the knife from the dirt, then lifted up the hobo's head by the hair. He drew the blade from one ear to the other, and then a rapid flow of blood started to blacken the dirt. "Think nothing of it, pal," Ezra said, extending a bloodied hand for Henry to shake.

THE NEXT MORNING they were drinking a cup of coffee at the counter of a place called the Pied Piper in downtown Los Angeles, waiting for breakfast. Henry was looking at a copy of the *Examiner*.

"Coulda knocked me over with a feather when you said you had a quarter eagle on you."

"That's what she gave me besides the hardtack. Thought I'd hold on to it until I got to California. Wouldn't have paid my fare on a passenger train."

A harried man with a paper hat brought them their plates. Ezra cut into his hamsteak, carving off a piece about as big as a man's ear, jamming it into his mouth and chewing with lust, rolling his eyes to the ceiling before closing them in exaggerated delight. Henry picked up a thick slice of bacon and bit off the end of it. It was cooked the way he liked it, still a little bit chewy. He tested the brilliant orange yolk of one of his eggs with the tines of his fork and found to his delight that it was liquid. He reckoned it had been ten days since he'd had an egg, and three weeks since he'd had any meat of any kind.

Ezra was almost done chewing when he spoke, ground-up chunks of ham sticking to his molars. "I much appreciate the meal, friend. Where you figure on sleeping tonight?"

"I ought to have two dollars and little more left after this, enough for a room for a few nights. By then I should have a job of some kind. Guess you'll be sleeping at home in your own bed?"

"You bet. Gonna give my sweet Trudy some of what for. I been missing that, I'll tell you what. Although truth be told I wasn't living an entirely bachelorly existence, while I was away, if you get my meaning." He swallowed the last of that morsel of ham and carved a large chunk out of an egg. "Only thing is, I hate to come home without something for her and the kids, and it'll be a day or two before I can get that money out of the bank I wired it to."

"Tell you what, Ezra, how about you give me your address and I'll lend you a buck out of my change."

"Would you really?"

"Sure I would. You saved my bacon back there in Bakersfield, it's the least I can do." Henry knew there wasn't any money, that likely there wasn't any family either, but he did owe the man a debt of gratitude.

THE LANDLADY STOOD in the doorway and shook her head at the sight of Ezra. The bags under her eyes had gotten redder since he'd last laid eyes on her and she looked even meaner. She didn't invite him in. "They been gone over a year. No forwarding. Owed me twenty-six dollars and twenty-five cents back rent." She smelled like mothballs and looked like a turkey hen.

"If you're trying to be funny you're not."

"And I don't blame that poor woman because you took off and left and never sent a dime. Far as I'm concerned you're the one owes me that money."

"I went to get work, Mrs. Broun."

She let out a snort. "According to her you went off to the saloon the night she went into labor and that was the last she seen you. Not so much as a post card. And her with two little children to support."

"Three of them."

Mrs. Broun shook her birdy head. "No. The morning after you took off she stillbore a little baby boy. No family to help her out and no husband either. And I don't know what she was doing to feed the other two while she was still here, but her hours were peculiar. Some kind of night work." She gave him a knowing leer, her lower, real teeth a yellowish brown in contrast to the bright white upper plate.

He hauled back his fist and aimed it right at the upper.

4

The young woman at the door was small and wore a smile that struck Flavia as bordering on imbecilic. "Good morning. May I be of service?"

"Morning, miss. Is Mr. Ogden here?"

"I'll go fetch him. Won't you come in?"

"Tell him it's Miss Purity Dove come to see him, won't you?"

She left the woman sitting in the foyer and went upstairs to the kitchen, where her grandfather was drinking coffee and reading the morning edition of the *Times*. "There's a girl here to see you."

"Can't you take care of whatever it is she wants?"

"Asked for you in particular. Strikes me as a bit dim. Says her name is . . ." She suppressed a giggle. "Purity Dove."

He sighed and stood up.

"Mr. Ogden," she said when he appeared on the staircase.

"Miss Dove, it's a pleasure to see you again. I see you've met my granddaughter."

She stood and grinned, and Flavia was struck by an odd set to her jaw. "Come upstairs and join us in the parlor, I'll have Mrs. Chen make some coffee."

IN THE PARLOR Miss Dove sat in a plush chair opposite the couch. "Did you see Jack made the paper?

Of course it would have been nice if they'd used a picture of the two of us, would have helped me out. But I suppose that's the nature of things when one half of a pair is a star and the other's just getting started."

The word "star" seemed a bit grand applied to Jack Strong, but he made sympathetic and encouraging noises nonetheless. "How many pictures have you made?"

Flavia brought in a pot of coffee and cups on a platter and set them down.

"I made three at Keystone, but I was in crowd scenes all three times. I don't think the fellow who was directing thought much of me."

"Where are you and Jack from, by the by? Arkansas? Tennessee?"

"My, you're sharp. McMinn County, Tennessee. How did you know that?"

"You sound like an old acquaintance who hailed from around there."

"That's why I'm in pictures. If I were to try to take to the stage I'd have to learn to talk like an English lady. I haven't the patience."

"It doesn't always come naturally."

She leaned forward and pressed her palms together. "I heard you discussing the camera business with Angus the other morning. You take show portraits?"

"Occasionally."

"Well, I sure don't like the ones I've got." She pulled a manila envelope from her handbag and took from it an eight-by-ten.

"How much did you pay to have these done?"

"Ten dollars."

He passed the print to Flavia. No aspect of it met any professional standard, from the lighting to the posing to the background to the printing to the fixative. "Lordy. I hate to say it, missy," he said, "but you've been robbed."

"Can you do me some that are better?"

"Why not look in the city directory? Lots of portrait photographers listed. Some specialize in show folk, even."

"You mentioned how your late wife was an actress. And you came up with that business about the city section being better than the motion picture pages, and Lord knows I felt a lot better when it happened than I might have if you hadn't set me straight. So I said to myself Myrna, that's the man you want taking your picture."

"Myrna," Flavia said.

"That's my given name. Purity was Jack's idea."

Bill looked over at Flavia, eyebrows raised.

"All right," Flavia said. "Can you come by the studio tomorrow at eleven? The sun will be coming through the skylight and I won't have to rely entirely on artificial lights."

"You're so kind. But tell me this." She hesitated. "How much do you charge?"

"For you, Myrna, it's free of charge. To make up for what this miscreant did."

AFTER PURITY LEFT, Flavia studied the eight-by-ten and the other poses from the envelope, and was stymied.

"They're badly enough done that they hide a stubborn problem," Bill said.

"How's that?"

"Her face is pleasant enough, and I suppose she might have been the prettiest girl in McMinn County, Tennessee, but something about the shape of her face just doesn't photograph well."

"Do you want to take her portrait then? You know more about these things than I do."

"I believe I'll take it as a professional challenge. Make her a set of portraits that will get her noticed."

THE NEXT MORNING Miss Dove returned to the studio, and Bill set about posing the girl and adjusting the reflectors and scrims. For a certain kind of portrait, natural overhead light still produced the most agreeable effect, and he still preferred it when practicable. This was particularly true when photographing children, or women like Purity Dove who sought an affect of innocence.

She was adept at taking direction, at holding her head or her hands this way or the other, and she maintained a sweet expression all the while that wandered from dreamy contemplation to childish joy. When it was finished Bill had high hopes for the finished product, and he told her to come back the next afternoon to have a look at the proofs.

One advantage of Los Angeles for a photographer of his vintage and habits was that he could do his rooftop printing nearly every day of the year without resorting to artificial exposure. As it was he was able to spend the waning minutes of the afternoon watching the day's images materialize on the printing-out paper. No longer having the patience to make his own albumen printing-out paper, he had a man in Burbank make it for him from eggs laid by his own chickens, which produced a more even coating than those manufactured papers he'd tried.

"HOW DID MISS Dove's sitting go?" Flavia asked him in the early evening.

"Disappointingly." He handed her a stack of finished prints and she examined one after another, brow knitted.

"She never shows her teeth, does she? Even with a big smile, her lips are together."

He showed her another print, one he'd kept separate. In that one he'd surprised her in midsentence for the express purpose of getting a shot of said teeth.

"Oh, my," Flavia said. "That doesn't bode well for a career on the screen, does it?"

Her teeth were very small and widely spaced, and her incisors turned inward. She must have been very adept at hiding it when in conversation, because neither of them had spotted it in person. Nonetheless it did something strange to her jawline that didn't photograph well.

"I have a notion, Flavey. I'd like to help that girl out."

EVERY ADVERTISEMENT HENRY had answered thus far had been filled, except for one as a multigraph operator for the city, which paid only twenty-five cents an hour. "And you are, I assume, at least seventeen years of age?" the examiner asked him.

"Twenty," he said.

"Excellent." The examiner was a tall, thin fellow with a prominent Adam's apple, a remarkably long neck, and a pair of round black eyeglasses. He kept his plump leather chair swiveling in nervous semicircles as he interviewed

Henry, gulping frequently as he did. "And of course you're an American citizen."

"Yes sir."

"And you've been a resident of Los Angeles continuously for at least the last year."

"Truth to tell you, mister, I just got in this morning."

The tall man's shoulders sagged and a look of profound disappointment settled on his skinny features. His glasses slipped a little down his beaky nose. "Now why would you come in here then? Surely you read the advertisement in the paper carefully enough to find your way to the office."

"Yes sir, I did, but I didn't see what that had to do with anything."

"And yet it was written right there."

"I intend to stay in Los Angeles."

"That's not what it says! It says, and I quote verbatim:"—he picked up his own copy of the *Examiner*, which was open to the classified pages, his own notice circled in pencil—"'Applicants must be American citizens *and have lived in Los Angeles continuously for at least the last twelve months.*' Plain enough, it seems to me." The skin around his collar was getting redder and redder against the white of the celluloid.

That proviso had figured in a number of the advertisements, and Henry hadn't seen the point of them. "How about we pretend I answered differently?"

"Out of the question!"

"Well, I guess it shows how honest I am."

The man rose out of his chair and pointed at the door with a long, thin arm. "This is the civil service and we tolerate no chicanery. Get out before I alert the police."

He put his cap on and sauntered for the door. He turned around for a brief moment as he opened the door and saw that the man had slumped to his desk, and it seemed to Henry that he was weeping softly. Folks were different in Los Angeles.

DR. BRADFORD OWED Bill sixty-three dollars for several sets of before-and-after pictures, which he had cheerfully made on credit, blown up to considerable size for streetcar advertisements and reduced for those in the newspapers. The son of a bitch tiresomely complained of being cash-poor whenever Bill attempted to get him to pay. Today he climbed the three flights of stairs and opened the door to the doctor's cabinet, in whose waiting area sat five of the most miserable-looking specimens he'd seen in a while. One old fellow's mouth was stuck in a snarl that revealed his left incisors and eyeteeth, his eyes watering at the pain of whatever had brought him in. A young man held an ice pack to his jaw, and a pregnant lady kept her eyes fixed to the tile floor with an expression of guilt. Rather than knock he opened the door to the surgery and shouted Bradford's name, which startled him into dropping the pick he was using to scrape the plaque off the teeth of a portly gentleman. They were on the fourth floor, and the top of a palm tree rocked in the breeze outside the window.

"Goddamn it, Ogden, now I've got to get a clean one. Miss Sturdevant, if you please." While she rummaged through a drawer for the appropriate tool he turned to Bill. "You can't be in here while I'm practicing."

"You ought to have it down pat by now," he said.

"Save it for the burlesque circuit. And come and see me outside business hours."

"This is business. I have a proposition for you." The man in the chair looked quite uncomfortable, frightened, even, and seemed relieved when Miss Sturdevant handed Bradford the pick and his cleaning resumed. "Say yes and I'll be on my way."

Bradford stared into the fat man's maw and scraped away. "I'm listening."

"There's a friend of mine who needs a new set of choppers. You provide them and I wipe the slate clean."

He looked up. "Is that all?"

"It's not all. I mean a really fine set, like you'd make for the First Lady of the United States. Not one of those ten dollar sets you see advertised in the papers. And she needs them as soon as possible."

"I can do that."

"And I'll enlist another dentist to check your work and verify that you're not cutting any corners."

He pulled his face away from the fat man, who was now sweating; Bill's presence seemed to make the entire experience even worse. "Listen here, Ogden, why don't you just get that other dentist to do the work if you don't trust mine?"

"Because you're the dentist who's in arrears." He arched his brows and the dentist retreated; wisely, he didn't want any discussion of their disagreement before his patients.

"All right. I assume this is a paramour of yours."

"She is not. She's a young lady wants to be in pictures. I'm just helping her out."

"Am I to understand then that she has rotten teeth at a young age?"

"Not at all. They're just unattractive."

"By God, you're not asking me to extract a set of healthy teeth?"

"I certainly am."

He stood a little straighter. "It's against every ethical tenet of my profession."

"I don't care," Bill said, and turned to go. As he went through the door the patient let out a yell, and Bill suspected a flustered Bradford's pick had slipped. Those waiting exchanged worried looks.

5

The *Examiner* had been full of notices for experienced salesmen and truck drivers and other positions for which he was unqualified. With a list of all the jobs he thought might suit him, he had planned the day's itinerary using a map of the city, which he had marked up with a stubby pencil he'd swiped from behind the cash register at the restaurant. He was getting close to the end of the day's leads. Tomorrow, he supposed, he could pick up a copy of the *Times* and see what they had on offer.

He got off the trolley at Spring Street and rang the bell at number 422.

Photographer's assistant. Experience preferred but not necessary. Lodging and board provided. Ogden Photographic Studio, 422 Spring Street, Los Angeles.

Might as well get the kind of work that would teach him a trade, he thought. Waiting for an answer, he watched the comings and goings on the street with interest. A car rattled by that had been converted to have a wagon bed in the rear instead of a back seat, filled with scrap metal and pieces of leftover broken wood, and on the door someone had painted SLIGO BROS JUNK HAULED on the side in a childish hand. A larger and fancier automobile than Henry had ever seen approached on the other side of the street, nearly silent, with a liveried chauffeur at the wheel and someone important seated behind. All sorts of people crowded the wide sidewalk, workingmen and businessmen alike, women dressed for office work or for domestic service or just out for a leisurely morning's shopping, he supposed. There were white people and Negroes and Mexicans and Orientals as well, and he found it terrifically exciting. He was turned away from the front door when it opened, and he spun back to face a pretty and stern young woman in a starched white blouse and long black skirt, her hair pinned up under a straw hat.

"Well?" she said.

"Ma'am, I came about the advertisement you ran in the *Examiner* this morning." For the first time that day he was acutely aware that he was not as presentable as he'd have liked, having only taken a birdbath in the sink of his room at the YMCA. His clothes, though rumpled from weeks in the knapsack, were unripped and clean; he'd kept one shirt, one pair of trousers, a jacket and a pair of socks unworn since his mother had washed them before his departure. His shoes were shined, if worn, and he understood that she was making a decision based partly on his external condition. He very nearly turned and walked away without awaiting a response.

"Have you ever worked in a portrait studio before? A darkroom?"

"No, ma'am."

"I'd prefer someone with experience. Are you currently employed?"

"No, ma'am, I just got into town this morning."

"All right. Come inside."

He followed her upstairs to a kitchen, at whose table sat an elderly man, expensively dressed and with a fine white mustache.

"Who's this? An applicant?"

"Yes, sir."

"No experience," the woman said. "He got to town this morning. Now you know as much as I do."

"You have a name?" the old man asked.

"Henry Seghers."

The young woman poured them each a glass of water and motioned Henry to take a seat.

"I'm Bill Ogden. This is my granddaughter, Flavia. Where you in from?" the man asked.

"West Virginia."

"You work in the mines growing up?"

"Yes, sir, after twelve."

"That why you came out here? Didn't care for it?"

"Not much."

"Any schooling?"

"I can read and do sums, if you're needing someone to do the books. My ma made sure I learned, even if my pa thought it was useless."

The old man tilted his head toward the young woman. "My granddaughter was a schoolteacher in Kansas before she decided to take advantage of the pleasanter climate here. Listen, you don't need much education to be a photographer's assistant. In fact over the decades I've employed more than one certifiable imbecile who made a perfectly adequate assistant."

Henry's offense must have shown on his face, because the man started laughing.

"I didn't mean to suggest that about you, my boy, just meant if you've got some smarts you might want to learn the trade yourself. It's not a bad business. I think you'll do."

"Gramps." The woman spoke in a low, carefully controlled voice. "If I'm to manage the studio, as was our agreement, then I should at the very least be included in the decision of whom to hire as an assistant."

The old man held up his hands in a gesture of wounded innocence. "Far be it from me to dictate. I was just making conversation. It's important to judge the conviviality of another's presence if one's going to spend hours upon hours in his company."

"May I ask him a few questions myself, then?"

With a moue and a sweep of his hands he handed the interrogation over to the granddaughter.

"Are you prepared to start tomorrow?"

"I am."

"Where are you staying?"

"I'm at the Young Men's Christian Association."

"The job includes room and board. Mrs. Chen cooks our meals and you'll find them satisfactory. Come in tomorrow morning by nine and we'll install you in the spare room and I'll start instructing you."

"I'll be here too," Ogden said. "I'll show you a few things also, if it's all right with her nibs, here."

Flavia turned to her grandfather with a fierce look, but his own expression got a laugh out of her instead.

IN THE AFTERNOON Myrna, or Miss Purity Dove, arrived to pick up her pictures. Bill and Flavia outlined the situation to her. At first she got a bit teary, but the more he explained himself the more she warmed to the idea.

"You see, you're a very pretty girl, but your teeth make you hard to photograph," Flavia said. "Your jaw will look fuller, and your chin won't disappear anymore."

"But how much will this cost?"

"It's taken care of. The dentist is in my debt."

"So, I'd wear these whilst being photographed and then remove them afterward?"

"No, you'd only take them out to sleep."

This confused her. "So they'd cover my real teeth all the time?"

"Your real teeth are coming out."

Startled, she took in a deep breath. "Out?"

"Extracted and replaced by a better-looking set."

"It sounds like a very generous offer to me."

Tears again filled Myrna's eyes, and Bill chose to interpret them as happy.

6

Grady was busy at the editing table cutting the new picture. Without having even run the finished product through the projector, he had a hunch he was going to have a hot item on his hands. He'd been afraid Trudy might not show up for the second afternoon's shoot, but show up she had, and she'd continued fingering the other gal like a pro, though when it came down to the cunt-lapping scene she'd flat out refused to go down on her, and in the end it was Victoria who went down on Trudy. This had worked like a charm, though, and the look on Trudy's face when she came—one of decidedly mixed emotions—would soon launch a thousand hard-ons all across the land of Liberty. It was a look of genuine surprise, almost astonishment, and Grady believed that her climax was both unfeigned and unexpected, maybe even a first.

Running the unedited raw footage through the projector earlier he'd seen something in Trudy, too, that he hadn't in person. She was certainly a handsome woman, with strong cheekbones and big, hooded eyes, but what he'd taken for fatigue and wear showed up on camera as strength of character. If he could only keep Trudy happy, he was certain his scheme to produce bigger and better blue movies would come to fruition. When he was done editing this one he'd start on a business plan. Might do well to hire a new cameraman, in addition to buying some new equipment.

The next day he stopped in at the West Coast Art Company on Spring Street and asked the girl at the front desk about having intertitle cards made. "Certainly, sir," the young woman said. "Most of the picture companies do them in-house, but we've done a few." She put the earpiece of her desktop telephone to her ear and leaned into the microphone on the candlestick, then plugged a wire into a switchboard. "Mrs. Buntnagel, there's a gentleman to see you about some cinema intertitles."

Mrs. Buntnagel. This would require some finessing. Then again, this Mrs. Buntnagel probably didn't know a damned thing about the ways of Sappho, and his titles would be mysterious gibberish as far as she knew.

"Mrs. Buntnagel is on the second floor, first office on the left once you get to the top."

THE HIGH-CEILINGED OFFICE was preposterously bright, daylight from tall windows shining on white walls with no wainscotting, decorated with charcoal sketches of nude women. He was surprised to see them in an office, but they were so well-done, and so unerotic, that no offense could be taken. Arising from a desk with an attached drafting board was a lanky woman with a very modern-looking pair of lavender Bakelite spectacles, which she removed as she approached him, right hand outstretched.

"Mrs. Buntnagel, I presume?"

"Call me Irene. And you're . . . ?"

"Clyde B. Grady."

"All right, Clyde. What do you need me to do?"

He was taken aback but not offended by the informality. It struck him that here was a modern woman who might not disapprove, exactly, of what he was up to. "Intertitles. For a motion picture."

"All right. Can you tell me if there's anything specific you want, any special typeface? Illustrations?"

"No, plain, just like you see at the movies."

"How many do you need?"

"There are seven of them . . . here you go." He took the list from his pocket and handed it to her.

Irene read the list, smirking immediately and then snorting and laughing out loud. "'Dearest Edna, I shall Die if you do not Apply your Dear Tongue to me this Instant!'" She looked back at it and giggled again. "Mr. Clyde Grady, are you making an obscene motion picture?"

"Of course not." His face was heating up and he grabbed for the list. She yanked it out of his reach.

"Don't be a dope. Listen, I'll have to do this on my own time, though, out of my place. Can't have the old firm associated with uncleanliness."

"All right," he said. His face was tingling, as were his fingers and his feet.

"I can have it done in two days, will that do?"

"That's fine."

"And do you need them photographed? I can do that, too, you'd just have to pay for the stock and chemicals."

"You do that out of your home?"

"I certainly can."

He had assumed he would have to stop into one of the

photographic supply stores on the street to purchase an animation stand, and he was uncertain whether a special lens would be necessary for that type of work.

"Then do it, Mrs. Buntnagel."

"I told you, it's Irene. If you'll give me your address I'll deliver them."

He froze for a moment. She might just be doing this in order to alert the postal authorities. "I'd prefer to pick them up here."

She smirked again. "Can't have the old firm associated, et cetera. And I've no intention of letting you know where I live."

"All right," he said, and he started writing down the address of the old paper warehouse.

THAT NIGHT SHE was in her studio working on Mr. Grady's intertitles when George stuck his head in. She looked him up and down. He wore one of his tuxes and his hair was brilliantined. "You look slick. If I were a different sort I'd be quite moved."

"I'm going out with Albert and Max," he said.

"Some husband you are. Leaving your wifey alone at home of an evening."

"Don't wait up."

"God knows I wouldn't. I suppose there's a party? And I suppose it involves chorus boys and transvestites."

"It might just. What's that you're doing there?"

"An assignment I took on, half as a joke. A fellow came in wanting to know if we did intertitles for the pictures, and look at the list he gave me."

She handed him the scrap of paper. He started

laughing. "'O Darling! Do Allow me to Suckle your Sweet Pink Cupcakes!' Good Lord. So I assume this moving picture of his is erotic in nature?'"

"And sapphic, to be more specific."

"See if you can get us tickets for opening night," he said before popping out again.

IT WAS ELEVEN before she was finished for the night. The borders were painted and the text penciled in. It was a better job than many a studio bothered to produce. She poured a glass of milk from the icebox and sat looking at an unfinished portrait; she'd started on the face three times over and was set to scrub it again if it didn't come together soon. She didn't want the sitter to come back—a disagreeable society lady who thought that her eccentricities and her money permitted her to behave badly—and she had enough pencil sketches of the old harridan to go on. It wasn't a commission, but Irene was certain the subject would purchase it if she made it known she might sell it to someone else. At eleven-thirty she went to bed and put in earplugs, just in case George came home tonight and stumbled drunkenly into his room with one or more of his boys. She had work in the morning.

TRUDY HADN'T BEEN able to stop thinking about what had happened the other night. She hadn't ever had that happen to her before and she was pretty sure that what she'd felt when Victoria put her mouth on her sex was a female version of what happened to a man in similar circumstances. She'd heard other women talk about such things before, but she'd dismissed it as braggadocio, thinking that the pleasurable but much milder sensations she'd always associated with sex were as good as it got for a woman.

She couldn't help but feel guilty about letting somebody put her mouth down there. She hadn't been to church in a long time but this was something that was going to call for confession for sure. It was against nature. Fine for some but not for her, a formerly pretty good Catholic mother of two children. It was one thing doing it in front of the camera for money, but to have enjoyed it as she had seemed to her unforgiveable.

Still, she had thirty-five dollars in cash for the deed, which was money to feed and house her babes. She never had to do it again, did she? She'd tell Grady next time she'd be up for doing it with a fellow or three but that she drew the line with that dyke stuff.

She wondered if she could get a man to do with his mouth what Victoria had done. She certainly wouldn't mind that feeling again. Then she tried to imagine Ezra acquiescing to such a request, and she started to giggle. Of course he wouldn't, and the thought of his rough whiskers scraping against the soft skin of her thighs provoked a grimace.

7

At six in the morning after his second night in a ten-cent flop Ezra had awakened to find the buck knife from the Bakersfield yard gone. The hammer and his money were still there, though, and whoever had pinched the knife was long gone. He left the place determined not to spend another night there even if he had to sleep under the stars, and that afternoon he made his way on foot to Los Angeles Street, a place he'd heard it said a drifter like himself might go and be unmolested by the police, as long as he wasn't scared of his own peers. That was funny. Ezra had spent a lot of the last couple of years in jungles and various urban tenderloins, and he had a few scars but he'd left more on others.

It was about as overcast a day as Ezra could remember in Southern California, the sky low and dark, and the sidewalks were crawling with the indolent and desperate, men who'd given up on everything. He was proud of the contrast between himself and these sad specimens of humanity. All of them were men, with the exception of a few haggard women leaning out their upstairs windows. One of them called out to him, a round-faced woman without much in the way of dentition.

"Hey, sport." When he didn't look up at her she raised her voice. She had on a high-collared red dress, faded in spots to pink, and her hair was pulled up in a disheveled, graying chignon. "You! Down there. You got a buck on you for a real fun time?" The window ledge she was leaning on was gray and splintering, the bricks around it fixed with crumbling tuckpoint.

"Nope."

"What you got then, champ?"

"Forget about it, I'm busted."

"If you could bring me a little bottle, I might could let you have a little discount."

"I told you I'm busted."

He went inside a saloon and bellied up. It was remarkably dark in there. Of the string of gas lamps hanging from the ceiling just one at the back of the room was lit, the front end illuminated only by the faint light of the day from the open door. Next to his right foot a spittoon was full to brimming. He still had a quarter left and he intended to get considerably drunker before he went back out looking for a job, or for Trudy and the kids. He could hardly stand thinking about the stillborn boy. Might just be Trudy had a good excuse to be sore at him, after all.

"What'll you have, Cueball?" The bartender barely looked up, a scowl plastered to his face. His mustache completely covered his mouth and his gartered sleeves were gray and thin with age.

"What'd you call me?"

"Calm down, Baldy. You want a drink?"

"Listen, you son of a bitch, bigger men than you've come to regret calling me names." Wishing he still had the buck knife, he took the hammer and placed the end of its handle on the bar. It still had some clotted blood on its claw from the Bakersfield yard.

The bartender came up with a double-barreled twelve gauge and gestured toward the door. "You can fuck right off out of here."

"Aw, now," Ezra said. "I didn't mean nothing by it. Just want a drink is all, and you calling me names and like that." He slapped the quarter onto the bar.

The bartender cocked his head back as if to assess Ezra's sincerity, then put the gun back into its place behind the bar. "This ain't the kind of place you can threaten people. And you got no friends here, none at all, and they all know me. You and me was to get into a scrape there's nobody outside who'd ever hear of you again."

Chastened, Ezra nodded. "Shot of rye and a beer chaser."

He guzzled the shot and nursed his draught. This bastard would go down quick as any man, he thought, if the circumstances were different.

Outside it started raining. In a minute or so it was coming down hard. "Fucking sunny southern California," the bartender said.

HE WAS ONLY a little drunker when he left the saloon half an hour later, not nearly enough. The rain had tapered off a bit and he raised the lapels of his jacket to his face.

"Hey, sport." He looked up to see the harlot from before. She stood up from her seat, placed a booted foot on the windowsill and raised her skirts to reveal her remarkably hirsute genitalia. As she reached down and inserted her left middle finger therein he could see her gleeful face through the grimy upper pane. She leaned her face down to the open part of the window. "Come on up and get you a taste."

"Told you I'm busted."

"Freebie, then. Just for today. You'll be back, I promise."

HAVING SPENT THE morning instructing the lad in the basics of the function of the studio and the better part of the afternoon demonstrating the use of the darkroom, Bill left him in the company of his granddaughter to watch her conduct a sitting. The sitter was an opera singer, a soprano who had arranged her sitting by telegram from San Francisco, where she had seen and admired a portrait of a rival singer with the studio's logo in its corner.

SEE IF YOU CAN'T MAKE ME LOOK BETTER THAN THAT OLD VIRAGO STOP

There wasn't much tolerance remaining in Bill's heart for show folk. He left late that afternoon for the Flying Scotsman, carrying a framed eight-by-ten print that he intended to offer as a gift to the house, a view of the bar with its curtained-over front window. Normally he would have offered one for sale, but there was no point to that at an establishment like the Scotsman. The barman was a dope-addled moron and the proprietress a senile pinchpenny, which led him to wonder how the business of the place got done—bills paid, bank deposits made. He had found himself a good deal more fascinated by the place than he'd expected.

The bartender on this warm afternoon was a tall, lanky fellow of fifty or so with a long and narrow face, heavily lidded eyes and a nose like a meat cleaver. He nodded at Bill.

Bill ordered a beer and once it sat sweating on the bar

before him he put down his nickel and handed the framed picture across to the perplexed bartender.

"What the hell's this supposed to be?" He squinted in the light from the front window. "I'll be dipped in shit if it don't look like this was a halfway respectable saloon."

"It's a gift for the house."

The man's look went from appreciation to distrust. "You know you're not even getting a free draught out of this, right?"

"It's a gift."

"Good, 'cause things been slow around here ever since the old Scotchman's been gone. If I could just get the widow to put up for an exterminator."

"What's infesting the place?"

"What ain't? Mice, rats, silverfish, cockroaches. Probably a thousand generations of houseflies been born, lived and died since I've worked here."

"Sounds like an exterminator's a good idea then."

"I looked into it. Had one come by and do an estimate. Son of a bitch wanted twenty bucks for a full fumigation. Twenty! With a guarantee, sure, but when I asked about houseflies he said, 'Now I can't speak as to houseflies, because if you keep that door open when it's nice outside they'll sure as hell come in and breed. But you keep a couple rolls of flypaper unrolled around the backbar and a couple in the shitter and you'll be right on top of that.' Anyway, the old woman upstairs is tight as a drum, she wouldn't have sprung for it at twenty cents."

When Bill had arrived he and the bartender were alone, but by six-thirty there were six tosspots in the place who seemed to Bill to be terminal rummies, dull and red-eyed and biding their time until the grave finally beckoned. "Where's Freddie?" one of them asked.

"Fired him," the bartender said.

"What for?" the man asked. He might have been forty or eighty, with an oleaginous tonsure of gray hair.

"Moral turpitude."

The man nodded, indifferent. "You'd get more customers if you brought back that free lunch, ever think of that?"

"The old lady won't bite. She's perfectly happy with the money the place brings in at the moment."

THE WHORE HAD been all right company, avid for drinking and fucking until she wasn't, at which point she started hallucinating, flailing her arms around and shrieking about bats and maggots. Ezra had seen the DTs before but not exactly like that, and he thought maybe she'd had a screw loose to start with. She started calling him Ozzie and threw out the window the bottle they'd been sharing, with nearly an eighth left at the bottom. Whatever this Ozzie had done it must have been pretty bad, because the look on her face frightened him something awful. "And where's my dollar?" she said, hissing, crooked teeth bared.

"Which dollar?" he said.

"The dollar you owe me for the swell fucking you just got out of me, you piece of shit."

"You said come up for a freebie!"

"I never did in my goddamn life," she said, very sure of herself. "I'll call the goddamn cops on you! They don't think much of whores but they don't like deadbeat johns either." She moved toward the window out of which she'd beckoned him earlier. "Help!" she yelled. "I need a copper quick!"

He had to dig around amongst her dirty clothes piled on the floor to get to the hammer. He grabbed her by the biceps and spun her around to find her laughing, and the look on her face scared him more than the idea of the cops. When he managed to connect the claw to her forehead her eyes crossed like that fellow Turpin in the pictures. When she landed on the bare mattress he swung again, still in a bit of a panic, and he hit her a few more times. Then he got dressed and left, feeling for the first time a little bit sorry for having killed someone.

BILL FINISHED HIS second beer and was about to go when the door opened and an elderly man stepped inside and looked around, nostrils flared. He addressed the bartender with outrage. "And who the hell might you be?" His accent was distinctly lowlands Scots. He set a threadbare mallet down onto the sawdust.

"I'm Roscoe," he said. "You left me in charge."

The man's eyes widened. "The hell I did." He was a big man, slightly bent by age but largely undiminished as far as the eye could tell. He picked the mallet back up and made haste for the door that had once led to the apartments upstairs. Before trying the knob he turned and pointed at the bartender. "I'm the goddamn landlord here!"

"Are you Ogilvie?" Bill asked.

The man turned to Bill with a scowl. "I am. What's it mean to you?"

"Nothing, but I was told you were deceased."

He stared at Bill with one plastered eye, the other shut in order to focus better. "Do I look fookin' deceased?"

"Not especially."

"And who told you that, by the by?"

"The previous bartender. He thought I might want to take the place over as a going concern."

Ogilvie looked penitent now, mouth hanging open, face pointed at the floor. "I had that one coming to me, I reckon," he said. "You see, when the missus croaked I locked the door and went on a bender, left 'em in the lurch. Took me a few weeks to get myself into a condition to come back. Like as not the coppers think I done her in meself."

"Mr. Ogilvie, it was your putative widow who tried to sell me the place on the cheap."

"Widow?"

"Your missus is alive. I don't know if I'm glad to tell you that or not."

"Yer daft. I seen her meself. Stiff as a plank, mouth stuck open. Undertaker must have had to break her jaw to get it shut again." He pondered for a moment. "Would have liked to watch that."

"A woman in widow's weeds came downstairs and made me an offer, summoned from upstairs by that hop-head barman. I couldn't see her face behind the veil but she represented herself as your widow."

"Could have been someone else."

"She referred to the place as a dosshouse."

That word had an effect on Ogilvie. "She can't be alive," he said, as though abandoning a cherished dream. "I swear she was dead."

"She seems to have thought the same of you."

"She came back from the grave just to fook me over one last time." Both eyes were wide open now, and his affect was that of a sober man.

THE APPLE-CHEEKED, PORKY little fellow at the desk of the Young Men's Christian Association on South Hope Street remembered Henry distinctly. "We thought Mr. Seghers might stay quite a while but as it happened he stayed only a night before finding work with a room. We were delighted for him, of course, but sorry to see him go."

How did a man stay that cheerful, Ezra wondered? Not that he should have been miserable, but what provoked that delighted smile, which didn't seem faked? "Don't suppose he left a forwarding."

"As a matter of fact he did. Mr. Seghers is working and staying at a photographer's studio on Spring Street." He reached into a drawer and grabbed a ledger. "Let me just find it for you."

8

GRISLY END FOR A TENDERLOIN PROSTITUTE
Felled by a Hammer-Wielding Maniac
MOTHER AND WIFE FALLEN PREY TO THE BOTTLE

The mutilated body of Mrs. Oswald K. Dinney was found this morning in the squalid Skid Row room she occupied at 178 Los Angeles Street in the city. Her cranium had been savaged, most likely, police say, by the claw end of a hammer. Her neighbors did not hear her cry out, which leads detectives to believe she was hit from behind, and that death or at least unconsciousness were instantaneous. Mr. Calvin Brokaw, bartender at the Paradise Saloon at 170 Los Angeles Street, believes that he served the killer a short time before the murder. A disreputable-looking character had brandished a hammer that day in a threatening manner. Mr. Brokaw thereupon administered him a sound thrashing and kicked him onto the street.

Mrs. Dinney, whose Christian name was Ramona, had been estranged from her husband and children for the better part of five years owing to

her dipsomania, and at the time of her murder they were ignorant as to whether or not she still drew breath. Mr. Dinney, of 1611 Armitage Street in Echo Park, commented that prior to her descent into the city's demimonde his wife had been a decent and respectable woman. "Then she started watching movies and reading magazines and she just went crazy."

"PICKING UP AN order. Under Provident's account."

"Just a minute," the clerk said, and disappeared into the back.

The intertitles had come out nicely—Irene had lavished more care on them than was perhaps warranted—and she'd had the idea it might be funny to frame them and hang them up around the house. George thought that was a hoot. He'd photographed the cards the next afternoon with the boxy old second-hand wooden camera he'd bought for home use after Provident switched to the new Bell and Howells. Seeing them printed so nicely in Irene's deliberately florid hand made them even funnier.

"Oh! The Strangeness that I am Feeling in My Nether Parts!"

It could have been awkward if anyone at the lab had taken a look at the titles, but in his experience they never examined their work unless you came back to complain about a botched job. It wasn't quite right, charging the processing and printing to the studio, but it was a little more money in Irene's pocket, and there was no way for anyone to know it wasn't part of the considerable business Provident did with the lab in any given month.

The clerk came back with a pair of flat canvas boxes and a sheaf of paperwork, with which he busied himself. George was certain he knew him from somewhere and equally certain it wasn't the film lab, but asking him about it could be tricky. It might have been at the studio in some capacity or it might have been at one of Burney's parties. Maybe he'd known him as one of Burney's kept boys. The clerk finished and looked up without any scrutable expression. He was handsome and young, but not too handsome or too young, and that lack of affect might have been the result of caution. There was something intriguing about his sullenness, and he decided to risk a faux-casual inquiry.

As he signed the receipts he looked up for a second. "Say, I don't mean to be forward, but I'd swear I knew you from someplace, don't I?"

"I was a grip at Provident, hoped to work my way up to operator, and you fired me. Didn't like the look on my face is what you said."

He remembered. That same almost blank, almost surly expression that just a moment ago he'd found so intriguing had annoyed him greatly during the filming of a Tommy Gill two-reeler. "That's right, I did, didn't I? Well, glad to see you've bounced back."

The clerk finished the paperwork without another word or meeting George's gaze.

THE THING ATE at him on the streetcar home. It hadn't been the clerk's fault. He'd been frustrated at Gill's performance that day, and at the knowledge that the picture was going to be a stinker, and it had been easier to fire a grip than to let the star know he was turning in a half-assed performance. Tommy was lazy and all he had to offer were minute variations on his Vaudeville routine, which had been funny enough ten years back but which every moviegoer in America now knew by heart. That son of a bitch was a lot less loveable than he thought he was, and if the exhibitors hadn't yet passed the message to Provident they soon would. Tomorrow he'd have a word with Kaplan about Gill's contract renewal. The date was coming up soon, he was sure, and it was time to cut him loose.

"YOU SURE YOU don't want me delivering these?" he asked.

"I'm sure. It'll be a fun lunchtime errand. I've never seen a blue movie studio before."

"How's about me coming along, then?"

Irene smirked. She had the kind of face that could do that without annoying him. "Are you concerned for my virtue, George? That's sweet."

"To be honest, he's a pornographer and I don't know anything else about the man."

"Well, if you want to come, stop by work at eleven-forty-five or so and we'll take a cab."

They were dining together for once, in the dining room, which was normally reserved for entertaining. It was just spaghetti with red sauce, and they were slurping as they ate and drinking dago red out of water glasses, but the grandeur of the room gave it a sort of shabby elegance.

"You remember that Tommy Gill from last year where he's a fireman?"

"Annie Maloney played his wife?"

"It was a piece of shit."

"I won't argue the point."

"I'm not going to work with him any more."

"Hold on. Haven't you made a couple, three two-reelers with him since then?"

"Each worse than the last."

"So why'd you ask about the firehouse one in particular?"

"Because I fired some poor son of a bitch off that one because I was sore at Tommy. Works for the lab now, saw him when I picked up the title reels. I'm marching right in tomorrow morning and telling Kaplan I'm through with Tommy."

She laughed.

"What's funny?"

"Just thinking it's a good thing that fellow didn't catch on to what was on that reel. Could have caused you a lot of trouble."

George's mouth hung open. "Oh," he said. "I hadn't thought of that."

FLAVIA WAS ARRANGING the third-floor skylight and its various scrims and volets in preparation for an afternoon sitting by a society matron by the name of Mrs. Arthur A. Palethorpe. Her grandfather had already taken Mrs. Palethorpe's picture two years ago, and she reported that she was happy with the work, but now for reasons unclear she wanted a new set. She specified that she wanted the older gentleman with the mustache to do the honors again, but Gramps declined. "You take her. I've photographed all the dizzy old rich broads I care to."

The bell rang downstairs and she wiped the dust off her hands before descending the ladder and then the stairs. Standing at the front door, hat in hand, was a man with most of his head shaved and a long eyetooth exposed by some sort of facial tic.

"Yes?"

"Sorry to be a bother, ma'am, I'm looking for Henry."

"How do you know he works here?"

"YMCA told me."

"He's off running errands this morning."

"Oh. You see, I owe him some money."

"He'll be back after lunchtime."

The man scratched his head behind his right ear. "I don't suppose I could wait for him inside, could I?"

"No, sir, you couldn't," she said, and closed the door.

THAT WAS DOWNRIGHT uncalled for, Ezra said aloud, though he wasn't aware he'd actually spoken it. He pondered waiting; Henry was the sort who might come up with a little extra to add to the original loan, now that he had a job in a fancy—by the looks of the outside—photographic studio.

IRENE'S STOCK ALWAYS went up a bit with the ladies on the first floor whenever George made an appearance. They all suspected something was up with her, what with the funny modern hair-do and her oddball friends who kept coming by to visit, but they were all taken in by his dapper look and his charm, and their genuine camaraderie made it possible for her to blush when the two of them headed out the door, arm in arm, for their ostensibly romantic lunch date. In the cab she relaxed a little.

"They sure did swoon," she said. "You'd make quite the ladies' man if you wanted."

He grunted, arms crossed. "Bunch of spinsters."

"Don't be a pill. Did you talk to Kaplan?"

He grunted again. "He says I'll take the assignments they give me and be grateful. But I'll bet you he starts thinking about it."

She understood that his charm and bonhomie back at work had been an act for her associates' benefit, and she almost put a hand on his forearm as comfort. He didn't speak again until they got to the old paper warehouse on Gower. "This can't be it."

INSIDE THEY CLIMBED two flights of stairs to a big room lit from a bank of high windows. There were lights on stands, but they were old ones, inefficient, hot and strong consumers of electrical current, and a couple of cameras older than the one George had shot the intertitles on. Grady was alarmed at the presence of a second party but relaxed when they were introduced.

"Boy, a real director, huh?"

"If Provident counts as a real studio," George said.

"It sure does," Grady said. "I love that Tommy Gill. Say, once we've got our business settled, how would you two like to look at my picture? You're a man and woman of the world."

9

During the war Bill had witnessed battlefield amputations without anesthetic and men dying with their viscera spilled in the mud. He'd disinterred murdered bodies from a makeshift orchard cemetery. Another time he'd watched a barkeep slice his thumb off into a cauldron of boiling slumgullion. Even beside those memories, the extraction of poor Myrna's teeth was an ugly, bloody thing, performed outside Bradford's usual hours of business. By the time it was over all involved were exhausted and bloodied. It would be weeks before her new set of choppers was ready. Though not unduly vain for a prettyish girl, she was horrified by the sight of her toothless, bruised face. Bill sent her home in a cab, along with a week's supply of morphine.

Earlier Bradford had had the gall to ask Bill to make a set of before-and-after pictures, a request he refused on the grounds that Myrna, or rather Miss Purity Dove, had a burgeoning picture career to consider and thus no interest in having her "before" picture plastered across bus stops and telephone poles. When he left the dentist's cabinet that evening the latter's dismissal was surly, due perhaps to that refusal or to a feeling of remorse at the professional sin of removing a whole mouthful of healthy teeth for aesthetic reasons.

◆ ◆ ◆

SEVERAL DAYS LATER he phoned Myrna's boarding house and spoke to a neighbor lady who informed him that Myrna, still unable to speak, was in considerable pain. In addition, Mr. Jack Strong had been unhappy about the whole business, likely because he hadn't been consulted beforehand, and after he made several uncalled-for, cruel remarks about her looking like the wife of a fishmonger, Myrna had ejected him from their happy home. His current whereabouts were uncertain, but the neighbor was certain he would return, since his steamer trunk was still in the apartment, filled with his clothes and belongings.

10

Tommy Gill had been born Francis Xavier O'Hara in Joliet, Illinois. His mother, Maeve O'Hara, had several months previous left the employ of the Gill family, whose patriarch, Thomas, had presented her with the sum of five hundred dollars and a promise to provide her with excellent references provided she leave town and take up residence elsewhere. She ended up opening a hand laundry in Elgin, Illinois, and feigning widowhood. Her son never questioned her marital status until he was twelve years old, when he asked her how it came to be that she'd married a man with the same last name as her own.

"What do you mean by that?" she asked back, without bothering to conceal her exasperation at his impertinence.

"The letters from the folks back in Ireland, the return address says O'Hara. So you were already an O'Hara when you married my father."

"There's plenty of O'Haras in Ireland." Her tone was short.

"Were you cousins?"

She laughed, a mean little laugh, accompanied by droplets of spittle. "That'd explain a few things, wouldn't it? No, we weren't cousins. Stop asking questions."

This had set the boy thinking, and he brought it up on a regular basis from then on. What part of Ireland was his father from? How had he died? Was she in contact with his family?

She did her best to deflect the questions, but she worked hard to support the two of them, and she was bone weary by the end of a day's work washing. One evening, at the end of her wits, she laid it out. "There was never a Mister O'Hara. You're the bastard son of a banker in Joliet by the name of Thomas Gill, who thought himself within his rights to have his way with a poor servant girl ignorant in the ways of men. When it was clear you were coming along soon he paid me to leave town."

He was fourteen by then, and already keen on running away. He spent every penny he made going to shows, and reckoned he could do better than some of the singers and comic actors he saw in the acts that came through Elgin. He left his mother a note explaining that she would be better off without him, and he did believe it, since she had always made it clear that he was an anchor and a burden, and he made his way to Joliet.

THIS WAS A gaudier bank than the one he and his mother patronized in Elgin. There was marble on the floor and massive columns, and velvet cordons marked the lines at the teller's windows. It was a busy time, those lines were long, and the clerks at the desks were all busy with clients. Rather than wait, he decided to approach a guard. "Is this the bank where Mr. Thomas Gill works?"

The guard stared at him. "He don't work here, he runs it."

He rose to his full height and pushed his chest forward. "I'm his son."

"The hell you are. Now fuck off or I'll let you have it."

At that moment a tall, gangly man with an elaborate set of chin whiskers and a pompous air was crossing the lobby. His slightly crooked, aquiline nose was a match for young Francis Xavier O'Hara's own, and the boy strode over to the man before the guard could stop him. He stuck out his hand for the banker to shake.

"Put her there, Dad," he said, and the look of confusion on Gill's face faded into one of horrified comprehension. He turned his back and hurried in the other direction.

He felt the guard's hand on his shoulder and shouted after the retreating figure. "I'll be going now, Father! I'll give Ma your best!"

Satisfied that the clerks, guards and customers had all heard and understood, he turned toward the entrance, shook off the guard's fist, and left the bank.

Within six months his assessment of his own talents had proved correct, and if not a star he was at least considered a promising young performer. He sang popular songs and told stories and did a knockabout act with another young comic actor who went by the name of Silas Beane. He billed himself as Tommy Gill, Jr., the pride of Joliet, Illinois, and the character he'd worked up for the act with Beane was proving to be a hit: a tall, pompous man with elaborate chin whiskers, forever attempting to molest women and girls and forever running from his responsibilities. Within two years of assuming the character, a stout middle-aged man approached him after the show and offered to buy him a drink. Tommy Gill never said no to free liquor, and shortly they were in a saloon across the street from the theater.

"That was the funniest goddamn thing I ever saw. Does Gill know about it?"

"Gill?"

The man slapped him on the back. "Tom Gill back in Joliet! That arrogant son of a bitch. You really nailed him, that walk."

"You know him?"

"Hell, yes."

"You expect to see him any time soon?"

"I don't make a point of seeing him, but I'll be back home in Joliet next week and I'm sure as hell going to needle him about this."

"Good. Tell him his son says hello."

"You're not really his son?"

"Tell him Maeve says hello, too." He grinned at the man, who ordered two more drinks and cackled.

11

Miss Ogden was cool when Henry got back from the photographic supply house. "You had a visit from a friend," she said. She stood in the parlor with her arms crossed and her lips pursed.

"I don't know a soul in California but you and Mr. Ogden and Mrs. Chen."

"Fellow with a permanent sneer and a jagged tooth. Said he owed you money."

"Oh," he said. He'd been sure he was done with Ezra. "That's just a fellow I rode into town with."

"A boon companion, I'm sure."

"Listen, Miss Ogden, you oughtn't to judge me by the looks of someone I barely know come around to see me."

"I haven't judged you."

"But you sure do blow hot and cold."

"Come on upstairs and help me set up the studio. Mrs. Palethorpe will be here any minute."

He followed her up the front staircase. Watching her climb, her skirts rustling against the velveteen wallpaper, he was sure he was wrong but it seemed to him that her rump was swaying more than was absolutely necessary and—even more unlikely—for his benefit.

WHAT PASSED FOR a screening room at the paper warehouse was a room with five folding chairs, a projector with an extension cord leading to the other room and a brick wall, painted white, for a screen. "Now this is just the work print, you understand, I put some black leader in the spots where the titles will go."

The projector was an old camera rigged with a bulb, and when the door to the outside closed Irene could see a flicker of a grin on George's face. Was he enjoying the loucheness of it, or was he smirking at Grady's pretension?

On the white wall an establishing shot showed two girls walking past a painted beach backdrop, the brick's uneven surfaces creating distorted patterns on the image. On second glance they weren't girls but grown women. A two-shot revealed them as hard-bitten and ordinary looking, and the one doing the seducing didn't seem honestly enthusiastic about the process.

Soon enough they were in a dressing cabana, playfully taking off one another's clothes piece by piece. The younger woman was laughing, seemingly having a high old time, but the older brunette wasn't as adept at faking the jollity. Yet something about her face when her hand went down into the blonde's lap made the blood rush to Irene's cheeks.

THE MAN BEHIND the candy store counter had on a straw boater and a bright blue vest and he didn't take kindly to Ezra's threat. "I suppose you heard of a man name of Matranzo," the fellow said. "I pay good money to see that this kind of thing don't happen."

Ezra smashed one of the panes on the display case with the face of the hammer. Behind the glass were big jars full of jawbreakers, gum drops and hard candies of all sorts of hues and sizes. He was distracted for a second by the sight of them when the clerk—or maybe he was the owner, Ezra didn't know or care—stepped around the counter and rushed him, a revolver in hand. He made a threatening gesture with it that didn't convince Ezra, who swung the claw end and hit the man in the throat, the hammer's momentum ending as it embedded itself in the esophagus.

Ezra ducked back as the man went down to the linoleum spurting blood from his carotid artery (though Ezra didn't know an artery from a vein from a fire hydrant) and ignored the horrified gurgling and choking as he busted the cash register open with multiple hammer blows. As always under these circumstances he was a little giddy, and he giggled involuntarily as he extracted three twenty-dollar bills, a ten, a fiver and three singles from their trays, and six silver dollars and another two seventy-seven in assorted coins. He looked down at the counterman, who had begun convulsing, and considered the revolver next to his right hand. That was a real weapon for a robber, not a hammer. Many was the time he'd hesitated to take something he needed because of the hammer's limited range, no further than he could swing his arm, and a gun would make things go faster. He might be able to threaten his way to what he wanted without actually having to use it. He took one last look at the hammer, at the blood dried and tacky and slick and fresh on its claw, and dropped it on the floor. He picked up the revolver, an old one by the looks of it, aimed at the candy man's head and pulled the trigger. It wasn't loaded.

"Dumb shit. Might have saved yourself some suffering

if you'd kept it loaded." He walked to the back of the store and exited into an alley.

TWO DAYS LATER Jack Strong made the papers again:

PRETTY GIRL IS ATTACKED
BY FILM STAR
Spectator Calls Pasadena Police to Aid of Maid Wounded in Struggle

Pursued by a hop-crazed maniac when she alighted from a Pasadena trolley car early today, Miss Agnes Calmont, a pretty young white girl employed as a maid in the home of a wealthy Pasadena resident, was attacked by the man, identified as picture actor Jack Strong, and shocked so badly she was taken to the Pasadena Hospital.

Miss Calmont is employed at the home of Mr. J. C. Bilbury and was on her way home when she alighted from the car. A man in the car saw the hop fiend leave the coach and pursue the girl. The man jumped off and ran after them. During the chase he fired four shots in the air, failing to frighten the maniac, who grappled with the girl two blocks from the car line. He ran to a phone booth and sent in an alarm to the police station. Although the scene of the attack was outside the Pasadena city limits, Officers Jerry McClurg, Ronald Boyce and Sam Ruskin responded and encountered the dope-head struggling with the girl. In a fight that followed the assailant was subdued when he was struck on the head by one of the officers with the butt of a revolver. In the opinions of the arresting officers he was under the influence of a stupefying substance, likely cocaine or morphine.

So disheveled was he that none present recognized him. At the Pasadena Police Station he gave his name as Edgar Robinson, and it was only after his processing that a secretarial worker recognized him. He was booked again under the name Jack Strong on a statutory charge.

This was excellent news, as it would certainly spell the end of Mr. Jack Strong's connection to poor Myrna. Bill had skipped the fitting of the new teeth when they arrived, but Myrna sent him a note in the mail to inform him that they fit well and looked fine, though her gums were still tender. It would take time to know whether she'd be able to wear them on a regular basis.

A few days after the article about Jack appeared in the papers, she telephoned to arrange for a sitting. Her voice, though recognizable, sounded different, and he booked her for the next morning.

During the session she allowed that she'd been shaken by the course of events, but was adamant in her resolve to be rid of him. "My word, Mr. Ogden, he phoned me from the police station and asked me to hire him a lawyer. He sounded like a wild man. I spoke to a policeman who told me he was hopped up on all sorts of things and not just my morphine."

"I hope this means you'll be keeping your distance from the likes of him."

"Oh, surely. I'll be moving into a flat building with another girl and leaving Jack's trunk in the basement of the building I'm in now."

"If you need any help moving, we have a company truck now."

TWO DAYS LATER she showed up to look at her proofs. She had on the same frock she was wearing in the photographs, a dark, high-collared thing at odds with her short, up-to-the-moment hairstyle. They sat in the parlor and Mrs. Chen provided tea and biscuits, and after a short polite conversation Bill produced a manila envelope and handed the proofs over. At the sight of the first image she let out a startled breath. "Oh, Mr. Ogden, this is lovely. What sort of a trick did you use?"

"What do you mean by a trick?"

"To make me look so pretty." She was on to the third print now, the one Bill liked best.

"Haven't you got a looking glass at home?"

"Well, surely, but I don't look like this, do I?"

"You certainly do."

Her lower lip was quivering, and he felt better than he had all week.

12

George and Irene, despite the unconventional nature of their union, did manage their finances as a married couple. After dinner the night of their visit to Grady's warehouse they had discussed the proposition at length. In the sitting room each of them had a reading chair with its own lamp, the rest of the room dark except for the light coming in from the streetlamp outside. Pale blue cigarette smoke rose in Irene's lamplight as they dissected their finances. They both made decent money and they'd been reasonably frugal over the last five years, and had enough set back that they could afford to take a reasonable risk.

"And it could be fun." That was Irene's final argument in favor, and so the next afternoon they arranged to meet with Clyde Grady.

THE WAREHOUSE WAS bright, direct sunlight coming in through the high windows of the storeroom, and it seemed to George that it might be possible to film there in the daytime. Put in a few big reflective panels and you could do without artificial lighting; maybe build four walls on the rooftop and cover the thing with canvas, just like when he'd started out. Grady was excited to see them again, and eager to discuss a collaboration.

"I've been thinking along the same lines myself," Grady said. "That's how come I wanted those titles made.

Thought about getting a loan to buy a new camera and some better lenses."

"For night shoots I could borrow certain pieces of equipment from Provident, as long as they were back where they belonged by morning. We'll have to bribe the guards, but they think I'm swell. Our production values will be as good as any. I started out as a camera operator and I've been a lighting cameraman too."

Grady nodded slowly, unsure of himself. "So what do you need me for?"

"You know who buys these things. We couldn't exactly take out an ad in the trades, could we? Plus you know how and where to get the talent."

Grady laughed out loud. "I hadn't ever thought of 'em as talent before."

"Those two in the picture we watched had some, I can tell you that," Irene said.

"And I could come up with some performers myself," George said, "for a different kind of picture."

"You mean like a regular motion picture?" Grady asked, intrigued at the notion of making legitimate movies.

"Not at all. In fact I'm thinking of a type of film that would be even more risqué than what you've been making."

"Dirtier than cuntlapping?" Grady said, aghast.

"I'm speaking of its male counterpart, among other things."

"Oh, I've shown lots of cocksucking. Victoria, the little blonde in the picture I showed you, she downright likes doing it." He snorted a short laugh. "Go figure, huh?"

"I'm not talking about a woman doing the sucking."

Grady sat in silence for a good five seconds with his mouth open, trying to grasp what George was implying. "You don't mean queer stuff?" he said, comprehension dawning across his big, flat face. Surely he was misreading the man.

"My dear Mr. Grady, there is a market for films featuring all-male casts that is currently only met by the crudest and most ill-made product, the performers strictly rough trade and the films, to be honest, fairly disgusting."

"I don't know, Mister Buntnagel. Seems to me we could get into a lot of trouble, promoting that kind of thing."

"Don't be ridiculous. You're already making and selling obscene materials, including lesbianism, which is no less illegal than male homosexuality."

"I suppose that's true. You say there's already stuff like that out circulating?"

"Nothing but amateurish trash. I'm well familiar with the market. Now if we can come up with something that was at once erotic and esthetically pleasing, we could corner it. And of course that's not all we could do. Masked women with whips. Orgies and such. All of it tastefully and artistically done with an eye to creating a product that will be synonymous with erotic excellence. Interested?"

"Mister Buntnagel, I am interested in anything that makes money," he said, hand outstretched.

"Then I believe we have ourselves a deal," Irene said. "Let's make some smut."

FLAVIA HAD NEVER yet altered a thing in the studio, hadn't even suggested any alterations to his lighting setup or the arrangement of the furniture or the various scrims and backdrops, and so it was a surprise to Bill when he came home at suppertime to find that the main flood had been moved to the west side of the sofa, and the smaller fill was on its left, which made no sense to him until he considered that the day's sittings had been scheduled for the late afternoon, when the skylight would illuminate the other side of the studio and allow the flood itself to serve as fill, permitting a smaller aperture to be used. If the sitter was old and vain this wouldn't do, but for the young and pretty it might be an advantage. When he sat down at the kitchen table he nodded at Flavia. "I see you altered the lighting setup."

She nodded at Henry. "It was all his doing." The young man looked up at Bill as though expecting a reprimand.

"I thought you didn't know anything about picture taking."

"Well, sir, I've been here a few weeks already. I guess I've picked up a few things."

"I'd say you have. Don't you two go changing things without asking me first," he said. "But I'll admit that was a clever layout."

"Wait till you see the proofs," Flavia said.

BILL RETURNED TO the Flying Scotsman that evening before dinnertime, curious as to the outcome of the Ogilvie's marital dilemma. Roscoe was tending bar again, and standing at the bar was the old woman who'd yelled "cocksucker!" on his first visit, a practice she was continuing while interspersing other epithets at random intervals.

"What ever happened to Ogilvie? Has he accepted the fact that he's not a widower?"

"Not sure. He went upstairs and fifteen minutes later came back down looking downright sick. Left and hasn't come back."

"And the widow?"

"I've spoken to her five or six times, getting her to pay bills and such like. She hasn't mentioned him."

A fat, bald fellow with big white sideburns at the bar spoke up in a vaguely English accent of indeterminate origin. "I'd have paid admission to see his face when he saw her up and walking around." He stuck out his hand for Bill to shake. "Feeney, Francis X. Actor by trade, relocated to Los Angeles in hopes of finding character parts in the pictures." He was about Bill's age, and his face had an uneven reddish hue that looked to be permanent.

"Have you found them?"

"Occasionally."

"I was married to an actress. Erstwhile, anyway."

"It's a manner of living that takes a certain temperament. And you, sir?"

Bill introduced himself and identified himself as a photographer.

"Splendid. Do you do portrait work?"

"That's the main part of my trade."

"Perhaps I'll arrange a sitting."

The two of them exchanged cartes de visite and Feeney started telling stories about the stage life. He claimed, among other things, to have trodden the boards with several of the Booths, including the assassin John Wilkes.

"I was young then, a child actor graduating to juvenile leads, and he took a liking to me. He'd nowhere near the talent his brothers and father did, but by God the ladies loved him. I'll bet he's got a dozen unacknowledged bastards up and down the Eastern seaboard. I ran into him once backstage in Baltimore with a pair of sisters, pretty and well-bred too, not show folk, and both of them nuzzling his neck like nobody's business." Feeney shook his head. "Why would you abandon such a life as that just to take a potshot at the president?"

THE WORDS CARMICHAEL PAPER CO. WAREHOUSE NO. 2 were carved into the stone arch above the doorway, and the front door unlocked as Grady had promised. Trudy found Victoria waiting on a wooden folding chair inside the foyer, shiny-stockinged right leg crossed over the left, absently working an emery board on the nail of her right ring finger. "Hi there, stranger," Victoria said, brightening at the sight of her. "Stairwell's locked and Grady's not here yet, so we're stuck waiting down here, unless you know how to work the freight elevator."

Trudy took a seat next to her and kicked at a scuffed, olive-colored linoleum square with a corner missing. "Hi," she said. She had expected to feel awkward in her presence, but Victoria's manner was casual and friendly.

She didn't know what was being filmed that evening, but despite herself she felt a thrill seeing that her co-star would be Victoria and not some pomaded, stinky gigolo. She had debated with herself whether or not she would be willing or even able to reciprocate Victoria's oral attentions, coming to different conclusions at different times, in one instance becoming so excited at the prospect that she locked herself in the bathroom down the hall from their tiny apartment and considered it so intensely she had to bite her cheek in order not to cry out.

"How are the kids?"

"Who told you I had kids?"

"You told Grady one night you needed to get home to 'em. Don't mind me, I'm not nosy, just making conversation."

"They're all right. I got a lady from downstairs taking care of them tonight. First time I've been able to afford that. Used to have to leave them by themselves."

Victoria shrugged and started filing her left hand. "I never once't had anybody watch me when my ma was gone and I guess I turned out all right."

GRADY WAS HALF an hour late, and Trudy found herself telling Victoria things she'd been keeping inside for quite a while: Ezra and the kids, the lost baby, the terrible months after Ezra's flight, the things she'd had to do to keep the babies sheltered and fed. Victoria's story, cheerfully offered, was worse, a tale of foster homes and evil-intentioned old men. "But look at us, here we are, making good money and having fun at it."

Before Trudy could formulate an appropriate response, Grady came through the door followed by a couple of swells, a tall woman with short hair and a fellow in a canary yellow suit. Trudy considered the possibility that there was going to be an orgy scene filmed that night, and she promised herself that if there was, she would not let herself be molested by this slick character.

"Hello, gals," Grady said, whipping off his hat and gesturing to the couple. "This is the Buntnagels, George and Irene." He turned to the Buntnagels and nodded at Trudy and Victoria. "I'm sure you recognize these two."

The tall woman smiled at them and replied that she certainly did. She had on a dress of burgundy silk that looked a little bit like a kimono.

"Where's the cameraman?" Victoria asked.

"He's already seen the picture."

"What do you mean seen it?" Trudy said, suddenly more afraid that there wasn't going to be any compensation for tonight's visit than she was of an orgy scene.

"Seen the picture. I wanted you to have a look before I start sending out prints."

"You mean you're just showing us our own dirty movie?" Victoria asked, her voice squeakier than usual. "We're not shooting?"

"Don't you want to see it?" The idea seemed to baffle Grady. "It's a heck of a show." He opened a padlock that secured a chain on the door of the freight elevator, then pulled it open.

"HOW'S COME THESE two get to see the picture?" Victoria asked as they took their seats. They were in the former storage room where they'd shot the thing, where the camera had been rigged up as a projector and a plain white sheet hung on one wall to serve as a screen.

"They seen it once already, they wanted to meet you."

Victoria glanced over at Trudy with an expression of exaggerated horror.

"I know that must sound strange," the tall woman said. "But we thought there was something different about it. About the two of you."

Grady, threading the film, nodded with enthusiasm. "I know, it's not just a dirty movie. It's got some . . . some feeling to it. I don't know."

Now the man spoke up. "It's quite well done, considering. We had some thoughts about helping you make some more of them."

Here it comes, Trudy thought. *Four in a bed, who knows what kind of other perversions, and me and Victoria just going along with it because what choice do we have?* "And I suppose we get paid the same as before."

"Sure thing," Grady said.

Trudy shook her head. "You don't understand. We want more if we have to do threesomes and foursomes."

The tall woman laughed. "That's not what we're here for."

"Let's screen the picture," the man in the yellow suit said. "Then we can talk."

WHEN THE PICTURE was over with and Grady brought the lights back up, Trudy's face was flushed and her blouse was damp with sweat. The swell gent turned in his seat to face them. "As I said before, it's quite well done, considering the standards of the genre." Trudy had a feeling this fellow didn't have any intentions toward her or Victoria, or toward his wife for that matter.

"Mr. Buntnagel here makes movies over at Provident. Real movies, and he's got some ideas."

"I have a notion that pictures of this . . . of this particular type could make more money if their production values were higher. Irene and I can help that to happen."

"Does that mean we'll get more money?"

Grady waved his hands. "Whoa, there, Vic. One step at a time."

Trudy crossed her arms. "Seems like maybe you ought to get us under contract."

"Contract!" Grady said. "Who do you take me for, Jesse goddamn Lasky?"

The tall woman spoke up and shook her head at Grady. "Of course there'll be more money. What say we give you each an extra five dollars per picture and, say, two and a half percent equity in the company?"

"I didn't know you had a company, Grady," Victoria said.

"Magnificat Educational Distribution Company, Incorporated," the man in the yellow suit said. "Not actually incorporated yet, but we're taking care of it."

Victoria looked at Trudy to assess the credibility of this claim, then spoke. "Oughtn't it be 'Something Something Productions?' Seeing as you're producing motion pictures."

"Ah, but we don't want to alert the authorities to the fact that we're producing anything," the woman said. "As for distributing, we could be dealing in sewing machine treadles or Baptist hymnals."

Trudy nodded. "When do we start the next one?"

"Soon as this one gets the scenario written," Grady said, indicating George Buntnagel.

Both the women laughed. "Scenario?" Victoria said.

"We're going to be a real professional outfit from now on," Grady said. "I got a story in my head where a traveling salesman stops at a farmhouse, see? The twist is the salesman is an innocent and the farmer's daughters are sex-mad."

"They're sisters in this picture?" the woman said.

"I guess."

"Forget it," Irene said. "That's incest. Even your smokers and stag parties won't like that."

"All right, then, maybe you're a couple of shepherdesses and you run into the boy who cried wolf."

"Where are you going to get the sheep?"

"Who knows, we'll use fake ones."

"We could film it outdoors with real ones," Victoria said.

"Why don't you let Irene and me worry about the storylines, Grady."

OUTSIDE, VICTORIA ASKED Trudy again whether she'd like to go get a drink.

This time she was happy to accompany her. "If you know a saloon serves unaccompanied ladies."

"Sure I do. Let's go."

13

Beatrice Gill never visited the studio. She'd never seen her husband's current dressing room, with its extra-long couch, and Tommy wasn't especially worried about her finding out about his habitual laying of aspiring actresses. She'd tolerated that reasonably well when they were on the road in the old days, working their way up into the vaudeville houses, when he'd occasionally go for a roll with a girl singing novelty songs or the female half of a dancing act. She claimed she had no ambition for acting any more, that she was happy to stay home and let him make the money. He halfway wished she were the jealous kind, because as it stood he didn't think she cared much about him one way or the other. This afternoon's girl was an ambitious redhead who, oddly enough, didn't seem to want anything in particular, just a roll in the hay same as Tommy did. She was a wardrobe girl and certainly pretty enough for picture work, though her eyes were a shade of blue that was hard to photograph. When she got dressed and left he decided he might as well leave for the day. He'd hit a saloon on the way home and socialize a bit. He was half in the bag anyway.

EZRA'S TAKE FROM the candy store had been enough for a bottle, a pack of Luckies and a week's rent on a room, with fifteen dollars and a quarter left over. He would have liked to find a cheaper crib on Skid Row, but reckoned he was persona non grata there for killing the whore, whose name he hadn't ever caught. And so he'd found himself in one of the cheap hotels on Hill Street that catered to the show trade and other disreputable sorts. It was still nicer than any room he'd ever rented, and he thought he might stay a few more nights. He read a story in the *Times* about the candy store clerk, whose name had been Hiram, and was relieved to see that no connection was made therein to the killing of the whore. He then put his mind to the problem of finding Trudy and the kids. He'd looked in a city directory from 1915 and found his own name still listed at their old address, but when he got to the city library he found that in the 1916 edition there was no listing for him or for her at all. She must have gotten some sort of job, but her skills were so few that he couldn't imagine one that would help him find her. She might have found work as a laundress or a waitress, but there were thousands of those in the city. If he had more money he might hire a finder of lost persons, but he'd have to stick up an awful goddamn lot of candy stores to get that kind of kale.

The fellow in the room next door was making a lot of noise, yammering at the top of his lungs some kind of malarkey Ezra couldn't make out. He rapped on the wall and yelled for him to pipe down. The noise stopped and he relaxed, lying down on the bed with his hands behind his head, and he stared at the high ceiling. It was dirtier than it had ever occurred to Ezra that a ceiling could get, considering that no one normally put their grubby hands on one. But besides the usual nicotine stains there was something that had dripped down from the room above and left a permanent orange-brown mark shaped like a cloud, darker at its center than at the edges. There were cracks, too, traced by colonies of black mold that had grown and died and grown again over the years.

There was a knock at the front door. He got up and stood next to it, wary. He'd known a fellow in Ohio, a big genial man who owned a small dry goods store, who'd gone to answer his own front door and got cut in half with a twelve gauge loaded for bear. The killer had been the current husband of the victim's previous wife, and the exact motive never became public, though rumor had it the wife in question knew so many esoteric practices in the boudoir that the new husband went mad at the thought of her engaging in such acts with a man other than himself.

"Who the fuck is it?"

"Your neighbor," said a voice on the other side. "I was rehearsing a role. You haven't got any smokes, by chance?" He sounded like an Englishman, or maybe like someone trying to sound that way.

"Go fuck yourself."

"I've got most of a bottle of rye if you do."

He stared at the door. A little company would be all right, and a few drinks from someone else's bottle would be better. "Don't try anything queer," he said, reaching for the knob.

"Never in my life, my good man," said the man in the hallway, an older geezer than he sounded. He had a bottle in one hand and in the other two water glasses of the kind the hotel provided, one per room. Ezra wondered how the limey had obtained a second.

◆ ◆ ◆

BEATRICE HAD GOT home shortly after five in the evening and found Tommy unconscious on the couch, his saliva leaving a large, dark stain on the satin upholstery. She went into the kitchen and returned with an ewer of cold water, which she poured slowly onto his head. After a few seconds of this he sputtered, shook his head and looked up at her.

"What the hell, you crazy bitch?"

"You were drooling on the satin."

He looked down. "And you poured water on it."

"Water can be cleaned. Saliva lasts forever."

She turned her back on him and left the room. She didn't know whether that was true or not, but she'd had the last word. She returned the ewer to the kitchen counter and rang the tiny silver bell to summon Mildred.

"Yes, Mrs. Gill?" she said from her quarters. "I'm fixing to start supper."

"It won't be necessary this evening. Mr. Gill won't require a hot meal and I will be dining with friends."

Mildred stepped out of her room. "It's no trouble for me to fix him something."

"Mr. Gill is on his own for the evening. You may have it off, with pay. Go home and see your children."

"Yes, ma'am. All the same I'll put something on a plate and put it in the ice box."

"Don't."

"All right, then, Mrs. Gill. Thank you for the night off." She went back into her little room without a word. Beatrice wondered once again what ever might the woman be thinking. Apart from the spoken words of thanks she showed no sign of gratitude. She was a regular sphynx, that one.

DESPITE BEING AWAKENED with a splash, he was revitalized by his nap on the sofa. After a long shower and a quick snort he was ready for anything. "Bea?" he shouted down the stairs. "What's for supper?"

He supposed she was pretending not to hear, so he yelled louder. "You dizzy broad, answer me when I call for you. What's for supper?"

He limped down to the ground floor. The kitchen was dark. "Mildred? Where's the missus?"

When Mildred didn't answer either he rang the little silver bell, then knocked on her door. "Mildred! Open up." When she didn't he opened the door and found the room empty, curtains drawn and bed made. He was sure it wasn't her night off.

He opened the ice box, half expecting to find a plate with a cold meal and a note explaining the women's absence, but he found only the usual staples. Nor was there a note on the dining room table, where Beatrice habitually left them.

She's walked out on me, he thought. *After all I've done for her. This nice house, the servants, the clothes, the trips.*

Just for the evening, probably, there was hardly a chance she'd actually leave him and the comforts he provided. Still, it would be a good laugh if she came home to find the locks changed and her belongings on the front lawn. That would be a good joke for the neighbors too. He was looking for the directory so he could call in a locksmith when the idea came to him that he might as well go out on the town himself. That had been his intention that afternoon anyway, after Kaplan had tossed him off the studio grounds.

He had parked badly. There was a wooden crate full of light bulbs wedged between the fender of the 30-35 and the back wall of the garage, and when he shook it there was a sound between a tinkle and the sound of sand going down an hourglass. Beatrice had had the bright idea of buying everything in bulk, in order to save a buck and also to reduce the number of times per year she had to go out and get things. The storage room in the house had similar crates of toilet paper, mothballs, cartons of dry laundry soap, Bran-Eata biscuits, razor blades, bars of hand soap, tins of salmon and myriad other items, so many that it was deemed necessary to store certain items, like the light bulbs and motor oil, in the garage.

He backed out into the alley and headed for the street without bothering to close the garage door, or even thinking of it. He was headed for the Rathskeller on Beverly Boulevard, where he might find a few of his fellow comedians. Dinner and drink would also be on offer and women would be present and presumably available, though after his morning's diversion with the redhead he wasn't sure he needed any further stimulation of that sort. He had been trained as a child not to be greedy and to accept what good things came his way with good grace and gratitude.

14

Ezra was face down, he knew that much. As he roused himself he became aware that his tongue was on the splintery wooden floor and that his face and shirt were wet with drool. He also realized that he wasn't able either to get his eyes all the way open or to retract his tongue into its customary spot in his mouth. His head hurt in a way he couldn't remember it ever hurting before, dull but fierce pain stretching from behind his eyes to his temples and around to the back of his head. There was daylight in the room but he couldn't focus well enough to say whether it was morning or late afternoon. It took him a minute to turn himself over onto his side, and a considerable while to get into a sitting position with his feet sticking straight out in front of him. The front of his pants was wet with piss, but as far as he could tell he hadn't shat himself, which was a small blessing.

He rolled over and managed with some wobbling effort to get onto his knees, after which he was able to pull himself up onto the bed and then onto his feet. The table next to the window was bare, and he stood for a minute trying to think what should have been there.

My smokes. My motherfucking Luckies.

A quick search of the room revealed that his remaining half bottle of gin was also gone, as were the fifteen dollars and a quarter he'd had left. The gun he'd taken from the candy store was nowhere to be found.

That limey cocksucker slipped me a goddamned Mickey Finn.

He swung his fist at the wall and, fortunately, got dizzy and lost his balance before he could connect. He fell against it and heard a tiny crack, either a piece of plaster or board, and slid to his knees.

He made his way downstairs and leaned on the front desk. The lobby smelled of mold and the artichoke green wallpaper made everything in it look even darker. A woman of sixty or so sat in one of the armchairs by the window, chairs a fellow tenant had advised Ezra to avoid. "Every sort of human effluvium has been deposited there and left to fester," the man had said, and even without asking him what effluvium meant, he knew better than to sit in one. The woman was fast asleep, face pointed at the ceiling and mouth wide open. *Bet if I waited long enough I could see a little piece of plaster fall right down her throat*, he thought. The desk clerk ignored him with a calm, sadistic demeanor, placidly scanning the interior of the *Examiner*. He was about fifty, balding and skinny, and everything about him exuded contempt for the hotel and its clientele. He looked to Ezra like someone who had once occupied a higher rung in life and hadn't accepted the fact that he was now as much a denizen of the Crosley Hotel as any of its roomers.

"Say, who was the limey in the room next to mine yesterday?" He had pounded on it long and loud until it occurred to him to try the knob. It was unoccupied.

"How should I know what limey it was?" the man said without taking his eyes from the paper. "I don't know what room you're in."

"525."

"Your right or your left?"

Ezra thought. "Left."

"523, that's the one pretends he's an Englishman. He just paid up and checked out."

Ezra slammed his palm down hard on the counter. The clerk didn't flinch. He had on a pair of pince-nez and a fussy little mustache and he smiled a little, eyes still on the paper. "Son of a bitch robbed me. Came over for a smoke and a drink and slipped me a Mickey Finn. Woke up and my smokes and my booze and my money and my gun was all gone."

"Didn't your mama ever tell you not to trust strangers?"

"So what was the fella's name?"

The clerk opened up the big old registration book, which looked unpleasantly to Ezra like a booking log. "Let's see, for the last few weeks number 523 has been occupied by . . ." He ran his finger down the page and laughed out loud. "Junius Brutus Booth."

"Is that supposed to be funny?"

"In my book it is."

"You mean to tell me you let people check in here with phony names?"

"Buddy, I'm sure sorry for your bad luck but if you let the man into your room it's your own damn fault."

AFTER SUPPER BILL had headed off for a quick drink at the Flying Scotsman, accompanied by Henry. At their departure Mrs. Chen had made a great show of her disapproval, because she saw in Henry an innocent being led into a life of iniquity. Flavia wasn't happy either, for reasons less clear to Bill. Despite her late husband's dipso-maniac tendencies she wasn't a temperance advocate and was known to tipple a bit herself. It didn't occur to him that she might have liked to be included in the excursion but wouldn't stoop to inviting herself.

"You'll find it edifying," Bill told Henry on the walk over. "The clientele is a splendid collection of cautionary tales, and the proprietor and his wife might have sprung from the pages of Edgar Allan Poe."

Henry spoke after they'd walked a dozen blocks. "Miss Flavia doesn't seem to have much in the way of suitors."

"She doesn't like that 'Miss Flavia.'"

"I know. Sorry. Way I was raised up. Her being my boss. 'Flavia.'"

"In any case, the matter of suitors."

"Her being a nice-looking gal with a good job. Smart too."

Bill looked over at him, eyebrows raised. "I don't suppose you're thinking of pitching her any woo."

The boy was taken aback. "No, sir. I'm her employee. Or yours, whichever it is. Wouldn't be my place."

"Wouldn't bother me in the least. You're a hard worker and a quick study. But I've got no say in it anyway."

"No, sir."

"Goddamn it, I already told you not to do that."

"Bill."

"All right. There's something you should know before you proceed. She's a widow. That's one reason she objects to the title 'miss.'"

"Oh," Henry said, not seeming to give it too much weight one way or the other.

"The thing about it is the manner of her husband's decease."

BY THE TIME they got to the Scotsman Henry had gone quiet, and Bill almost wished he hadn't decided to have a little fun with him. He doubted that Flavia had any interest in the kid, but if anything were to start it would be good for the lad to know what he was getting into. In the sparsely attended bar, talk was of the presidential election.

Dr. Franklin "Shorty" McAllister, well into his cups, was holding forth about President Wilson's deficiencies as a politician and human being. "I suppose you're voting for the pointy-headed son of a bitch," McAllister said to Henry, who stood silent next to him.

"He's too young to vote," Bill said.

"That pinch-nose-spectacled bastard." The doctor propelled a good-sized hocker into the spittoon. Bill had introduced his personal physician to the Flying Scotsman not long before and was a trifle concerned at the man's current state of insobriety, but he didn't suppose his drinking habits had begun with his first visit there.

"You oughtn't to say things like that about the president," Henry said.

"I'd say he puts his trousers on one leg at a time same as me."

"I mean I think it's against the law."

A man standing on the other side of the doctor, and considerably drunker than he, poked at the air in front of him. "You tell him, kid. Little respect for the office."

Behind the rummy stood the actor, Feeney, who was in a cheery mood. "It's untrue, lad. In this great land we've every right to call people all sorts of names. Even the President of the United States."

"That sack of pigshit," McAllister said.

The night bartender looked unnerved. "Better knock it off, doc. I don't want any trouble."

Feeney knocked back the last of his beer and placed the glass back on the bar. "Gentlemen, normally I would bid you goodnight at this point in the evening. However, I recently completed a role in a motion picture and I am celebrating. A round for the house, landlord."

"Landlord's not here," the bartender said.

"It's an anglicism, lad. Just pour the drinks."

Bill's old drinking companion Lil stood at the end of the bar, or rather leaned on it, repeating the words *you son of a bitch* over and over. The bartender set up the drinks and sat back while Feeney went on about his day at the studio, about how he'd worked with the likes of Francis X. Bushman, Mabel Normand, Constance Talmadge and Blanche Sweet.

"All in the same picture?" Henry said.

"Certainly. Connie's a dear friend, she recommended me for the role, knew I'd suit it to a T."

Dr. McAllister regarded Feeney with disbelieving contempt. "That's one hell of a cast. Must be a big picture."

"Unfortunately I can say no more," Feeney said. "I gave Mr. Griffith my word . . ." He stopped speaking, and shuddered. "Dear me, my tongue is too much loosed by drink! Please forget everything I've said."

Henry leaned on the bar, quite pleased to have a

picture star amongst his new acquaintances. Imagine fat, red-faced old Feeney with his big white muttonchops, running around with the likes of Blanche Sweet!

"You son of a bitch," Lily said, addressing her glass.

FEENEY REGRETTED ROBBING the stranger but he was an artiste and it was vital he be able to eat, keep a roof over his head and maintain a healthy and prosperous appearance for auditions. He didn't regret checking out of the Crosley, where he had spent months in a miserable state, sneaking past the desk clerk when he was in arrears like a scoundrel in the lowest sort of one-reel comedy. The revolver, an old one, had only netted five dollars, but he now possessed upwards of eight, and in comparison with his recent penury that felt to him like a lot of money indeed. He didn't regret leaving Hill Street either, with its constant stink of desperation and failure, the constantly replenishing swarm of old hams and naïve youngsters come to Los Angeles to revitalize dead careers or create new ones. He'd run into an old love one night in the corridor outside his room and hadn't recognized her. Sukie Lufkin was her real name, but she was known on the stage as Maud LeClerc, her specialty playing women of class and breeding. By the time they'd met she had already progressed from playing debutantes to society matrons, but she was still a lovely and delicate creature, and many a leading man despaired of ever bedding her. And she'd chosen Feeney, an eccentric character player, as her paramour all those years ago!

"You don't know me, do you, sweet thing?" she'd said to him in the dismal gaslit hallway of the Crosley.

She was in a dressing gown of tattered and not particularly clean satin, featuring faded images of old Japan, and her face was puffed and discolored, her eyes baggy, and he was certain he'd never seen the woman before in his life. Still, the voice was reminiscent of someone's, as was the sobriquet *sweet thing* . . .

"It's me, Sukie, you nitwit," she said, and laughed loud, her mouth open wide enough to reveal a number of teeth broken or missing. "I see you ended up here same as me, trying to catch a break in the flickers."

"My God," he said, trying to make his astonishment sound like joy.

"Now I'm in the character business like you. Playing charwomen and fishwives. Can you picture me as the queen of France now?"

When they'd met she was playing Marie Antoinette, and Chester Arthur was president. "You'll never lose that regal carriage, my dear," he said.

"I'm widowed now, sweet thing. Did you know I'd married Curtis Danville? I met him playing his Lady Macbeth."

"I wept for a week after I heard," he said. Danville was known for his wide range of Shakespearian credits and for a tendency, which got worse with the passing years, to overact. His Lear was said to have been side-splitting.

"I've not remarried, in case you're wondering."

"Ah. Well, I'm certain an artist of his calibre is a hard act to follow. So to speak."

She placed a coquettish index finger on his sternum. "I don't plan to remarry, if that's what you're scared of."

He fled the scene with a muttered excuse, shamefully, and called out in his retreat that he'd look forward to their next meeting. That was when he started forming a plan to steal, if that was what it took, to get enough to leave the accursed Crosley.

HE DIDN'T EVEN have the goddamn hammer any more. How was he supposed to make a living? If he ever caught up to his neighbor he'd use his bare hands, but in the meantime he needed money and it was damned hard strongarming it without a real weapon.

The least he could do was start with another claw hammer. He walked around downtown for three hours before he found a hardware store. The day was hot enough for the overhead fan to be running, and it made a whispery sound as Ezra approached the service counter on the left-hand wall. Behind it was a sliding ladder to facilitate the retrieval of merchandise, which hung on the wall on hooks all the way up to the high windows. They were toward the rear of the store, and the overhead bulbs did a poor job of illuminating it. It was a good fifteen yards to the front of the store and its sunlit entryway.

The man behind the counter looked at him like he was some sort of insect who might need to be swatted. "Say, listen, mister, I know I don't look so good. I got robbed last night and the son of a . . . the fellow what did it took my tools. I'm a carpenter's helper. Now I got a job lined up this afternoon and all's I need is a claw hammer, the boss ain't going to be there so I got to bring my own. I got fifty cents, you got a hammer for that much?"

The sales clerk's expression softened. "I have one for forty-seven cents, as a matter of fact."

He took a hammer off of a rack on the wall and set it down on the glass counter in front of Ezra, who picked it up and hefted it in one hand and then the other. "Well, sir, I suppose that this one'll do me just fine." Then he bolted for the front of the store.

"Esteban!" the clerk yelled. "Thief!"

Ezra looked over his shoulder to see a very large man exit the stockroom and give chase. He should have kept running. The brief turn of head took his eye off the front door and freedom, and he bumped against a stack of paint cans, which crashed to the linoleum. He let loose an involuntary yowl of fear as he yanked at the door and, for an instant, it didn't budge. When he made it onto the sidewalk he sprinted, as nearly as he was capable, up the street. He was half a block away and certain he'd made good his escape when a stunning blow struck his back and he went down onto the clean, hot concrete. He looked up to see a giant standing over him, a good six and a half feet tall, with a full head of black hair, a Cossack's mustache and a pair of massive fists held in a threatening manner. Ezra swung the hammer at him. The man feinted, reached out and grabbed his forearm. He squeezed it until Ezra yelped and dropped the hammer on the sidewalk.

"I'd say it's your lucky day," Esteban said, picking up the hammer. "Mr. Theakston said not to hurt you. I ever catch you around here again, I surely will, though."

WHEN HE GOT back to the hotel the same clerk was on duty. "You best make sure you can pay your bill by noon or you're out of here," the fellow said. Adenoidal and high in pitch, something about his voice made Ezra think of a comic actor he'd seen onstage in a burleycue show once.

"Go fuck yourself, shorty."

"This isn't like some of the fleabags along here," the clerk said. He poked at the ledger three times. "Says here you paid for two weeks and they're up and I'll be damned if you get a night for free."

"This morning you was acting like you didn't know any of us from Adam."

"Well, sir, as soon as you walked out the door I checked on your account."

"Say, I don't see you harping on anybody else around here. What makes you think I won't pay and they will?"

"Cause you got robbed is why. You told me as much your own self."

"Robbed by one of your own tenants! For all I know the house was in on it, stealing from law-abiding customers. I by God ought to call the cops and tell 'em what kind of a gyp joint you're operating here."

A feline smirk formed slowly on the clerk's face. "Well, why don't you just do that? You won't even need a slug, I'll let you use the house phone."

Taking the stairs to his room, Ezra considered his options. His one advantage was that he had registered under the name Bobby Talbot, with whom he'd spent time in a New Buffalo, Michigan, cell, both of them locked up on burglary charges. Upon their release he'd declined to go along with his new friend's plan to hold up a Benton Harbor drugstore, a solid decision on his part as the effort had ended in gunfire and a pauper's funeral for Bobby.

There was nothing to recover in his room except for the rucksack containing his other shirt and trousers, and he picked it up and left.

15

There was no sitting scheduled for the afternoon, all print orders had been fulfilled and the darkroom was in fine order. Henry stuck his head into the parlor and listened for a minute without announcing his presence. He hadn't ever heard anyone who could play the piano like Flavia. Lots of people back home could play, and Mrs. Thorndyke at the church was good on the old pipe organ, and even his mother would take a turn at the neighbor's old, out-of-tune upright, but they played hymns and old chestnuts like "The Turkey in the Straw" and "Beautiful Dreamer," not the kinds of things Flavia did. Hers were lovely and complicated and they sounded like they were devilishly hard to play. The piece she was playing now was simple-sounding in comparison to what she usually did, but it was sublime nonetheless, and her playing seemed to him extraordinarily subtle.

When she was done he applauded, startling her. "Oh," she said. "I didn't know you were there."

"That was some really good playing. What was it?"

"A Polonaise."

"I don't know what that is."

"It's a dance. A little bit like a polka." She was still looking over her shoulder at him.

"How come you don't play for show?"

"I wouldn't dare."

"Really? I know a dozen people back home play the piano, and you're better than any of them."

"Oh, I'm not good enough to play professionally." She shut the lid to the keyboard and closed the sheet music, turned her face back to the wall.

"You could even play in church."

"That's very sweet."

"Darkroom's all set, just wondered if there's anything else needs doing."

"No, you can go ahead and take the rest of the afternoon off."

No employer had ever given him a paid afternoon off before. "All right, there's a Farnum Western I was wanting to see over at the Alhambra."

She turned on the piano bench to face him fully and crossed one leg over the other. "There's a Norma Talmadge at the Palace, if you'd rather see that."

He stood there for a moment, unsure why she'd think he'd want to see a Norma Talmadge instead of a William Farnum. Then he saw that she was a mite flushed and favoring him with a coquette's nearly imperceptible smile.

"If you'd care for some company, I mean," she said.

THAT NIGHT HENRY brought up the subject of church at the dinner table after Flavia had left the room. "My father was a minister and a hypocrite who hanged himself after he got caught messing with a parishioner. Soured me on the whole business," Bill said.

"He was a what?"

"He professed things he didn't believe."

"In God, you mean?"

"I couldn't say, but by the end I don't think he believed in the resurrection or the holy trinity or any of that. After he killed himself I turned atheist out of anger, I'll admit that, but after the anger dimmed I found I just couldn't make myself believe any of it again. Just didn't seem very likely to me."

"And people didn't look askew at you for staying home Sundays?"

"I didn't give a damn."

"Mrs. Chen gave me another pamphlet yesterday. I think she gave the same one to Flavia."

"She's a damned fine cook. If you don't want the pamphlets, tell her so."

"Don't want to hurt her feelings."

"Then don't tell her. Won't hurt to throw them out, discreetly. Long as she's not proselytizing the customers, I'm fine with her trying to save you and the girl."

"She doesn't try and save you?"

He shook his head. "She's got me sussed out."

OVER THE NEXT few days Henry gave it a lot of thought and finished by deciding that he was not on the lookout for a friendly church in Los Angeles after all. He was not prepared to admit this to his mother, however.

Ma,

Greetings from your son in sunny CAL. I am still working at the photographic studio and learning valuable new skills. The folks I work for say I am doing all right and seem content with my work. I have been attending services at Broadway Church of Christ a DOC church headed by Pastor Hutslar, a very fine fellow who preaches just like Pastor Dunwoodie back home nice and loud. I am looking to meet a nice Christian girl don't worry about those racy motion picture gals turning my head (ha ha). I do have one aquaintence who is in the pictures though. He is making a picture with Blanch Sweet and Mable Norman but he is a very nice moral fellow and assures me that the talk of actors and such being wicked characters is a lot of bunkum. I hope you will give the little ones and Pa my affectionate best wishes and inclosed is ten dollars. I will send more later.

Love your son,
Henry

He'd taken the name of the pastor and the church from the city directory, and he justified the deception with the thought that his mother would have been distraught at the idea that he was giving up church. But the idea that he never had to go back was thrilling to him. And he hadn't stopped believing, not exactly. He'd just given himself permission not to feel bad about skipping church. And no matter what Pastor Dunwoodie back home might have said, Henry felt certain that God forgave him.

THE LOOK OF shock on the landlady's face would have been comical if not for the disfigurement of her lower jaw. "Mrs. Broun, what happened to you?"

She spoke with difficulty, upper and lower jaws staying

clenched. "That husband of yours came a-looking for you and he didn't like that you'd gone."

"Oh." Trudy felt something tighten in her chest. "He hit you?"

Mrs. Broun nodded, eyes shut.

"I come by with the rent I owe from a while back, and an apology for skipping."

The old woman's eyes opened wide. "I don't blame you for none of it."

Trudy handed her an envelope with a twenty and a ten inside. "I hope you called the police on him."

"Made a report and everything." She tucked the envelope into her apron. "Things going all right for you and the tots? Better, anyway?"

"Yes, ma'am. Things are coming out all right."

"Good. I hope they catch that son of a bitch before he catches up to you."

On the streetcar ride home she consoled herself with the thought that Big Ezra was a dumb bastard and the odds of him finding his own cock in a dark room were slim indeed.

BUT IT ATE at her all through supper, and once she got the kids to bed she got the jar of medicine from its hiding spot. It was running low, though she'd been using it less than usual the past few weeks, the money coming in having done a great deal to salve her jangly nerves. She was developing friendships, too, with the Buntnagels and also with Victoria, with whom she'd made another picture. In that one they took turns sucking and fucking a newsboy and then the boy was getting blown by Trudy while

Victoria licked Trudy and the whole thing had been fun, of a sort. Irene had sat watching while George directed, and even poor sidelined Grady had seemed to enjoy himself. The reedy, redhaired fellow who played the newsboy thought himself pretty lucky.

"Got my dick sucked, fucked two girls and got paid five bucks for my trouble! Holy shit, if this ain't the greatest country in the world."

Irene had paid him with a bill from her own pocketbook, having cautioned Trudy and Victoria not to let on how much they were making, lest he decide he was worth more.

"You see, most men would do this for free. So we could replace him on a moment's notice, but he's got a nice camera presence."

"You mean he's got a cock like a horse's," Victoria said.

"That's what I meant, yes," Irene said.

TONIGHT, THOUGH, THE thought of Ezra's possible return had made her yearn for a little chemically induced peace. She mixed it into her Fox's U-Bet to hide the taste, and shortly she was experiencing an ecstatic sort of reverie, a certainty that Ezra would never find her, that she'd stumbled into something wonderful whose existence she'd never suspected, and she was consumed then with a certainty that she would in fact reciprocate Victoria's oral ministrations. On camera or off, it didn't matter. What a wonderful selfless person Victoria was! How unlike anyone else she'd ever been to bed with. Her eyes were closed, and her hand began to stray downward, but before it reached its destination a voice aroused her.

"Mama, Ezra's wet the bed again."

She opened her eyes and found her little girl standing there in her nightdress.

"That's all right, sugar," Trudy said.

"I can't sleep because the sheets are wet."

"Then you can sleep in Mama's bed tonight." Her eyes were closed.

"What about Ezra?"

"Is he awake?"

"No."

"Then let him sleep. He'll be fine."

BILL STOPPED IN at the Flying Scotsman at seven-thirty in the evening. He was alone, Henry having declined his invitation in favor of staying in and reading, which, Bill noted, had earned the lad a furtive smile from Flavia. Mrs. Chen had retired to her room already, so perhaps it was best to let matters take their course.

"Evening, Feeney," Bill said. He laid his *Evening Herald* down on the bar and nodded at Feeney, who was staring into his habitual bourbon and soda, and the actor said nothing. Bill tapped at the front page. "Been reading about the fellow Barrett, killed his wife and stepson and claims he was hypnotized. 'Brain-clouded,' it says. What you think of that?"

Feeney took his drink in hand and took a vigorous swig rather than his customary sip. "Friend, I have lost several acquaintances and one former sweetheart." He nodded at the paper. "You read the lead story?"

"That hotel fire? Skimmed it."

"The Crosley. Well-known among show-folk as a

welcoming establishment, friendly to those of us in the worlds of theater and pictures. I lived there until just a few days ago, when some vague whim for which I can't account caused me to pack up and move."

"Now there's a lucky break."

"Not so for some of my boon companions. Of the eleven dead, four were friends of mine, including Maud LeClerc, the leading lady. I once called her my sweetheart. I'm sure you've heard the name."

"I do recall the name. Seems to me I saw her onstage in San Francisco, late nineties. Playing Salomé, a mite too long in the tooth for it but not bad overall." He picked up the paper and returned his attention to the front page. "Says here it looks like arson. 'Fire Chief A. J. Eley tells the *Herald* the firebug, when captured, will surely be charged with no fewer than eleven counts of murder in the first degree.' It also says the Crosley advertises itself as fireproof. Guess that shows you have to take some things with a grain of salt."

Feeney finished his bourbon and called for another. It was the fastest Bill had ever seen him drink.

"How's that picture of yours coming along?"

"Oh, swimmingly." He didn't seem very interested in pursuing the subject, so Bill went back to Barrett, the murderous hypnotist.

The bartender poured Feeney another drink.

16

Grady hadn't ever seen such a thing before. He'd slept with plenty of women, and watched plenty of sex—he'd been arrested twice in his native Akron, Ohio, for window-peeping—but he'd never laid eyes on a fellow putting his mouth on another fellow's tallywacker. And here these two were going at it like it was the most natural thing in the world. And the Buntnagels just watching the whole business, as clinical and disinterested as though they were filming a bicycle race or a dog show.

The production had started off late in the afternoon with a truck from Murphy & Duckworth Theatrical Supply delivering backdrops and furniture. "You sure we need all this?" he'd asked George. "I got chairs and a davenport and a bed and some painted backdrops, you seen 'em in the last picture."

"Those won't do for this picture. We're aiming for something approaching a studio level of verisimilitude, and what you've got stored here is more fit for a seaside tintype maker. No offense meant, of course."

"But what it's costing . . ."

"Irene and I are covering the cost, remember?"

Then the truck arrived with the equipment from the studio, half a dozen men carrying it up and unloading it, the same half dozen who'd be back before dawn to pack it up and sneak it back into the lot. And then the tuxedos showed up. Grady didn't even want to think about the expense involved.

By the time they were set up and ready to go the two young men were in their tuxedos, for which—Grady had learned—Buntnagel had had them fitted. The tuxes, he explained, were part of the salary. "I happened to know that neither of them owned any proper formalwear, and they travel in the sort of circles where such a thing is sometimes called for."

"How do you mean?" Grady had asked.

"Debutante balls, society weddings, et cetera. They're well-bred but end up spending a lot of money on tuxedo rentals. These are second-hand, I know a fellow who made me a special deal."

Grady shook his head. The set was a gentleman's library, with a big stuffed chair and divan and a giant globe, and he had to admit it was going to look pretty swell on the screen. The scenario was perfectly simple— one fellow claimed he had the biggest dick in high society, and the other told him to prove it. The intertitle:

—Say, that's not so big, Hubert.
—Give it a rub and I'll show you.

Before long they had proceeded from a hand job to cocksucking in just three camera setups—Grady had to admit that as a director George knew what he was doing—and then they broke for a minute to discuss the choreography of what George referred to as "the evening's main event." He seemed quite familiar with the business involved.

For the first time Grady was feeling a little uncomfortable with the stag film business, and he allowed as much to Irene between takes of the main event. "Don't be silly, Grady," she said. "You don't get to pretend you're a prude after all the things you've photographed."

They were standing in a corner, out of earshot of the cast and crew. "Say, Irene, it's none of my business, but it seems to me your husband's pretty well-informed on the mechanics of . . ." He stopped, in a vain search for a way to say it to a lady, then gestured toward George, in huddled conference with the tuxedoed, brilliantined youths.

"Anal sodomy?" she said.

"Well, I reckon that's one way of putting it."

"You're only just now figuring this out?" she said, a gentle smirk on her face.

He was starting to, but he didn't know if he ever really would. These were stranger people than he'd ever dealt with.

EZRA WAS FLAT busted, without even the price of a flop, and he was damned if he was going to panhandle. Having hopped a couple of streetcars without paying he'd ended up in Pasadena, where he wandered around downtown as inconspicuously as he could until he saw a limping man in a wool suit and straw boater disappear into an alley. His only weapon was his own razor, which he had heretofore avoided using as a weapon because of a deep-seated fear that, having tasted human blood, it would no longer be safe to use for a shave. With luck he wouldn't need to use it, just threaten the gimp with it.

The limping man stopped halfway down the alley and

turned to look at Ezra, then turned back around and continued on his way. He was old, with a crooked yam of a nose and a look of disapproval on his face which made Ezra want to slit his throat.

"Excuse me, sir," Ezra said.

"I carry no cash," the man yelled, waving him off without a glance backward.

"What makes you think I want a handout? I'm no bum." He could feel his face getting hot.

Now the man turned, mouth pinched nearly to a single point, and he hurried. Ezra increased his stride and in a few paces had caught up to him. "Listen here, pal, I want your billfold and your watch." He opened the razor and brandished it inches from the man's throat.

"Murder!" The man had a loud, strong voice, a lot louder than Ezra would have guessed, and despite his bum leg managed a decent attempt at a run.

"Stop, goddamn you!"

"Help! He's going to kill me!"

"Shut your hole, I ain't gonna kill you long as you give me your billfold."

He had nearly pulled abreast of the man when, at the other end of the alley, stepped a pair of boys, twelve or thirteen by the looks of them. One of them yelled down the street. "Someone's fixing to kill Mr. Marsden!"

He dropped the razor and ran in the other direction. At the mouth of the alley he collided with a stout woman carrying a paper bag full of figs, which exploded onto the sidewalk as they both hit the ground. Ezra managed to arise, but as he was castigating the woman for being a stupid cow he stepped on one of the figs, crushing it into a slimy mass that sent his shoe flying skyward and his ass back onto the sidewalk. Now a crowd started to gather, just as the old man and the two boys stepped into the cool evening light out of the alley. "Hold that man down! He tried to kill old Mr. Marsden!" one of the boys yelled, and from behind him Ezra heard a policeman's whistle. Someone laughed.

"Did you see that geezer tumble? Ought to be in the pictures."

17

They were in a tea parlor, dressed like smart house-wives in fashionable bonnets, eating lemon pastries and sipping coffee from china cups, poured from a silver pot. "Well, that's it. I'm sure about it now."

"What the hell, Trudy. Who did it?"

"How should I know? The redheaded kid? Or one of those two sissies, when we did the orgy scene. Maybe the bohunk played the plumber."

"Well, how'd it happen?" Victoria said.

Trudy glared. "Is that supposed to be funny?"

"No. I just meant ain't you been douching after? Or using some kind of cream?"

Trudy shook her head. "I guess I never used to do it where I wasn't more or less planning on the possibility of a kid."

"How about when you were on the street?"

"That wasn't long. Maybe six weeks before I took Grady upstairs and he asked me if I didn't want to make dirty pictures."

"And you weren't using any kind of . . ." She held her tongue as the waitress passed behind them. "Hygiene devices back then?"

Trudy shook her head. "Just got lucky, I guess. I hadn't even ever done it before, except with Ezra."

Victoria shook her head. "Before you got married, you never did it?"

"Nuh-uh. Not even a kiss with my mouth open."

"Don't that beat all. I'll tell you what, though, Trude, you ended up pretty good at it."

"What's that supposed to mean?"

"Nothing. Just, you seem to have gotten to like it lately. More than at first, anyway."

This wasn't strictly true. With her male counterparts it was strictly mechanical, nothing more or less exciting to her than it had been with Ezra. With Victoria it was different. She'd been fighting the urge to suggest that they try it sometime when they were alone and out of the lens's reach.

"So what you want to do about it?"

"What do you mean?"

"I mean you want it took care of?"

She understood then the reason she'd decided to confide in Victoria. "Yeah. You know how to get it done?"

"I know a lady dentist in Echo Park, she's just about good as a doctor. I'll set it up for you."

TWO DAYS LATER they were finishing a picture about a bride who sleeps with the maid of honor, the bridesmaids and her groom's sister. Between takes an elderly gent was taking stills with a stereoscopic camera. The idea, Irene said, was to maximize the amount of material stemming from each production, and the girls were to receive a portion of the proceeds. The first batch of movies had done well—not by the standards of regular motion pictures sent out to motion picture theaters, but they were smashes in the world of lodges and bachelor parties and brothels. "Mr. Ogden here has been taking dirty pictures for a long time, haven't you?"

"I believe I took my first dirty stereo pictures in 1872 or three, Mrs. Buntnagel, a long while before anyone else present was alive," the old gentleman answered.

Trudy stood there in a rather nice wedding gown, the veil hiding her features in a way that the photographer assured her some would find provocative. "Now, if you'll just hike the skirt up the way you did when the groom took you leaning against the armoire . . ."

"All the way up so's you can see some hair?"

"Let's do one just above the tops of your white stockings, and then we'll do another where we see it all. You'd be surprised how many fellows prefer the more modest sort of obscenity."

They moved on to a scene between Trudy and Victoria, the latter dressed as a bridesmaid, and when it was done the photographer had them recreate it. "You're quite flushed, miss," he said.

"Oh."

"Now if you'll move your hand slightly to the right so the camera can see your friend's nipple as you squeeze it, I'll have a nice stereoscopic effect."

She felt her face flush harder than before as she followed his instruction. He was a genial old bird, though, and there was no mockery in him. He had long white sideburns and a mustache that curled down alongside the corners of his mouth and he seemed perfectly at ease with the proceedings. His young assistant, on the other hand, was flushed and seemed robbed of the capacity of speech.

"So we'll be able to look at these in a stereoscope and see it like real life?" Victoria asked.

"Yes, miss, in three dimensions."

"My ma's got a stereoscope in her parlor. Used to anyway."

"Doubt she'll want to see these."

Victoria let out a laugh, a loud one as always. People said the laugh didn't suit her, but she was born to it and nothing was to be done. "Nah, most likely not. She was keen on pictures of the Holy Land and Jesus and like that."

"You wonder how they got old Jesus to pose for those pictures," the old man said, and Victoria laughed harder.

THE BOY WAS silent at the wheel of the van on the way back to the studio. It was late afternoon and he was zigzagging in a vain effort to avoid the road apples that dotted the bricks on the wake of the horse-drawn buggies, outnumbered now by motorized vehicles but stubbornly refusing to pass from the scene. "You're uncharacteristically without a running commentary," Bill said. "Am I to assume the afternoon's work wasn't to your liking?"

"I don't know what to make of that back there." Still new to driving, Henry kept his eyes carefully on the road, and he kept his speed at a cautious and steady twenty-five miles per hour, whereas other drivers raced past at thirty-five or dawdled at a timid ten or twelve, soliciting angry honking and vocal derision from more daring motorists.

"They were making a dirty moving picture." Bill let his arm dangle out the passenger side window and waggled his fingers at a matronly lady standing on the sidewalk next to a pair of perfectly coiffed Pekingese. She gave him a surprised, friendly smile in return.

"I know that. What were we doing there?"

"We were photographing the proceedings in full stereoscopic glory."

"I mean why would you accept a job like that?"

"Apart from the money, because it sounded like an amusing and edifying way to spend the afternoon. Mrs. Buntnagel approached me . . ."

"Mrs. Who?"

"The tall woman in the hat, the one who remained fully clothed. She knew I had a good stereo rig, and she also knew I'd taken such pictures in the past."

The boy shook his head. "About that . . . people were really making dirty pictures way back then?"

"I was a photographer on the wild frontier, my lad. You took work where you found it. And I didn't mind it. You met some interesting people in those trades." They slowed at the intersection of Sunset and Vermont as a trolley passed. Henry didn't like coming to a complete stop for fear of stalling, though this had only happened to him once. A gaggle of assorted pedestrians crossed in front of them and Henry wended his way slowly through them, occasioning resentful stares and a cry of "Go get yourself fucked" from an elderly man carrying a scrawny, half-feathered bantam rooster, which squawked as the van crept past.

"And how did this Mrs. So-and-So know about that?"

"We're old chums. She works at West Coast Art Company down the street."

"I don't know, I just wish I hadn't been a part of it."

"I needed an assistant, and I couldn't very well ask my granddaughter to help, could I?"

Henry's driving gloves squeaked as he tightened them on the wheel. "What are you going to tell her about it?"

"She'll figure it out in the darkroom."

"You're going to have her work on that filth?"

"Filth?" He let out a snort. "I didn't get half of what they were up to. Couldn't have if I'd wanted too, emulsion's too slow. Anyway, part of her job is managing the darkroom. I've had my fill of that for a lifetime."

"Ain't right."

"How you figure that?"

"Well, she's a woman. A decent lady."

"She's no babe in the woods. She was married back in Kansas, remember."

Henry took his eyes off the road for a moment and stared at the old man. They came close to sideswiping a Lippard-Stewart delivery truck with INNES SHOE COMPANY marked on the side panel, and its klaxon sounded three times in quick succession.

"Watch the goddamned road, that van's a lot more expensive than this one is."

Henry returned his gaze to the street ahead. "How'd her husband die, anyhow? Accident or sickness?"

"He was no good, so she brained him with a baseball bat."

"That's not funny."

"Isn't meant to be. He was a rotten son of a bitch, came

home drunk one night and got a little fresh with her, he took out a gun and she knocked him into the company of the great majority of souls."

Henry grew quiet. He'd been wrestling with it for months, but now he was certain of it: he was in love with Flavia.

FEENEY WAS IN his room at the Belltower Arms, a hotel marginally more genteel than the Crosley had been, watching the early evening passersby on the sidewalk below and contemplating his remarkable good fortune at having vacated his room at the latter establishment. Most of his floor had been gutted, and though he couldn't be certain of his missed appointment with the Angel of Death, the timing of it seemed more than coincidental. Pity about poor Sukie, but he had to admit it had been a bit of a relief to hear that she hadn't escaped the building alive to give him chase once again. That morning he had bought a new jacket, two pair of pants and some fresh celluloid collars, and he hoped to begin making the rounds at the studios once again in a day or two. His luck had changed since he'd robbed the poor moron back at the Crosley, and he was going to make everything he possibly could out of it.

"SHE'S A CROSS old pill but she knows what she's doing. She helped me out once and a couple other girls I know."

It was seven in the evening. Arm in arm, Trudy and Victoria approached a building with a tobacconist's on the ground floor and offices above, all the windows dark except for two at the end. A sign on the main entryway read:

DR. GRETEL ALBRECHT

CREDIT DENTIST

THIRD FLOOR

"That's her. Don't worry, she might as well be a doctor."

They climbed the stairs in silence, and at the end of the third-floor hallway a light shone through the pebbled glass of a door, also painted in gold leaf with the name of Dr. Albrecht. Victoria knocked three, one, two and they waited. The sound of wheezing accompanied those of heavy footsteps on a wooden floor, and presently the door opened to reveal a stern woman, much thinner than the footfalls had suggested, wearing pince-nez glasses and a white smock. Her expression was blank except for thin eyebrows that arched upward.

"Office hours are ten to five." Her accent sounded German.

Victoria spoke. "Mrs. Zondervan sent us in regards to an extraction."

Dr. Albrecht looked Victoria up and down and gave a short nod. "I remember you. No need for that. Come in." She turned and walked down a hallway and entered a room on the right. "Close the door behind you and bolt it."

18

Tommy knew he was as good as Chaplin, better, even. He'd seen him onstage more than once, the first time with Karno. Good as Arbuckle, too, and those were the only two he even considered his rivals. If he hadn't yet achieved their level of fame or financial success that was the fault of Provident Studios, which hadn't put him in the kind of vehicle that would really showcase what he could do. And the writers and directors they assigned him were as hapless a lot as he'd seen, without a gag among them that hadn't been done better onstage or in other movies. The director Buntnagel in particular was a pain in his ass. He'd been making his disdain known in myriad ways for the last six months or a year, and he'd heard a rumor that the man had tried to refuse to direct any more of Tommy's pictures, which the boss had scotched.

Fine with me, he thought. *I ought to direct my own, that'll be in my next contract for sure.*

Today's mess was set in a shoe store. Various customers were to come in and try on shoes, with various mishaps, both plotted and improvised, providing the laughs, if any were to be had. The basic premise was stolen from, among other sources, an old vaudeville bit by a forgotten comic by the name of Hiram O'Brady, whose career had ended with him falling drunk out of a moving train. His carcass wasn't found until a couple of days later, half-eaten by coyotes and turkey buzzards. Tommy had been on the bill the night they realized Hiram hadn't shown, and he'd been taken aback at the callousness of his fellow performers, who had seemed friendly with the man.

"Hiram's a sot, kid," the female half of a brother-sister dance act had told him. "The more shows he misses the further down the ranks he goes. You can't get too worked up about it because you can't stop it, see?" And yet a day or two later when word came about Hiram's sacrifice to the scavenger class, the woman cried for a good ten minutes, which further mystified Tommy.

Anyway, here was Tommy trying to make something out of Hiram's shoe salesman routine. "Say, George," he called out to Buntnagel when the latter passed his makeup chair. The director stopped and stared at him, expressionless. "Here's the thing, old Hiram used to be the one buying the shoes."

"Who?"

"Hiram O'Brady. This is an old bit of his. The salesman was the straight man, see, and I've got a notion I could be the customer instead."

"I don't know who Hiram O'Brady is, and we're not borrowing anyone's act. This came from our boys, and anyway if you're the only customer there's not enough for a two-reeler."

Tommy spat on the floor. "Horseshit if you say you're not stealing from old Hiram."

"Got no time to argue. How drunk are you, anyway?"

"I resent that." He'd barely gotten into it, just a little pick-me-up to calm him down before the shoot.

Buntnagel didn't even bother to reply, just went down the hallway to the set.

AT IRENE'S INSISTENCE George had agreed to allow the tots to accompany him to the studio. She'd been bringing them to West Coast Art Company the last couple of days, and the ladies there had cooed over them and teased Irene about when she and her handsome husband were going to have some of their own, but today was set to be a busy day with a lot of running around from department to department, and besides, she'd said, think of the fun the children would have watching a picture getting made. As it happened Mrs. Bochner from the secretarial pool was available to watch them and since Kaplan wasn't there that day—he would have been apoplectic at the notion of company time going to babysitting—the kids had come to the studio with their Uncle Georgie, as Irene had them calling him.

He didn't mind it much, in fact found that he rather liked them. They watched in courteous silence as he ordered the crew around, getting the set ready for shooting. "Do you kids know who Tommy Gill is?"

"No," the girl answered.

"Good," he said.

GILL WAS HALF-CROCKED, of course, and after an hour of take after unusable take with the ethereal, ectomorphic Olive Dreyden trying on a pair of enormous clodhopper boots, George told everyone to take ten.

The cameraman was a young hotshot named Travis who wanted to be a director instead, and he pulled George aside. "We're not going to get anything out of him like this. We've got to get Olive to do something to him instead of the other way around."

He considered it and beckoned Olive. "I want you to give him the goo-goo eye and then no matter how he reacts I want you to slap the hell out of him. Hard as you can." Olive, a veteran of the stage who detested unprofessional behavior, was delighted at the prospect. "And hit him so's he falls to his right. If we're lucky we'll see his face."

On the next take, Olive batted her eyes at Tommy, who, unprepared and unable to react in the moment, just sat there looking surprised. His costar rose to her feet and swung her purse straight at the left side of his head, knocking him onto the floor with a loud cry of protest. "Jesus Christ, she slugged me!"

The crew laughed as loud as any audience, Travis cranking and giggling at the same time, and Tommy got up and stormed off the set, his gait unsteady in retreat.

"Now that's the stuff right there. What you have in that bag of yours, anyway?"

Olive beamed with pride as she extracted a two-pound sashweight from her purse. "It was a pleasure cracking that son of a bitch upside the head."

A stagehand had been sent to negotiate Tommy's return to the set. It was established that Miss Dreyden was not to be on the premises, which was fine because her scene was done. George considered the next situation, in which an elderly man was to be made a fool by Tommy. But what was funny was seeing Tommy have to eat shit, and the scenario as plotted out had Tommy getting the upper hand. He knelt down and called Mrs. Bochner over with the children.

"Kids, have you been having fun watching the shooting so far?"

"It was funny when the lady hit the fellow on the head," the girl said.

"It was, wasn't it? Now how would you like to do that yourself?"

"Hit him with a bag?"

"Something like that. So what do you say, you want to be in a moving picture?"

"I DON'T WORK with kids or animals," Tommy said as the scene was sketched out for him, unaware that the version he was getting differed from the one George had given the children.

"Listen here, you soak. You've got me behind half a day already and there's not one soul on this set who won't tell Kaplan it's your doing. I intend to get this one in on time if it means I have to replace you with some old juicer straight out of the gutter who'll at least do as he's told."

Tommy, who'd tossed a few back during his walkout, was sufficiently cowed to agree to a scene in which a mother, played in a pinch by Mrs. Bochner, brought her children in for a fitting. The camera rolled and Tommy, already seated as he was having trouble with his balance, greeted the mother and invited her to seat her tots across from him. He held the Ritz stick up and prepared to measure the little girl's feet, and his astonishment when the girl took the measuring stick unexpectedly from his hand quickly turned to a drunkard's apoplectic fury.

"That's not what you're supposed to do, you little bitch!" He swiped at the stick to retrieve it, but his reflexes were no match for those of the little girl, who had been told to laugh at whatever the man said, even if he seemed cross with her. The entire crew was in stitches, and so was Mrs. Bochner. The little boy watched the scene with curiosity, awaiting his cue.

The girl kept the Ritz stick just out of Tommy's reach, and she seemed to have a natural understanding of where to hold it in order to keep Tommy's face in camera range. George couldn't have been more pleased, and when the action seemed to have gone on long enough and when Tommy was in just the right position he called out, "Now, Ezra!"

And little Ezra, all of four years old, marched right up to Tommy and punched him right in the balls, though from the camera's point of view he might have hit him in the belly. Tommy went down to his knees, howling.

Now little Pearl descended upon Tommy, whaling on his skull with the Ritz stick until George, breathless with laughter, told her to stop and then yelled cut.

"Are the whole lot of you out of your fucking minds?" Tommy moaned, rising to his knees.

"Your language, Mr. Gill!" Mrs. Bochner said, shielding young Ezra's ears. "There are small children present."

"Those vicious little bastards, that's what you call children?"

Pearl looked up at George, concerned. "Wasn't we supposed to do that?"

"Of course you were. He's just pretending to be sore. He's a famous comedian, you see, and he's being funny."

"I don't have to put up with this shit. I'm the star of this picture." Mrs. Bochner was still covering Ezra's ears.

George looked over at Travis, who smirked back at him. "Don't be too sure of that."

"Nuts to the whole bunch of you," Tommy said, rising with difficulty to his knees and then to his feet. "I'm done for the day."

Travis looked at George again and shrugged. When Tommy had staggered out of earshot he spoke. "Seems to me we've got all the Tommy we need for today. We've got Chester Hotchkiss and Marie Dolenz on deck, right? Let's play the kids against them."

George nodded, feeling better about the picture than he'd felt about any Provident production in a very long time.

19

They were alone in the parlor and she had just finished playing an absurdly difficult étude by Liszt. Flavia was dissatisfied with her progress on the piece and annoyed at how taken Henry was by her playing. "If you don't know the notes that's one thing, but can't you hear how I keep slowing the tempo every time I get to one of the harder passages?"

"Well, I guess that's how you learn to play the rough parts, slowed down, isn't that so?"

He wasn't wrong about that, which grated even more. She closed the keyboard lid, turned to him and made herself smile. Through the window the afternoon sun was getting low, and she went over to the davenport and sat next to him.

"So I suppose you developed those pictures," he said.

"Which pictures? I develop a lot of them." She couldn't help teasing him. Her grandfather had let her know about Henry's horror at the thought of her seeing the dirty stereographs, and she thought it sweet.

"The ones your granddad and I, I mean your granddad did, I was there but I didn't operate the camera." Her eyebrows raised, awaiting more detail. "The ones from the movie shoot, the, the . . ." His face was red now, and she took pity.

"The dirty pictures, you mean."

"I sure wish he hadn't let you see those. I would have developed them myself."

"It's my job. You're still an assistant."

"But they're dirty."

"I've seen dirty pictures before, Henry."

"How?"

"Gramps used to have a whole stash, I found them going through his files one summer when I went to visit him and his wife up in San Francisco. Pictures he took in brothels." Henry looked at his feet and she chucked him under the chin. "That's not to say I got a charge out of looking at them. It was a strange thing to discover about your grandfather. But he explained to me that those pictures were for lonely fellows without any outlets for their urges."

His face was even redder. "Urges."

"And I didn't just fall off the turnip truck either. I was married back in Kansas."

He looked up at her. "That's what your granddad said." She had the impression he'd been hoping that was a joke on the old man's part.

"He tell you how I got out of it?"

Henry nodded.

"Well that's true too. He was a rotten son of a bitch and I'm not glad I did it but I'm not sorry either."

Her use of the word shocked him, but something told her he liked it.

"Haven't heard a lady curse before?"

"Just two. One was touched in the head back home and she walked around town cussing something awful. The other's a customer at that saloon."

"Well just so you understand, I don't do it in front of just anyone."

"HOW WILL YOU get home, Bill?"

"Streetcar, I suppose. Maybe a taxi cab." Her bed was bigger than some rented rooms he'd occupied over his life. The walls were covered with French paintings, the blurry but colorful sort, and the ceiling a good fifteen feet from the floor and carved with detailed filigree that must have taken a master woodcarver months to finish.

"Didn't you tell me you'd bought an auto for the business?"

He was pulling on his boots, and he felt a twinge in his back. "I don't know how to drive it."

"Why on earth did you buy it then?"

"The lad who works for me drives it."

"Seems to me if you own it you ought to learn to operate it." She was sitting on her bed in her nightclothes, her feet dangling over the carpet. Her long, dark hair was undone and came down past her waist, and she was twirling a long strand of it in her right hand.

Her house was in one of the nicer parts of Pasadena. It was Tuesday and her servants were off, and her husband, as always, would be at his insurance office until six or seven in the evening.

"I suppose I'll see you in a week," he said.

"I expect so. Listen, why don't you have the young man drop you off and pick you up next time? He could amuse himself downtown in the meantime." They allowed themselves only a couple of hours per assignation, with the understanding that if any neighbor happened to notice

his arrivals and departures, the distinguished old gentleman would be identified as her French tutor. No one
had ever remarked on it, though; apparently the notion
that a distinguished society woman of forty-seven would
be cavorting in bed with a man well into his seventies
didn't occur to them, or maybe no one had noticed him.
Perhaps they didn't even care.

"And what would I tell him I'm doing here?"

"Why tell him anything? Is he a servant or no?"

Bill resisted the temptation to lecture her and shook his
head. "He's an inquisitive lad."

"Tell him the truth then. Why not? He doesn't know
anyone I do. Who's he going to tell?"

"I've shocked the boy enough recently. I had him assist
me taking some pictures at a dirty movie shoot and he
was scandalized."

"A dirty movie!"

"Would you like me to describe it?"

"Next time, dear, yes. Beforehand."

"He's sweet on my granddaughter, that's another thing."

"So you mentioned."

"I scandalized him with the story of her widowhood
the other day. I fear he may desert us if his notion of us
is sullied any further." He brushed off his coatsleeve. "I'll
see myself out, then. Until next week."

KAPLAN SAT AT his desk with his head in his hands
and his elbows on the blotter. "You didn't get the kids' parents' permission? That's what you're telling me?"

"I didn't think of it until later," George said, still
standing. Irene was there with him. Kaplan liked her and

sometimes he'd listen to her when he wouldn't George, so she'd come along to advocate for the kids.

He raised his head and looked straight at Irene. "I can't argue with the end result. That's the funniest picture we've put out in months if not years. Shit, what are we going to do about this?"

"I'm certain their mother will sign, but you're going to have to do better than a standard contract," Irene said. "She's quite shrewd."

"Here's the thing, though. I find myself wondering if I find it especially funny because I can't stand Tommy and I just enjoyed seeing him get a real kick in the pants."

"Sure," George said, "but I'm pretty sure our audiences feel the same way about him. Think about the poll they ran in *Screen Stars*, the fifteen funniest screen comics."

"I don't read that kind of shit," Kaplan said. "I'm slightly appalled that you do."

"You know where Tommy came in?"

"Enlighten me."

"He didn't. So Irene called up a pal of hers at the magazine and asked about it."

"Tommy was number twenty-one, just behind Harry Gribbon and just ahead of Clyde Cook," she said. "Three years ago he was number fourteen. I have a sneaking suspicion that the public is ready to see him taken down a peg."

Kaplan snipped the end of a cigar and lit it. "If you look at it one way we're doing him a kindness. This could mean a whole new direction for his career, instead of straight into the shitter."

Irene sat on the corner of the desk. "About that contract."

"The standard starting contract is quite generous."

"She'll never go for it. And word's already out from the day players that these kids are a real find. She could take them over to Keystone or just about anywhere."

He took in a lungful and exhaled it slowly, looking crosseyed at the cigar in front of his face. "I'm a gambler at heart, Irene."

ON THE STREETCAR home from Pasadena, Bill sat next to a handsome woman wearing spectacles, a basket full of vegetables at her feet. After a while she turned to him and spoke. "You hurting, mister?"

"What makes you say that?"

"You keep wincing."

He hadn't been aware of it. "I pulled a muscle in my back."

She looked him up and down, mouth pinched tight. "You look like a man's been up to some mischief."

"How's that?"

"You have a look I recognize. A cheat."

"I beg your pardon."

"I can smell her eau de cologne on you. And I'll bet she's married, too, isn't she?"

He turned away and looked out the window. He didn't wish to engage her any further. But he was curious as to what had made her judge him thusly. Surely he didn't smell any more of Matilda's perfumerie than any other man who'd embraced a woman, nor was hers any stronger than any respectable woman of her social status wore. Finally he spoke. "And what makes you think the woman whose eau de cologne you smell isn't my wife?"

She turned her head toward him. "You have an air. My late husband had it. He couldn't help himself. He was a charmer and the ladies liked him and he had an expression just like the one on your face after he'd done something wrong. Just like he couldn't believe he'd gotten away with it again and wasn't he the luckiest fellow in the world."

Neither her expression nor her tone of voice were hostile, and he decided to take a calculated risk.

"Your late husband, you say. Do you miss him?"

Her smile was faint but fetching, like a little secret between them. "I didn't begrudge him his excesses. As I say, he was a charming man."

20

"I don't understand what I'm signing, Mr. Kaplan."

"It's a contract, Mrs. Crombie."

"I know that, I just don't understand what it is I'm signing over."

Seated next to her, Irene put a hand to her shoulder. "It's for Pearlie and little Ezra. For the movies."

"You told me about that already, but I don't remember saying they could be in a picture."

Mr. Kaplan growled in Irene's direction. "See, Mrs. Crombie, we didn't realize at the time that you hadn't agreed to allow them to be in the picture in question. And we'd like to release it."

Trudy shook her head in consternation at the gall of it. "I ask you to take care of my little ones for a few days . . ."

"I explained to you how it happened, and I apologize for it," Irene said.

"What if I say no? Your picture doesn't get sent out to the movie houses?"

"It's more than that, Mrs. Crombie," Kaplan said. He was a short, dapper fellow, and sitting behind his desk he looked like he could have been an actor himself. "There's also the question of all the other pictures we want to make with them."

"What other pictures?"

"We want to sign them up on a regular basis. A hundred dollars a week."

"A hundred dollars a week?" Trudy had never considered such a thing possible.

"Apiece," Irene said. "With a raise if it's renewed in a year."

Trudy became aware that her mouth was hanging open and she snapped it shut. "More pictures?"

"Would you like to watch the picture?" Kaplan asked. "Projection room is set up."

THE SIGHT OF her own kids on the motion picture screen nearly made her fall out of her chair. Kaplan and Irene were both laughing and Trudy realized that she was too. The thing started with that googly-eyed, goat-bearded comedian she didn't like getting whipped by her very own Pearlie and Ezra, and as mean as it was she had to admit that the kids were funny.

When it was over she stood and reached across Irene to shake hands with Kaplan. "I guess I can't say no to that kind of money," she said.

In the taxi on the way back to the Buntnagel residence she turned to Irene. "So I suppose this means I don't have to be in your pictures any more."

"Not if you don't want to," Irene said. "You can be a proper stage mother."

THEY WERE LIVING in a little bungalow in Echo Park now, a nicer place than she'd ever lived, and watching the children play on the floor of the parlor she thought it had been worth it, all the things she'd done to afford such a place. Now they'd be able to afford something even nicer and she wouldn't have to screw near-strangers on camera any more either. She wondered if she'd still be getting her share of the profits from the dirty movie company, but it almost didn't matter.

21

A traveling show he'd seen as a boy had made a great impression on him. For the price of a nickel one was ushered into a tent of black cloth, outside of which stood a painted sign reading:

**The Mer-Maid of Panjandrum!
AS REAL AS YOU OR I!**

Henry and three of his friends had skipped the last hours of school for the express purpose of seeing the mermaid, and eagerly conjectured as to the nature of the beast.

"The bottom half is fish, the top half a necked woman," claimed his friend Frank. At twelve he had an avid interest in the mysteries of reproduction, but a sad lack of actual knowledge, especially for a farm boy.

"What if it's the other way around, a woman's bottom half and a fish's head?" Henry asked.

"Reckon you'd do it from behind so's not to have to look into the fisheyes." Leon, the boy who spoke, was a year older than the others and claimed to have had experience with a prostitute on a trip to Wheeling, as well as with his own cousin Frances on a more regular basis.

The tent was the smallest among seven, and the

cheapest of the lot. The boys were uninterested in the Human Matchstick, the World's Fattest Boy, the Tattooed Lady and the rest. The man who ran the Mermaid attraction was quite drunk when they showed up at the tent flap and forked over their nickels. He had on a sweat-stained Stetson hat that had lost its shape after years of wear, and his nose was deep red and pocked. "Take a good look, boys," he said with an accent like none Henry had heard before.

Inside the tent was lit with an oil lamp so dirty it seemed to Henry its fat-encrusted glass might catch fire at any moment, illuminating in its dingy brown light a plain pine box with a glass lid, two feet by three or so and eight or nine inches deep. Inside rested a hideous creature a couple of feet long, its dead face contorted in a permanent howl of pain, the top half of the body covered in mangy fur, the second half plainly the taxidermied tail of some sort of bony fish. The ends of its arms had claws clenched in seeming terror, and Henry suspected that in life the mammalian half of the thing had been a monkey. There were curling, yellowed photographs surrounding the corpse showing fishermen posing with it, purportedly dating from the moment of its removal from the deep, but the creature looked precisely the same in the pictures as it did in the box: the same exact position, the same moth-eaten fur.

They all examined it in something like awe, and finally Frank spoke. "You suppose a monkey fucked a fish or the other way around?"

Outside, Frank expressed his disappointment to the old man in the Stetson. "Thought I was gonna see some bosoms at least."

"Monkey tits is all you get for a nickel, kid," he said. "If I had one with a woman's top half I'd sure as shit be showing her off in a better place than this."

IF SUCH A mermaid existed, Henry thought, Los Angeles is where they'd show it off. Driving the photo van, the city's scale seemed a bit more manageable to him than it had, but it retained its capacity to intimidate him. He was more capable behind the wheel than he had been, and he was learning to plot a route between one part of it and the next, but it was so much larger than Wheeling—the only other big city he'd ever seen—it beggared belief.

He was in Pasadena today, dropping something off for Bill, and though the package was marked OGDEN PHOTOGRAPHIC STUDIO he had the distinct impression that it was in the nature of a personal gift and not a business delivery. The house was palatial, located on the grounds of the most splendid piece of property Henry had ever laid eyes on. It sat at the end of a winding driveway, and wasn't even visible from the street.

The woman who answered the door must have been a great beauty at one time, and she bade him enter with a grand gesture of her left hand, guiding him inside.

"You must be Henry," she said, taking the parcel from him. "May I offer you a refreshment?" She smelled of rosewater, but not, he thought, in a vulgar way.

"I've got other stops to make, thank you, ma'am."

She was dressed in a manner that looked at once very expensive and somewhat out of date. Silk and velvet rustling with every movement, she tried to give him a quarter.

"Oh, I can't accept gratuities," he said, though there was no rule against it per se; it just felt awkward to him.

"Very well. I thank you kindly for your prompt service, and please give my very best to Mr. Ogden." Her eyes widened and her voice dropped to a whisper, full of portent. "And to his lovely granddaughter."

Then, to Henry's astonishment, she winked as she opened the door to let him out.

"IT SURELY IS strange seeing you without your chin-whiskers, Mr. Gill." Whishkerzh, she pronounced it.

Not as strange as it is seeing you without your teeth. Her voice had a curious sibilance and her empty jaws made her look like a dreadful chimera of a newborn babe and a crone, but her tone was still that of a young woman. The overall effect was off-putting.

"It must be difficult to talk without your plates in."

She nodded and, without speaking, replaced her dentures, top plate first. Once fitted she tapped the two against one another and she was transformed as if by miracle back to her previous lovely self.

"Bet you never had a sucking like that before," she said, still sitting side-legged on the ground, one silk-clad ankle crossed over the other.

"I haven't, no," Tommy said. "I hope it wasn't too big for you."

"Oh, well, it's pretty long, but not too big around, so I was all right."

The glow from his climax was beginning to dissipate. "Were you in an accident of some sort?" he asked.

"No, but my real ones just weren't right for the pictures.

I got a portrait done to show studios and such but they were no good. The next photographer I went to told me there was just something wrong with the way my teeth set. Made my face crooked. So you know what he did? He called up a dentist owed him some money and told him he'd be off the hook if he took them all out and made me a first-class set of choppers." She clacked them together again, pointing at her mouth. She truly was a very pretty girl, with a sweetness of affect that didn't strike Tommy as false in any way.

"And he charged you nothing, this dentist?"

"Nope, and neither did the photographer."

"I guess there must have been some other kind of horse-trading going on, then."

"Shame on you, there was not! The photographer was just a sweet old gentleman who wanted to help me."

He shifted his weight and buttoned up his fly. She got up from the floor and took a seat on the couch next to him. "Your dressing room's kind of small, isn't it?"

"It's not," he said.

"I just meant a star like you ought to have something grander is all."

It was all right, he told himself, she was just a star-struck young thing who imagined that the world of pictures would be more glamorous than it actually was. "And where did you come here from?"

"McMinn County, Tennessee. Came here with my young man—my fiancé—and we got started going around to the studios looking for work. He went by Jack Strong."

This came as a surprise. "He was in some pictures."

"He sure was. He was doing much better than me until

I got my teeth pulled. Then he got into the morphine the dentist give me and oh, boy, that was that. Next thing you know he's loaded on that or something else all day and night. He ended up molesting a lady on a streetcar in Pasadena and got arrested and I hope he never gets out."

"Well." She really was a pretty girl. If he could advance her career a bit in exchange for the occasional sexual favor that might just be worth the trouble, as long as his wife didn't tumble onto it. "How would you like a small part in my next two-reeler? I can think of something for you to do."

"Oh, Mr. Gill, that's so sweet of you, but Mr. Kaplan wouldn't allow it."

"Why ever not?"

"Well, he's got to approve of every role I take, and he's got in my contract I'm only to play leads."

"You've got a contract?" The world seemed turned on its head. Surely this girl was a walk-on who, seeing a star, decided to parlay her not inconsiderable erotic skills into a few screen appearances?

"My first one came out last month, didn't you see it? *Winner Takes All.* It did quite well."

"You're Magnolia Sweetspire?" It was inconceivable that the studio's newest and brightest star had just gummed him to the most satisfying orgasm he'd had in years. He was so far beneath her in the studio's pecking order that it seemed wrong for her to even address him as a peer.

"Really it's Myrna Bogle. I wanted to call myself Purity Dove, but when I signed my contract Mr. Kaplan said that kind of name was old hat. So then I was Magnolia Sweetspire."

"Myrna . . ."

"Didn't you know that when I came up to you at lunch-time?"

"I'm afraid I didn't."

"I saw you sitting there all by your lonesome and I said to myself Myrna, girl, there's your favorite, Tommy Gill hisself, and here's your chance to meet him in person. And now here we are."

"And here we are indeed."

"By the by, don't mention what I said about Jack being my fiancé. Mr. Kaplan doesn't want that getting out, him being in the papers and all with that streetcar business."

IT WAS NICE from time to time to get a chance to get to know someone as perfectly charming as Miss Magnolia Sweetspire, and now he started thinking strategically. If he could join up with her professionally or personally—Bea be damned—she might just turn out to be his salvation. He went to Kaplan's office and marched straight in.

"Say, Kaplan, I have a notion."

Kaplan looked up from his newspaper, his feet on the corner of his desk, cigar smoldering in his right hand. "Miss Lipscomb let you in here without announcing you?"

"I just breezed past her without letting her stop me."

Miss Lipscomb, in her thick spectacles and her long blond coils of hair, appeared in the doorway. "I'm sorry, Mr. Kaplan."

Tommy waved her off. "This is worth it. Have a listen."

"Tell me why I shouldn't kick your ass out into the hallway."

"Me and Magnolia Sweetspire."

Kaplan laughed. "Go fuck yourself."

"I'm serious. I met her today at lunch, she's a big fan. And she'd be a natural. She'd do fine in comedy, she could be the next Mabel Normand."

"Forget it."

"I'm telling you, with that sweet face . . ."

"With that sweet face she's going to be getting rescued and swept off her feet in dramatic roles on a regular basis."

Tommy pulled at the corsage in his lapel. "Just let us shoot a test."

"Do you have any notion of how much money *Winner Takes All* made last month?"

"I'm not the goddamn accountant."

"Are you smashed at three in the afternoon?"

"Of course not."

"I can smell you from here. Now go home and sober up and don't bother me any more."

THE TWO FIGURES in the image were mostly in focus but slightly blurred at the feet, which must have been swaying during the exposure. They stood out in stark relief against the storefront from whose eaves they hung, the spectators unable to keep still sufficiently to record any recognizable visage. Along the right half of the stereoscopic image was written in white "Hanged Men Cottonwood KAS 1873. Copyright 1873 W. Ogden." Henry was using Bill's own fancy viewer, manufactured for ophthalmological use. He slipped another card in place, a view of a tent city with a group of women standing in front of a large white canvas and wood structure. "Working Women Cottonwood KAS 1873," this one read.

He sensed someone's presence behind him but continued to concentrate on the image before him. The women in the stereograph would by now be either elderly or dead, a notion that made him rather sad.

"I don't suppose you've got anything better to do of an afternoon," Mrs. Chen said.

"Truth is I don't."

"My late husband never let a moment go by idle."

"That's an admirable quality," he said.

"It were from necessity, young man. He come over from China and worked on the railroad."

"I always wondered how you came by a Chinese name like that."

"He was a good Christian man, make no mistake. He never was a heathen, his mother made sure he was raised right, even over there. Well, I met him at a Christian Aid Society meeting and we was engaged before you knew it. My folks never spoke to me again."

"That's too bad."

"They would have preferred anyone to a Chinaman as a son-in-law. After we wed we opened a restaurant and do you know we ran that eating house for thirty-two years slinging chop suey and the like before he slipped into the arms of the Lord. And he took nary a day off, not even Christmas. And our children, how do you suppose they are?"

"The same, I wager?"

"Not in the least! They work bankers' hours. The eldest one plans to retire at sixty, and his father would be appalled at such thinking."

"I suppose if he works hard enough he ought to be able to retire."

"He's an accountant! Works with numbers all day. If you call that hard."

"Sounds plenty hard to me."

"Now Mr. Ogden, he may have his faults, and he's slowed down a bit, but look at him, still working at his age. It seems to me you might benefit from a bit of his gumption, young fellow," she said. "You won't go far looking at pictures in the middle of the day."

22

Who thinks this shit is funny?

Tommy was seated in the middle row of a smaller movie house in Glendale, watching Billie Ritchie playing a variant on Chaplin's tramp character. Everyone in the business knew Ritchie had done it first, just like everyone knew Chaplin did it better. Tommy was looking for something he could purloin, and he couldn't steal from Chaplin or Arbuckle or Mabel, because even the dolts who ran Provident would recognize the theft. But there wasn't anything here worth taking that Chaplin hadn't stolen already, and after taking a good-sized nip from his flask he blew a raspberry loud enough to be heard over the piano accompaniment.

"Knock it off," someone said from behind him.

"Go fuck yourself," Tommy said, and to his great surprise he felt a slap to the back of his head, hard enough to knock him halfway out of his seat.

"Watch your language. There's ladies present."

He stood and turned to face his assailant.

"Sit back down and watch the show." He was a lanky fellow with a lean face and white hair, and seated next to him was one of the smallest women Tommy had ever seen. She was unquestionably an adult, but her feet didn't reach the floor, nor did the back of her head reach the top of the seat back. In contrast to her tetchy companion she had an expression of serenity and calm.

"You hit me again and I'll give you a show," Tommy said.

"Down in front!" yelled a high-pitched voice.

"I'll sit down when I've had some satisfaction."

The white-haired man shook his head in disgust. "I'll hit you again you don't sit."

Tommy reached out to backhand the man across the face, but as he swung he lost his balance and went over the back of his seat, provoking a bigger laugh from the crowd than any the picture had gotten. Using his skills as a stage acrobat he overcorrected and went all the way over and onto the floor next to his nemesis, who stood and kicked him in the shoulder. At that point an usher came down the aisle.

He shone an electric torch in Tommy's face. Tommy looked up from the floor and pointed.

"He started it."

"I did not! Escort this man out of the theater."

"All right, mister, get up. Some of these folks paid to see a show."

It seemed to Tommy he'd given them a pretty good one, but with a certain degree of difficulty he managed to pull himself upright and exit the auditorium with a modicum of dignity.

On the drive home he went over it in his mind, but not in the bitter manner such a humiliation would normally have inspired in him. It wasn't a bad idea for a picture, was it? It wasn't entirely original, but the audience had laughed hard enough, hadn't it? He'd run it past the boys at the studio in the morning. Hell, maybe he'd write a sketch of it himself and hand it to the son of a bitch George Buntnagel, maybe get a little respect out of him for once.

Night had fallen and he'd made it to Burbank. The streets were quiet, the traffic almost nonexistent. Fantasizing about Buntnagel's rhapsodic reaction to his yet-to-be-written outline, he took another long pull from his flask, and as he turned from San Fernando Road onto West Olive he felt a distinct thud and lurched forward onto the steering wheel as the car careened out of control, off of the street and onto the sidewalk. His right front tire had made a hell of a crunch as it hit the curb, and he hoped he remembered how to put the spare on. Bea was going to be all over him when he got home. What happened to the bumper, Tommy? You drunk again, Tommy? Laying day players again, Tommy? Cursing at his empty flask, which had fallen and spilled onto the floor of his 30-35, he cut off his engine and stepped gingerly out of the vehicle to take a look at what he'd hit.

BEATRICE GILL MADE note of her husband's condition upon his return home that night and, noting the injuries to his face, unobtrusively checked out the condition of his car once he'd gone to bed. Finding the right front tire mangled and the spare still bolted to the rear of the carriage, and serious impact damage to the grille, she came to the obvious and unsurprising conclusion that her husband had crashed the car under the influence of alcohol. When he went to the studio next morning he called a taxi, and had a Provident employee drive him home. As far as she could tell he hadn't made any move to replace the tire or have the grille fixed.

A tireless reader of newspapers morning and evening, she spotted an article in the *Examiner* the morning after next which suggested to her why Tommy might not have been in a hurry to get back behind the wheel.

WOMAN KNOCKED OVER IN BURBANK DIES
Police Seek Identity of Hit-and-Run Driver

Burbank police say the elderly pedestrian hit Tuesday evening on West Olive in Burbank has succumbed to her injuries, making the identity of the driver of the automobile who knocked her over a more serious piece of business, as it is now considered a case of vehicular homicide. Mrs. Augusta Malvern, aged 77, a widow living on her late husband's GAR pension, passed away last night at the Hospital of the Good Samaritan. Burbank Police Captain A. J. Burnside reports that based upon evidence at the scene the automobile in question sustained some damage as it ran into the kerb. Auto garages are currently watching for carriages showing suspicious damage.

She clipped the article out and put it in her handbag. Life with Tommy Gill had been a trial for some time, even before he started working in pictures. He made good money—five hundred dollars a week!—but he was drunk with increasing frequency. In that state it was not unusual for him to hit her, and physical intimacy was no longer a part of their marriage. She didn't know whether this was a result of his drinking or whether it was because he'd taken a mistress, but it was not a sacrifice she was prepared to make for much longer. She was still a reasonably young woman and good-looking to boot and she was damned if she'd waste these years on that tosspot. His career appeared to be suffering as well, the reviews in the papers and the trades having descended from unenthusiastically favorable two or three years back to indifferent or occasionally downright caustic the last few releases.

She'd been an actress, a singer and a dancer, but she'd always remained a devoted Catholic girl, and divorce was anathema to her. But if Tommy was now a killer in addition to a sot she saw no way or reason to remain.

23

Agnes something.

He hadn't thought of her in years, decades, maybe, but there she was, every bit as young as she'd been when he saw her last. When had that been? Kansas, forty or forty-five years before. And here she stood, looking no more than twenty-five or thirty, and him all of seventy-two, neither of them with a stitch of clothing.

"Strange thing you showing up just now," he said. "I was just in the process of writing you a poem." He recited for her the first lines of it.

> *Her Christian name was Agnes*
> *But she'd nothing of the ovine*

"Quiet, you old goat," she said. "I didn't come such a distance to listen to you rhyming. I've got something important to tell you."

A truck backfiring in the street outside woke him with a start before she could finish what she was going to say, and he sat up with a start and looked around his room. As usual it took Bill a moment to get his bearings and remember that he was in California. He reflected on the dream, and considered that he'd composed a pretty good poem in his sleep, the first two lines thereof, anyway.

Agnes. A slender little thing with hunched shoulders who'd come into town one day, found him eating breakfast at the Cottonwood Hotel and announced that she wanted a picture made for her husband, who traveled for a living selling musical instruments. She'd given him directions to their little house on the outskirts of Independence, and asked that he come at precisely three the next day.

"Not trying to talk myself out of a job, but why don't you have your picture made there? Two or three decent photographers in town at least."

"I heard you was awfully good."

"Is that so?" he said.

"Opal Renfrew says so." She said this with her eyes wide, leaning forward to ensure that he wouldn't mistake her meaning.

"Ah. And how is Mrs. Renfrew?"

"Husband's home all the time now. She regrets that."

Opal Renfrew had welcomed him into her simple farmhouse several times the year before and shown him considerable hospitality while her husband was off tending to winter business. "I hope you'll give her my best."

The sitting had begun that next afternoon as though it were all there was to the visit. As he worked setting up the camera she talked about marriage and how difficult it was for a woman who had become accustomed to certain aspects of wedded living to do without them.

"I haven't any money to pay you for the pictures," she said.

He hadn't yet daubed the foul-smelling collodion onto the glass plates yet. "There's plenty more work for me to do before I set you down on the couch to take the picture. Chemicals and such."

She made her way over to the couch and patted the seat next to her. "Why don't you come sit next to me for a spell before you get started, then."

After that he started making his way to her little house outside of Independence under cover of night, and they maintained a lively weekly rendez-vous until she received a letter announcing that her husband had socked away enough money to buy a farm outside Cottonwood. The same letter brought the news that he would be home on or about June the first, and the day it arrived was May the thirtieth. With some regret he stopped visiting her, though he spotted her in town with her husband and baby—a boy, he believed—a few times before he himself left Cottonwood. The husband was a round, red-faced fellow, prematurely bald and unusually cheerful of mien.

Agnes Arglist, that was the rest of her name. She'd told him she'd nearly called off the wedding because of the name.

"I HAD A funny dream last night," Bill said when he came down for breakfast.

"I put no stock in dreams," Mrs. Chen said. "Nothing but heathen nonsense and deviltry."

"Everybody has dreams."

"But they don't mean anything. Anyone who says they do is promoting the devil's work."

"I seem to recall God visiting old Abimelech in a dream."

"That was in olden times." She put his scrambled eggs and flapjacks on a plate and served him. The old man was himself a heathen, never went to church and neither did his granddaughter nor young Henry, and yet here he was referring to scripture as knowledgably as a preacher.

"Well, I didn't think this one was prophetic. Just a visit from an old lost friend. Probably dead by now anyway."

"Neither Miss Ogden nor the boy are in at the moment."

"That's all right."

"Mr. Ogden, things are afoot in this house of which you should be made aware."

"Are there."

"Those two are engaging in . . ." She struggled for a decent way of putting it. ". . . sinful activities."

"Idolatry? Falsely testifying against the neighbors? Coveting their goods?"

"Stop that. You know perfectly well what I mean."

"I do not. Spell it out."

She looked away, furious at his glib pleasure in her discomfort. "When they are alone in the house, or think they are, they lock themselves in her room."

"And?"

"Mr. Ogden, when an unmarried man and a woman sequester themselves it's quite clear what the intent is."

"Maybe they're composing a sonnet."

"They certainly are not! You know exactly what I'm talking about."

"Are you suggesting that my granddaughter and Henry are engaging in carnal relations?"

"You know that I am."

She looked back to see him. The eggs and the flapjacks were gone; it was a wonder how fast the man could eat. "You know, it's funny. The very friend I dreamt about once told me that once a woman's been married she might find it hard to do without physical intimacy. Flavia's a widow, as you may know."

"So am I, and you'll notice I don't go running after men." In fact she had rather enjoyed the marital bed, but since Mr. Chen's decease she'd never been tempted to marry again, certainly never to lay with a man to whom she wasn't wed in the eyes of Christ.

"I thank you for informing me of the situation, Mrs. Chen."

And that was all he had to say on the subject. It amazed her that the man could take such a cavalier attitude to his own grandchild's lack of chastity, but then again no one ever said evangelizing would be easy.

WHAT TOMMY HANDED George wasn't a scenario, precisely, just some scribbled notes on a piece of unlined paper, in a hand that suggested that of a small child just learning his block letters. He was right for once, though, it wasn't a bad idea for a picture. There was no need to build a set, just dress the screening room as if it were a commercial theater and light it. The kids could be the instigators, and the same batch of character players from the shoe store two-reeler could finish it up. "How'd you get the shiners, Tommy?"

"Walked into a door," he said.

Fell down shitfaced was more like it, George thought. *And I wish I'd been there with the camera running.*

"This'll be a good second vehicle for you and the kids," he said, and horror crossed over Tommy's face.

"Those goddamn little bastards, I won't work with them again."

"If you want to work here at Provident you'll work with them. Admit it, Tommy, the last one was a howler."

He scowled but didn't argue.

24

————— • —————

Flavia had been celibate since well before the end of her marriage, which had gone mostly sexless a couple of months after the wedding. That was a good thing, she reasoned, because with a child or two in the picture the dispatch of Albert Purcell would have been more difficult, maybe even impossible. She'd thought for a while that it might be possible to go on that way indefinitely, but recently her thoughts had drifted in that direction with greater frequency and intensity. So she'd gone and seduced young Henry, and she didn't regret it at all. He was reasonably new to it—though she was sure it hadn't been his first time—and he had things to learn, but he was eager to please and certainly enthusiastic about the whole business.

Now she had to apply herself in order to concentrate on the business at hand, the taking of a formal portrait of a society lady. This was the sort of job her grandfather had only recently begun to delegate to her, as these were the most lucrative of assignments, and the sort of thing that led to other work, for these ladies were competitive to the point of viciousness; if one of them had a truly distinctive and flattering photographic portrait by Ogden Studios, then her friends must have them also.

This one insisted on being photographed in her home, next to a fireplace big enough to roast a bison. "It's lovely,

Mrs. Atchison," Flavia said, "in fact I don't think I've ever seen one so impressive in scale. But it will make you look small. The lower edge of the mantel is above your head."

Flavia had learned from her grandfather how to talk to such nabobs, which tone to take and how to ensure they understood that her concern was for their vanity and how best to flaunt their wealth and beauty. Mrs. Hobart J. Atchison nonetheless had to make her best effort not to scowl, unaccustomed to her orders being questioned by tradespeople. But she sensed that the young woman knew of which she spoke.

"There is a smaller one in the den," she said. "Hoskin will show you the way."

Hoskin was the majordomo, short, furry and as wide across the chest as a bear. Bald, with strands of black combed over the pink skin of his pate, he looked like a troglodyte with his animal skins replaced by a morning coat. He was unable to conceal a seething contempt for the interlopers, and Flavia detected a bit of the same aimed at his employer, who was cheerfully oblivious. She and Henry followed him down a long hallway to another enormous room whose hearth was large enough only to contain a large hog, and she directed Henry to set up the lighting while she prepared the camera.

When the time came for Mrs. Atchison to pose, she had changed into a different dress than the one she'd started out in. The first had been a conservative frock with lace and brocade work over the poitrine, its skirt puffy and coming down over her feet. The second clung to her generous figure, revealing a goodly amount of décolletage, and the pointed toes of her silk slippers emerged like mice from beneath the hem. All that remained of the previous outfit was a prodigious amount of jewelry: diamond earrings heavy enough to stretch her earlobes half an inch, an enormous gemstone pendant on a platinum chain, and a tiara with what Flavia took to be emeralds. She suppressed the urge to suggest that less might be more in that area. From her movements, her improved mood and the smell of her breath it was evident that the change in wardrobe had had its origin in the consumption of a cocktail or two, and Flavia was determined not to make her regret her alcohol-fueled daring.

"I'M DIVORCING YOU," Beatrice said over dessert, a chiffon pie that Mildred had baked that afternoon and which, up to that point, Tommy had been very much enjoying. He served himself another piece in order to feign an air of aplomb. The pie server was sterling silver and had his initials engraved in an elaborate, dainty script, which he'd never before noticed. He hadn't ever had to get his own slice before, not since they could afford such silverware. He was suddenly aware of the heat from the candelabra on his face.

"The hell you are," he said.

"I am." She looked up at him and then back down to her plate.

"Look here, Bea, that could do me some damage."

"It certainly could. I'll do it quietly if you'll cooperate. Otherwise I'll talk to the newspapers." She took another bite. "This really is good pie," she said.

He blew a raspberry. "What the hell you got to tell the press?"

"Your excessive drinking, for one thing."

"No one gives a damn about that."

"Skirt-chasing."

"Prove it. And again, no one cares."

"Then there's the matter of the dead woman."

He put his fork down on the plate. "What dead woman?" he asked, very slowly.

"You knocked over a woman with the 30-35 the other night. She died in the hospital a day later."

"You can't prove that."

"Can't I? I notice you quit driving. Though maybe you didn't want anyone to see the fender."

"Maybe I just want to trade up to a Model 30."

"I suppose you've got it parked in there right now."

"Just maybe I do." He looked in the direction of the garage.

"Wonder what the police would have to say if they saw that blown radiator."

He got up and strode toward the kitchen, napkin still tucked into his collar. He opened the door and stepped outside without closing it. The evening was beginning to cool, already getting dark. He swung the bottom of the garage door upward and was greeted by the worst sight he could imagine. The 30-35 was gone.

BEATRICE WAS JUST finishing up her slice of pie when he stepped back into the dining room. "Mildred really outdid herself, didn't she? This filling is just as light as air."

"You crazy bitch."

"You're going to miss her cooking, I'll bet. But you're

a successful, famous man. I'm sure you'll find someone almost as good wherever you end up."

"What do you want from me?"

"I want you to check into a hotel tonight. I had Conchita pack you a valise. I'm keeping the house and I want three-quarters of the money."

"You're out of your goddamn mind."

"You'll make up for it quickly enough. Remember, you've got a ready source of income and I don't."

"Provident wants to get rid of me."

"Nonsense. This new picture's a hit, you said. And just last week you were telling me how they want to give you a feature."

"That was just talk."

"Three quarters of what's in the bank and what you've got invested or the police get the word on where your car's being stored. And don't try to hide any of it, my attorney's got his men on it right now and they'll know if you try and cheat me."

"Aw, Bea, honey, don't. You know I love you."

"Aw, Tommy, honey, you know that isn't true. We got married because we had a successful act together on the road and I was under age."

"I loved you," he said, a high-pitched, plaintive tone creeping into his voice.

"You lusted after me and you were scared of getting arrested. I thought I loved you, but after a few years I got to know you."

Across from where he stood hung a painting of an eighteenth-century lady. Beatrice had bought it on a trip to New York City and she got a kick out of telling people it was her great-great-grandmother. She wasn't looking at him any more and for the first time Tommy noticed the look on the face in the painting. The woman was smiling at the viewer in a conspiratorial manner, a secretive look that verged on a knowing smirk. He had the sudden intuition that the lady and the painter had been lovers.

Beatrice snapped her fingers to bring him back into the present. "Quit your dreaming about how goddamn unfair it all is and go upstairs and fetch your suitcase. I'll call for a cab."

THAT EVENING AFTER Flavia washed up she looked into the mirror and considered her face. She had a wide mouth, full lips and prominent teeth, and though she'd never cared much one way or the other she had never considered herself particularly good looking, and apart from keeping herself well-groomed she did nothing to make herself more so. Other people liked her face well enough, though; Henry certainly did, and Alfred had at first. So had other boys in her adolescence and at teacher's college. Her grandfather had ended up alone, or unpartnered, at least, and he was perfectly content. So could she, she was sure of it. In the meantime she'd play house with Henry until she felt like something different.

25

"Burney claims this fellow was trained by the very psychic who used to conjure up Honest Abe for the widow Lincoln, way back when."

"I don't believe in such things," Irene said, though she was afraid she did. The occasion was a party at Stan Burney's at which a séance was to be held before dinner. Burney's parties didn't always include women, but she'd found the ones that did reliably entertaining. They were in a taxi cab and getting close enough to Burney's house that Irene was getting the fantods.

"Think I'll ask to talk to my sister Mina," George said. "That should be fun."

Irene looked out the open window. It was getting dark already and people were moving en masse along the sidewalks, carrying groceries and walking dogs and living in their sealed-off little worlds. George had, of course, no sister at all, alive or dead. He was just going to try and fool the medium, who, Irene supposed, faced such challenges at every séance he threw. She'd have liked to ask for a word from her grandmother in Connecticut, but she was too frightened, lest she get an actual message from the Other Side, which would have terrified her.

BURNEY'S VALET LET them in and they joined the other guests, who included Victoria and Trudy, in the salon, where champagne cocktails were being served. The former was deep in conversation with one of the gigolos who'd screwed her onscreen, a slender and charming chap whose name Irene failed to conjure. She waved and they both reciprocated. Victoria had his full attention, and she had an odd notion that he might be one of those rare fellows that really will go after either sex; she'd never known anyone like that, but George swore he knew dozens.

She headed for Trudy, standing by herself next to the unlit fireplace.

"Evening. Having fun?"

"Oh, I am," Trudy said. "Good booze." She held her champagne flute out as if to prove it.

Irene gestured toward a man in a white tuxedo. "That's the fellow there who's going to try and raise the dead."

"Oh." Trudy looked repulsed. "I don't think that's right."

"I'm sure it's a humbug, don't fret."

"Back home in Maine I knew an old woman who said she talked to the spirits. She was tetched, everyone said, but one time she told me where to find my cat who'd gotten herself lost. In the loft of a barn a mile away, she said, and I was so scared I'd lost the cat I upped and went to that barn and what do you think I found but my little lost kittycat?"

Irene didn't know what to say, so she just widened her eyes to indicate that she was struck by the tale.

"Anyway I was always nice to her after that. Most weren't." She looked over at Victoria and the gigolo. "She seems to like him, doesn't she?"

Irene glanced over her shoulder at the pair, who did

seem enraptured by one another. "I wouldn't take it seriously. I believe he prefers the company of his own sex."

"Really?" Trudy was incredulous. "He certainly seemed to have a good time atop her and me the other week."

Irene looked back over her shoulder. Was she wrong? No, she'd seen him here at Stanley's parties before, drunk and cavorting. Maybe he really was one of those men who switched back and forth. Wonders never ceased. "Anyway, I wouldn't worry about him."

Trudy's face was flushed. "Why ever would I worry?"

THE SÉANCE WAS held as soon as it was dark outside, though Irene hadn't known that that was one of the conditions for summoning the departed; she supposed it should be enough just to draw the shades.

Haha, the shades. I made a funny.

They seated themselves around a massive rosewood table, twelve in total, leaving half a dozen off to the side watching, including Irene and Trudy. This, too, struck her as incongruous. Shouldn't everyone in the room be holding hands or something? Candles were lit, and all electric illumination shut down. Oil fixtures, of which Stanley still used a surprising number, were also extinguished.

The medium explained himself at great length. He was but a vessel, and in his trance states he was often unaware of what had gone on and what the spirits had conveyed through his instrument, as he referred to his voice. He went on for a while about ancient Egyptian religion and medieval philosophies and the mysteries of the orient and the ether and the longer he talked the more he sounded to Irene like a carnival hawker trying to rope people into his tent for a look at the world's fattest baby or the dog-faced boy. His voice was mellifluous and he had clearly studied elocution but he could have used some acting lessons as well.

Soon enough he stopped talking and began moaning, at which point a couple of Stan's friends giggled. They stopped when he raised his voice, and its tone deepened considerably.

"There is a spirit who wants to make himself known. He was quite old when he passed and it was long ago. His name is . . . Joseph. Known to most as Joe. But to one here he was known as . . ." Here he paused and squinted in deep concentration.

"Uncle Joe?" said one of Stan's young men friends.

"Yes. Your Uncle Joe wants to tell you that he's all right."

Irene shook her head. This character wasn't even a good charlatan. She could have faked such a presentation herself and done a better job of it. This went on for another half hour, with a couple of the supposed spirits getting no takers at all, and the general mood of the room was one of ennui and tension.

Just as the séance was winding down, the seer let out a low moan quite unlike the noises he'd been making thus far. He stiffened and held the hands to his right and left much tighter, startling his neighbors, and he rose out of his chair a little bit. Then he pointed at George.

"You know him what done it," he said in a voice unlike his own, feminine and indignant. "You have to get him to make it right, what he done. It ain't right. He knocked me right over with his automobile and drove on away."

Irene felt her back muscles quiver.

"Who is this?" Stan said.

"I'm a widder woman. He ought to be in the jailhouse. And he was drunk as a skunk, I can still smell it on him."

WHEN THE LIGHTS came back up, all agreed that the last visitation had been an unnerving experience, and the medium affected not to remember it. Upon having it described to him he was plainly unsettled. George, unflappable, said he didn't know anything about anybody getting knocked over by an automobile, though, and by the time dinner was over the matter had been dismissed or forgotten by everyone but Irene.

26

Another dream about Kansas.

He was just outside Cottonwood, standing in the yard of the farmhouse he'd built for Flavia's grandmother. It was in better shape than the house had ever been in reality; he had done an indifferent job building it, and in keeping it up, and the one time he'd been back since abandoning it he'd found an Exoduster living there with his family. The man had chided him for his shoddy craftsmanship and lack of pride in his work.

The man stood there now, in front of the house, somewhat older, and still shaking his head at the piss-poor job Bill had done building the farmhouse.

"I had to pull down that barn you made and build another. The flooring in the kitchen was starting to rot right through."

"I already told you I was sorry. Anyway it wasn't me that sold it to you, was it?"

He touched his hand to his neck. "Reckon it wasn't. But it was your poor workmanship caused me all that grief."

"Were you ever a slave?" he asked. It had been a question he'd wanted to ask the day he'd met the man in real life, though he hadn't dared. Then as now he was impressed at the man's bold way of speaking to him, which would not have been without risk, depending on whom he was addressing.

"Born into it."

"I suppose there's not much you take for granted."

"Only a fool takes anything for granted." He pointed at the front door. "Look there, I put you up a mailbox."

"What for?"

"You've been getting mail here ever since you left. Surprised you never came back for it."

He approached the box and stuck his hand inside. When he withdrew it, it held a sheaf of envelopes, maybe twenty of them, and many more remained within. The top letter was from an old school chum he hadn't thought about in fifty years or more. The second was from a cousin in France.

"I'll be damned."

"Don't swear. Why don't you clear those out so's I can take the mailbox down."

The dream soon degenerated into gibberish involving calf-sized pollywogs in a pond and a vain attempt to board a train to San Francisco, and upon awakening he paid the rest of it no mind.

"I HAD A funny dream last night," he said at breakfast.

At the stove Mrs. Chen snorted. "Dreams again. I put no stock in them and neither ought you."

He made a face behind her back and Flavia snickered. "Flavey, do you recall your grandmother's old place outside town?"

"Not really. I heard plenty about it, how it leaked and

how things were always coming apart, starting around the time you ran out on her."

"I didn't run out on her, I was being pursued by unfriendly forces."

"Have it your way. Dad and Ooma always said you ran out on them."

Henry appeared to be scandalized.

"That's not how it was, lad. I'll tell you the whole thing someday."

He appealed silently to Flavia, who gave him a knowing nod, a promise to spill the whole lurid story outside of the old man's presence.

Mrs. Chen laid a platter of hotcakes on the table and took her own seat. She studied Flavia and Henry for a moment, their physical gestures toward and proximity to one another so different than before, and the old woman shook her head so hard her jowls vibrated, closed her eyes and said grace, while the rest of the table sat in silence, waiting to dig in.

AT NOON THE mail brought a letter from Miss Myrna Bogle, from whom he hadn't heard since shortly after her fiancé's run-in with the law.

Dear kind Mr. Ogden,

You will be happy to hear that I have made a splash in the motion pictures thanks to your kindness regarding my bent teeth and getting them fixed up straight. I am under contract now and have made a picture already! I will certainly be sending everyone your way when it comes time to take their picture! That scowndril I was engaged to is in prison now and I thank you for your assistance with him too. If you want to see my picture it's called Winner Take All and it's doing well. My name for the screen is Miss Magnolia Sweetspire.

With grattitude,
Myrna Bogle

By 2 P.M. he was sitting in the big chair in the studio reading by the skylight, a rare overcast day out making the light perfect for deciphering the tiny typeface of his father's 1802 Isaiah Thomas edition of the Greek New Testament. He was rereading a particularly difficult passage for the fifth or sixth time when Flavia knocked and, without awaiting an answer, entered.

"What are you reading?"

"Scripture. Acts, to be precise."

"What on earth for?"

"I can sense my Greek rusting, and I have an unseemly and vain need to continually remind Mrs. Chen of my mastery of the Bible in all its forms."

"Mrs. Chen is a disagreeable old virago. Lucky she's a good cook."

"She's on to you and the lad."

"I see you are too."

"Wasn't hard to dope out."

She sat down on the canapé. "What do you think?"

"Why should I think anything?"

"Because I'm your granddaughter, a decent and respectable woman, who's risking her reputation in a sinful dalliance."

He snorted. "A respectable murderess."

"What do you think of it, though?"

"I assume Mrs. Chen and the object of your affections are out of earshot?"

"She's provisioning and he's off picking up some borax for the darkroom."

"All right. You know perfectly well I don't care if you answer nature's call without a marriage license. So as to Henry. He's a young man of good character and cheerful disposition. Why should I disapprove?"

"He's not very well educated."

"But in no way unintelligent. Probably a bit late to start him on his Greek conjugations, but he's not your intellectual inferior, or mine either."

"Just so you know, I'm not looking at trading in my hard-won status as a widow. Just wanted to hear your thoughts." She stood up.

"If you need a young man with whom to keep company in my home, you have my blessing. Ignore Mrs. Chen's dirty looks and go forth and sin some more."

BACK AT HIS reading of the passage that had so troubled him—Acts 21:3—he found a typographical error. Some hapless typesetter a hundred years earlier had mistaken ἀναφάνεντες for ἀναφάναντες, and Bill hadn't misunderstood the passage after all. He felt a certain petty satisfaction in noting the long-dead printer's careless botching of so simple a job. It gave him a warm feeling to know that his Greek had not deteriorated as badly as he'd feared.

27

"A vote for Hughes or Wilson is a vote for war. Benson's the man."

"Balls."

An elderly burglar named Buddy spat onto the ground of the yard, a big glob with a mucousy, pale yellow center. "I thought that was Wilson's slogan. 'Kept us out of the war.'"

The big man looked down at the grass and shook his head. He had a big skull, dented and scarred, and he ran one huge hand over his scalp. "No, no, no. That's just his line. It's a lie. The banks want us in the war, you see?"

Ezra looked at him dead in the eyes. "Tell me why I should give a shit if we get into the war."

"There'll be a draft, for one thing."

Ezra laughed, long and hard. "They gonna draft the likes of me? A convict?"

"You'll be goddamn surprised," the Red said. "They'll be drafting anyone over the age of sixteen with two legs and one ball."

"You're forgetting something else," Ezra said. "We can't vote."

"I know goddamn well we can't! I'm just trying to get you to use your heads."

Ezra's fellow prisoners knew him as Alvin Spack, as did the state of California. Those cops back in Pasadena hadn't much cared who they had in hand and neither had the courts. He took the name from a fellow he'd known during a long ago summer misspent in Providence, Rhode Island. Alvin was a thief with aspirations toward the confidence game, but he was a charmless man with a long, skinny neck that led to a head that was always cocked to one side, and that made him look as though he was lying even on the rare occasions when he wasn't. One night after he and Ezra had broken into a warehouse only to find it lined wall-to-wall with lumber far too large for them to steal, Alvin had broken down blubbering about his bad luck in his scratchy, high-pitched voice.

"Ain't nobody ever loved me 'cept my gram and she croaked when I weren't but eight. I can't catch a break and I don't even know what we're going to eat tonight. Nothing, it seems to me."

Ezra had found himself in the uncharacteristic position that night of comforting Alvin Spack and promising him that things were bound to turn around. He even sprung for a pint of some of the worst booze either of them had ever drunk. They slept in a hayloft on the outskirts of the city, Ezra wondering how soon he could get away from this squirrely character.

As it transpired he woke that night to find Alvin opening the barn door with the intention of making away with both their bindles, and he set out after him and beat him unconscious. To that very day Ezra couldn't put into words why he'd left him alive.

Why the Red was wasting his time trying to convince them that Benson was the one deserved to be president was a mystery to him. Maybe he just couldn't shake the habit, trying to get people het up about the class struggle and all that. Ezra didn't buy any of it. He'd seen his old man getting his skull busted by Pinkertons and it hadn't improved their lives any, had it?

The one-eyed kid was laughing, at what no one knew. He'd lost the eye when the wife of the butcher whose shop he was robbing pulled a revolver from the till and shot him. He'd fired more or less at the same time and his bullet finished her, whereas hers only took his stereoscopic vision. The Red took his laughter the wrong way.

"Keep laughing I'll knock your other eye right out the goddamn socket."

"Hell, I was just laughing thinking of that Wilson. He looks just like he's got a goddamn stick up his ass."

"See that one over there?" Ezra said. "Used to be a picture star. Raped and strangled a woman right on the trolley car is what I hear."

"Looks like a bum to me," one-eyed kid said. The man was sallow of complexion with speckles of beard and his face was slick with a layer of sweat, and he looked less like a screen idol than a dopesick vagrant.

A con strolled across the yard in their direction, and the putative motion picture player made haste to stay out of his path. The con's crossed eyes bugged out and he had his hands in the pockets of his trousers, and he was no more than five foot four inches tall and a hundred thirty pounds, but the four of them shut their mouths as he neared, and no one dared look at him except the Red, who was new to the prison.

"The hell's the matter with all of you?" He jerked his head at the little con. "That little dink?"

"Pipe down. That's the meanest man in Folsom. Offenbach, the Little Tiger."

The Red snorted. "Little Tiger, my balls."

Ezra snickered. "Dare you to go up to him and call him squirt."

Buddy grabbed the Red's arm. "Huh-uh. Don't you go doing that. He's a killing son of a bitch, that one."

The Red stared after Offenbach. "Huh."

"Huh is right," Buddy said. "He's in for killing five people, and I happen to know he's finished three cons since he's been here and in San Quentin. That and he damn near killed a turnkey last year."

"What for?" the Red asked.

"He didn't need a reason."

THE FOLLOWING AFTERNOON Ezra saw a chance to purloin the contents of a tin of Mail Pouch. The rightful owner was Al Schnurr, a hapless yegg doing three years for aggravated burglary. Ezra swiped the tin from Schnurr's bunk and rolled a smoke in front of a guard and three other inmates and lit right up, laughing about it. Word got quickly to Schnurr, a man not ordinarily disposed to violence, and he knew he would have to defend his honor in order not to appear weak and vulnerable. Over the course of a week, using a tiny scrap of sandpaper pilfered from the wood shop, he honed the bone handle of his toothbrush to a sharp point.

A full week after the theft of the tobacco, Schnurr crept up behind Ezra in line in the mess hall and stuck the business end of the shiv into his back, right between the shoulder blades, nearly up to the bristles.

Ezra let out a roar of pain and indignation and spun, the weapon still in his back, to face Schnurr. "You son of a bitch," he said, and he picked the smaller man up by his collar and shoved him against the concrete wall.

"That's what you get for nicking my tabacky, you sack of pigshit," Schnurr said, and it must have occurred to him at this point that his plan hadn't been thought quite thorough, that a more lethal entry point might have been more appropriate for his hand-made weapon, for Ezra had his big hands around his neck. He spun him around and bashed his forehead against the edge of one of the long mess tables.

When the guards and then the warden had come into the mess hall to investigate, every inmate present swore that the poor fellow had just tripped and hit his forehead on the edge of one of the long mess tables, hard enough to cave in the frontal bone. The prison doctor noted that the victim seemed to have arisen and fallen again with great force on the same exact spot seven or eight times, but no convict felt strongly enough to finger Ezra. In his written postmortem the doctor settled for a conclusion of accidental death and left it at that.

EZRA KNEW HOW to make friends among his fellow prisoners, and he knew not to keep them at arm's length. He'd been in prison before, a two-year stretch in Maine, and he didn't care to spend any more time locked up than was absolutely necessary this time. Early on he'd established his place in the hierarchy. Out of sight of the guards—or maybe with their tacit approval—he'd broken the cheekbone and jaw of a furry behemoth who was trying to cornhole a skinny little embezzler. The behemoth himself, who had been relying on his mere size to intimidate his way into the top spot, was a wretched pariah afterwards. After this Ezra was determined to keep out of trouble, working diligently in the prison laundry and angling for an early release, because he wanted nothing more than to return to Los Angeles and to the bosom of his little lost family.

28

"Henry, why don't you take my granddaughter out to a Vaudeville this afternoon." He took two silver dollars out of his pocket and gestured.

"Thanks, Bill. Don't you want some help with your portrait session this afternoon?"

"No, this is something for my own use. A lady friend wishes to be immortalized *à poil*."

"What?"

"In the altogether." Henry's expression was still baffled. "Naked."

"I've taken pictures of whores with you before."

"This is a distinguished widow woman from Pasadena who wishes me to have a remembrance of our time together. It's Mrs. Chen's day off, now I just need you and Flavey out of the house."

"The lady I met?"

"Another one."

Henry shook his head in something like admiration.

THEY WENT TO a picture show instead of a vaudeville. First on was a comedy about a shoe salesman getting the hell beaten out of him by one customer after another, and the both of them were laughing hard by the end of it. The feature was a William S. Hart and Henry enjoyed it more than Flavia did. After the show they went walking and he bought her an ice cream cone.

"You think it's all right to go home yet?" she asked.

"How do you mean?"

"I mean you think he's finished with his lady friend?"

"How do you know about that?"

"I know my Gramps well enough to guess that when he makes an effort to get everyone out of the house then he's entertaining a lady."

"Oh. Well, he's taking dirty pictures of this one."

"I don't know that there's a woman he ever set his sights on that he didn't manage to take dirty pictures of."

"Huh. His wives even?"

"Oh, I'm quite sure there are compromising photographs of my grandmother somewhere."

"How can you say such a thing about your dear old grandma?"

She laughed. "She'd probably tell you herself if she were here. She's a pretty candid sort. And as far as his second wife, Maggie, I'll bet it was her own idea. Well, if he was taking pictures of this widow first, they probably didn't get into bed until two or three."

She offered Henry a lick of her ice cream. It was pistachio, a kind he'd never tried before and he hesitated because he didn't think ice cream ought to be green. But he didn't want to look any more like a rube than he already did, so he licked it right where she had and found that he liked it very much.

"For a fellow his age your granddaddy sure has a way with the ladies."

"Always has. Never knew him not to have something going on with a widow or three."

He couldn't get over how she'd started talking to him about sex once they'd gone to bed; from the start he'd thought of her as a Wichita schoolmarm, prim and innocent, and now she was speculating on the sex lives of a couple of elderly people.

"How would you like to take some pictures of me?" she asked. He had no reply. His life had taken a turn he couldn't have imagined back in West Virginia.

MRS. LATTIMORE WAS enthusiastic about the picture-making session, but apprehensive at the same time. "You give me your solemn promise that no one but you and I will ever see these pictures?"

"The negatives and prints will all be kept in a file marked 'TO BE DESTROYED UPON MY DECEASE.' My granddaughter has given me her oath that my instructions will be followed to the letter."

She lay on the canapé with only a sheet draped over her abdomen for cover. She was shy about her belly, convinced as she was that the bearing of children had distended it, and no amount of assurance from Bill would convince her that it was a perfectly normal midriff for a woman of fifty-six. That same enigmatic smile that had intrigued him so on the streetcar played across her mouth, and she lowered her left hand to her genital region, middle finger primed for insertion therein. "How about a picture of this?"

He replaced the film holder and activated the mechanical shutter. "Perfectly delightful."

♦ ♦ ♦

WHEN THE PICTURE-MAKING was done they had repaired to Bill's bedroom, and once they were finished with what they did there she pointed her right leg at the ceiling, toes *en pointe*. "You surely are limber," he said.

"How come a fellow like you isn't married, Bill?"

"That's a hard question to answer. I have two wives back in Kansas."

"Two?"

"The first I abandoned in my youth. Flavia's grandmother. She remarried long ago, though we never officially divorced. The woman who left town with me considers herself my wife, though we never officially married."

"Why's she in Kansas?"

"Because she can't stand my presence. She's got bats in the belfry, writes me letters every so often, ordering me back to Kansas. I ignore them. My family there takes care of her, including my first wife."

"They're friendly?"

"Thick as thieves."

"I don't suppose you'd like to try for a third? We could join the Mormons."

"I don't think I'm up for it. But I'll buy you dinner at Cole's."

29

"You in the shabby bowler."

Feeney looked up, uncertain it was he who was being addressed. He still thought of the hat as his new one. "I?"

"Can you play drunk?"

He rose and staggered, then froze. "Funny or not?"

"It's a melodrama."

He willed a sad look onto his face and staggered in a pathetic manner toward the casting director, then stopped and leaned against an imaginary lamppost, looking dreamily upward, as though contemplating loves lost.

The casting director handed him a slip of paper. "Report to wardrobe. You freeze to death in the first reel."

He straightened up and gave the man a slight bow. "I shall do, eliciting a maximum of pathos."

"Piss off, bud, before I change my mind."

At the door of the wardrobe room he stopped cold at the sight of Maud LeClerc, also known as Sukie. His face felt hot and his hands started to tingle.

"Feeney," she shouted from across the room, where a cranky seamstress was fitting her in a charwoman's ashy gown.

It was she, there was no question of it. Steeling himself, he strode to her side.

"Sukie, my dear. I understood from press reports that

you'd succumbed in the blaze that overtook our former mutual residence."

She cackled, her jagged yellow-gray teeth showing. The seamstress scowled and yanked her slightly forward by the fabric of the gown. "You didn't read the next day's paper, then. Wasn't me got roasted, it was some other old broad they counted as me. Good publicity."

Another seamstress, younger and in better spirits than Sukie, approached Feeney with a tape measure. "You're our sot, I suppose?"

"That I seem to be," he said.

THE LUSH'S BREATH was like the bottom of a rye barrel if you'd been thrown in it headfirst and the lid nailed shut.

"Those kraut cocksuckers are planning to give Texas back to Mexico! I got half a mind to head down to the recruiting station myself tomorrow morning."

"You're almost forty years old, Abner," the bartender said, "with a glass eye and a limp."

Abner was a big man who looked as though someone had shaved his head with a set of dull hedge clippers. He stuck a fat finger in the bartender's face and shook it, slightly harder than his alcoholic tremor already had it shaking. "Otherwise I'd be down there."

"Bill, you're a war vet, what say you?"

"I'm agin it."

Abner turned to face him. "Did you hear me say they want to give Texas back to Mexico?"

"I did, and I've been reading about it in the papers too. Mexico said no thanks."

"Don't matter, they made the offer."

"Seems to me Mexico's neutral and so should we be."

"That's a chickenshit attitude, mister."

The bartender shook his head. "Don't you talk like that to Bill. He was in a war and you wasn't."

"All being a vet means to me is I have a yardstick to judge whether it's worth it or not. Looks to me like this is a family squabble amongst a bunch of inbred European royalty and as a democracy we don't have much at stake therein." He took a long drink of his beer.

"Texas! That's our stake in it. And I guess you don't care how many Americans drowned on them ships they sank."

"My understanding is they stopped doing that in order to keep us neutral."

"They're playing possum." Abner's left hand was in a fist on the bar and was about the size of a grapefruit. He looked around Bill, to whose left stood Henry. "You, young man, how come you ain't in uniform?"

"Draft will take care of that soon enough, I'm afraid," Bill said.

Henry took a sip of his beer. "Might enlist if it comes to that. Haven't quite made my mind up yet."

Bill glanced over at him with some alarm. "Don't do anything rash, now, son."

"There you go!" Abner yelled. "Get the kid a beer and a shot on me, barkeep."

The door swung open and in walked Feeney, accompanied by Sukie, who was back in her civilian garb and looking quite dignified, almost regal. He had been surprised at how glad he'd been to find her still alive, and if he was honest with himself he had to admit that the notion of carnal relations was not without its attractions. He was no great catch, he knew, and if she was willing to sully herself with his touch, then who was he to disdain hers?

Bill called out a greeting. "Who's your charming consort, Feeney?"

He led her to the bar by the elbow as though she were a countess. "Bill, may I present to you the celebrated actress Maud LeClerc?"

"Call me Sukie," she said, "everyone does."

"Miss LeClerc, I saw your Salomé, it was superlative."

"You're far too generous, sir."

"Not in the slightest. That John the Baptist never knew what hit him."

"The wax head was so realistic we had people fainting when they saw it."

"I nearly did myself." He introduced her to Henry and to Abner. "Perhaps this is a delicate matter, but the newspapers reported your death in a hotel fire."

"You may safely disregard as untrue anything the newspapers have to say about me."

Feeney beamed. He sometimes suspected that his drinking companions thought him an exaggerator if not an outright fabulist, and now here they were, interacting respectfully with his old love, a true star of the stage. For this one night the pride he felt was genuine.

30

Melvin van de Kamp was a frequent habitué of Mrs. Spencer's brothel around the corner from Union Station. In Melvin's opinion it was the finest whorehouse in all Indianapolis, rivaling the best houses in Chicago or St. Louis. The girls were clean and friendly and the entertainment first rate. On this evening he'd made it there despite a blizzard that had shut down most of the city, and he was looking forward to an evening of amusements with one or more of the ladies employed there. Maybe, he hoped, he'd get a little something extra for it being such a slow night.

Mrs. Spencer herself let him in to the foyer, resplendent in a maroon robe of a silk so smooth and glistening he had the urge to reach out and caress her considerable bosom, a transgression he knew better than to allow himself. "I've fucked enough of these idiots for one lifetime," she was fond of saying to the girls, "now it's your turn." She was still a handsome woman, though, and if she'd wanted to she still could have done a considerable trade herself.

"Good evening, Melvin, what a surprise to find you out on an evening as inhospitable as this." She had a funny way of talking that was hard to place, somewhere between German and hunky. The maroon of her gown was a subtle echo of the bright red velvet covering the walls, nearly the same shade as that of her lip rouge.

"Evening, Mrs. Spencer."

"The girls are all up in their cribs, none of 'em's done up for trade this evening, I'm afraid. Seeing the weather out I gave them the night off."

"I see. Golly, and I came all the way over here." He stomped his galoshes on the welcome mat for emphasis, knocking chunks of ice onto it. "I don't suppose you could entice one of them to go back on the clock."

"I never give those girls a night off, not even Christmas. It'd be cruel to tell one she's got to come down after all." She cocked her head and gave him a sly look. "I know something you might enjoy, though." She beckoned with a scarlet-taloned index finger and headed down a hallway.

The lamps were all burning low. He'd never been down this corridor before; it was for bigger spenders than he, and he still didn't know exactly what went on back here in the recesses of the big old house. All he could imagine wanting there he received in the embraces of Mabel, Esther, Lenore, Letitia and the rest of them.

She entered a doorway at the end of the hall and lit the lamp next to the door. He hardly dared hope that she was going to make an exception to her rule and allow him access to her person, but he could feel his heart rate quicken and he felt certain he was in for something truly special.

There were richly upholstered benches, all facing a wall that was jarringly unadorned except for a coat of white paint. In the center of the room was a mechanical contraption that he thought might be a motion picture machine.

"You're in for a treat tonight, Melvin. Only the high rollers normally get the chance to take a gander at these."

He fully expected her to remove her robe at that point. Instead she started fussing with the motion picture machine. "Go over there and turn the lamp down a ways, then have a seat."

Disappointed, he dimmed the lamp. "Bit more," Mrs. Spencer said. He turned the key a tad further and she called for him to stop. He took a seat.

"You got you a hankie?"

"Of course I do," he said, taking offense.

"Good. See that you don't get any jism on the brocade, it's a hell of a thing to try and get out. Worst regret of my career was when I ordered these goddamn benches and didn't think to ask the upholsterer what's the easiest fabric to clean spunk off of."

"Mrs. Spencer?"

"Yeah?"

"What's about to happen here?" He was aware of a quaver in his voice, and of its pitch having risen slightly in fear, though fear of what he couldn't have said, exactly.

"My boy, you are about to see something that'll make you glad you were born a man."

There was a clattering sound, followed by the illumination of a bright light within the motion picture machine. He looked back and saw Mrs. Spencer turning the crank. "Don't look at me," she yelled, "look at the goddamn screen!"

A title came up, white letters on a black background, that looked like any other movie title card, except that the words read:

SALLY GETS HER PUSSY EATEN
A Busy Beaver Production

Onscreen a girl, good looking without being pretty, exactly, sat on a bale of hay in front of a wooden fence and fondled her left breast through an open blouse with both hands, a faraway look on her face. Just as she was starting to move her right hand down to her skirt another girl showed up, prettier but somehow not as interesting to Melvin, and laughed. The first girl, embarrassed, moved her hand back to her lap. The second girl sat down and took the hand in her own. A title card appeared:

"Why, Sally, You Mustn't Be Shy About Pleasuring Yourself!"

Melvin, who had just begun his own self-pleasure, had never dreamt such things existed. He had to exercise considerable restraint or he would have ejaculated long before the film's own climax, during which the second girl lowered her face to Sally's mons veneris and took to licking. He was a bit surprised at the amount of ejaculate on his handkerchief, and indeed on the wooden floor of the screening room.

The light in the machine dimmed, and the clattering continued for a bit before slowing and finally stopping, and then Mrs. Spencer was standing beside the lamp at the door, bringing it back up to its previous level.

"Now you tell me that wasn't something to see!" she said. "Aren't you glad you came up tonight, even with the girls on furlough?"

Suddenly ashamed to have committed the sin of Onan

in her presence, he rose and stuffed his pecker back into his trousers, which he then buttoned. "I suppose I'd better get headed back home, thank you very much for the show, Mrs. Spencer."

"Now don't be like that. Just because you came doesn't mean you have to go home. Tonight you get a brandy on the house, just for making the trip down here through the snow."

"I don't partake of alcohol, Mrs. Spencer."

She gave him a look that suggested it would be better not to argue. "Mr. van de Kamp, if you knew how rarely I offer a john a free drink in this house, you wouldn't decline the offer. Now come join me in the parlor and we'll have us a drink and a chat."

KAPLAN HAD THROWN a party after the screening of the new picture the kids were in. It had turned out that audiences loved watching them torment Tommy Gill, who in this one played their bachelor uncle, shanghaied into babysitting them and then brutalized by a shovel, a large cast-iron skillet, a hockey stick and several other dangerous items wielded by little Ezra and Pearlie. On the taxi ride back to Trudy's new place Victoria giggled, tipsy on champagne provided by Mr. Kaplan, whom she'd found perfectly charming. "That was certainly my idea of a fine time," she said.

"It was all right," Trudy said. She'd been nervous as hell, even though she saw most of those people nearly every day at the studio.

"That Tommy Gill sure turns out to be a pill in person, don't he?"

"He was just plastered."

"He didn't like you much, did he?"

"No, he certainly didn't."

"That actor with the mustache, the one who plays the villain all the time, he seemed nice. Asked me out on a date but I put him off. Played a little hard to get."

"He asked me out, too."

Victoria looked disappointed, but only for a moment. "We could go out all three of us. He'd never know what hit him."

Trudy smiled. It took some effort. In the rear-view mirror the cabbie met her eyes and raised his brows as though confirming whether an invitation was somehow being extended his way. She looked hurriedly away.

AT HOME THE children were asleep and grumpy old Mrs. Cullen took her dollar twenty-five and left. She was a white-haired, matronly, devoutly Catholic lady who liked to inquire as to the children's baptismal states as well as Trudy's despite never getting a straight answer, and she made no effort to hide her distrust of Victoria. She didn't approve of the children being associated with the picture business, either. Trudy caught a derisive snort as the old termagant left the house, but Victoria either didn't notice or didn't care.

"It's awful nice to see you again, kid."

"It is. I've meant to get together more, but all day with the kids at the studio . . ."

"Say no more. I understand."

They sat down on the canapé instead of the larger

couch. "You've bought more furniture since last time I was here, ain't you?"

"I guess I didn't have enough of it at the old place so I'm making up for it."

"I don't blame you. I'd do the same."

"I guess I ought to light a fire. It's a little chilly in here."

"It is. And here I'd always heard winter never came in California."

Trudy got up and set about starting a fire in the hearth.

"So at least you're not making dirty pictures any more, eh, Trude?"

"True."

"I'll bet you don't miss that."

"I miss some things."

She got the fire crackling and moved back to the canapé and snuggled a bit closer with Victoria, who gave her a curious look. She leaned in for a quick kiss on the mouth, and after a second Victoria pulled back. "I thought you didn't go for that stuff."

"I reconsidered it," she said.

THE SCREENING HAD been a success, and as the assembled revelers left Kaplan's house one by one Tommy had cornered Myrna in the dining room.

"Honest, Mr. Gill. Tommy. I think you're just about the funniest person I've ever seen, on the screen or off, but that day in your dressing room, that was just the one time."

"It could be a lot more than that, Magnolia. My wife's gone and left me."

She put her hand on his shoulder. "Aw, I'm sorry. Call me Myrna, would you?"

"Myrna, then."

"How come? You didn't tell her about the blow job, did you? I didn't know you were married, by the by. I don't want you thinking I make a habit of doing that with married men."

"Of course I didn't. No, she just admitted to me that all she'd ever been was after my money."

"The hell with her, then. You're a fine man and any woman would be lucky to be with a gentleman like you."

"It could be you. We could make pictures together. Be a team."

"Aw, no, Mr. Kaplan wants me in dramatic pictures, not comedies."

"I could do drama."

"And waste that talent of yours? That picture tonight, you were a real hoot."

"I don't wish to continue making that type of thing, where I'm the constant victim of indignities."

She whacked his left biceps with her palm. "Tough toenails, Tommy, you've hit a gold mine with them two kids. You're part of a trio now."

THE ROOM WAS much like the rest of the house, red velvet wallpaper and dark paneling, and it was barely lit. The chairs were nicer than Melvin had ever seen in his life and he guessed they must have cost about a month of his salary each. "Oh, the johns are just wild for that shit," Mrs. Spencer said, on her third brandy and slurring a little. "Although I made the mistake of showing one without watching it myself first and it turned out to be two fairies! No girls at all. Looks like they'd sent me the wrong one. I just about had a riot on my hands, I'll tell you that. Truth be told though I think a lot of those fellows would have been just as happy if I'd kept on and showed the rest of the picture."

Melvin was still working on his first glass, but the more of it went down the less off-putting he found it, and he did perceive, as she'd predicted, a certain warming effect in his chest. She sat across from him at a table in the sumptuous parlor, that silk robe looking dark brown in the lamplight.

"I don't need to see any of that queer stuff," Melvin said, surprised at how slow his voice was coming out of his mouth, how his tongue wasn't obeying his brain's commands as quickly or precisely as usual.

She cackled. "You sure enough like the queer stuff when it's two gals, though, don't you?"

"Guess I do. Hadn't really put much thought into it before."

Another cackle. "I like you, Melvin," she said. "Not that way, don't get the wrong idea. But you're a regular fella. You treat the girls right, there's always a little something extra for her afterwards. You're polite, not like some of the shitheels we get around here. Especially some of the high rollers. Had an assistant City Attorney in last week, thought he was owed a freebie because he heard the cops got 'em. Had to oblige him or he said he might have to start listening to the church groups want to shut the whole neighborhood down."

"That's no good." He swallowed the rest of his glass, and she poured him another.

"Listen. You can't go home tonight, you're liable to

fall down in a snow drift and freeze to death in your condition."

"My condition . . ." He stopped, genuinely baffled by the length of time it took to get out the four syllables.

"Now you finish that and I'll put you up in one of the spare rooms. By yourself, mind. But you'll be happy enough. Now tell me this, Melvin, you're clearly not a regular drinker. But have you ever tried morphine?"

31

Tommy was headed home in his new Model 30, having spent the night in Kaplan's guest room. The house was still his, for the moment. Beatrice's attorneys had convinced her that a play for the bulk of the estate would be more likely to succeed if she didn't take sole possession of the house immediately. His own, a wily codger by the name of Cudahy, advised him to play along and to keep as quiet as possible the news of his new contract. If they could settle the whole business based on his worth at the time of the separation he had a good shot at screwing her over.

Despite Miss Sweetspire's rejection—which he persisted in thinking of as mere reluctance, a thing to be gradually overcome, rather than an outright refusal—and despite the brutal pounding in his head, he was feeling optimistic as he crossed the town with the top down, despite the early morning chill. Before the pictures with the brats, he was sure Kaplan had been planning to cut him the minute the old contract expired. And Kaplan never would have allowed him to stay overnight before. Hell, this was only the third time he'd ever set foot in the mansion. Now he had a raise and a new car, and the more he thought of it the gladder he was to be done with Beatrice, who had been grating on his nerves for years now. Who knew what she'd been up to over the years, anyway? Probably fucking the gardener and the iceman and the greengrocer. God knew she hadn't done it with him in long enough.

The nerve of her, threatening to expose him. He hadn't done anything wrong back in Burbank. As soon as he'd realized it was a person he'd hit, he'd gone straight to a police box and called it in. "There's an old woman here's been knocked over by an automobile." He would have stayed to wait for the officers or the meat wagon but there was always the chance someone might drive by and recognize him, even out of costume, and besides, what could he have done? He was no doctor.

"JESUS, DID YOU hear the news? Boss let a john spend the night."

Mabel was washing her face. "Thought we were closed last night."

"Van de Kamp showed up in the middle of the blizzard last night and she let him in."

"Who had the honors?"

"Nobody, she just showed him a blue movie and gave him a drink. He's snoring up a storm in the trophy room."

Once her morning toilette was finished Mabel wandered down to the trophy room, so called because Mrs. Spencer had furnished it in honor of President Roosevelt, with stuffed moose and elk heads on the wall and a moth-eaten cougar mounted above the headboard. Melvin was sleeping beyond soundly in the big bed, so deep in slumber that if not for his raspy, slow breaths she would have felt obliged to check for a pulse.

Mrs. Spencer appeared in the doorway behind her.

"How desperate for pussy do you have to be to go out in a storm like that?" she said.

"Poor fella," Mabel said. "He must have been awful lonesome and horny both."

HE WAS VAGUELY aware of the women's voices, but he wouldn't have been able to speak if he'd tried. Good God, what had that woman done to him the night before, and why were they here in his house?

His house.

He wasn't in his house. He was in the whorehouse. And there was cold winter light coming in through the window, so it was morning. He'd watched that disgusting film about the degradation of two innocent young women and abused himself to it and then he'd accepted liquor from Mrs. Spencer and then more liquor. And now he felt quite sick, his head pounding and his stomach turning. And it was Wednesday, which meant that he would be unable to get to work on time unless he went without a shave or a change of clothes, and getting those would require going home anyway, which would require an accounting of his evening's activities. His wife would most assuredly not be amused or mollified no matter what sort of lie he told.

Making his way down the corridor toward the front of the establishment he crossed paths with one of the girls, a petite blonde in a sateen bathrobe of cerulean blue.

"Hiya, Melvin. Word is you had a rough night." She giggled, and the tinkling sound of it made her seem like an innocent child. A fresh wave of shame came over him, and as she distanced herself her laughter continued.

32

After the death of Al Schnurr, Ezra had kept himself mostly out of the sort of trouble that would have interested the parole board, and he was released for good behavior after only eight months of his two-year sentence. On the day of his release, he received two silver dollars and a cheap suit, and he began making his way slowly southward.

Two days into his freedom he was in the seaside town of San Buenaventura. An auditorium downtown advertised boxing matches that evening, and at dusk he climbed the fire escape to the roof. There he watched the fights through a big skylight. They were welterweights and though the first bout wasn't much the second was a good one, the fighters well matched and scrappy, and Ezra took an occasional pull from a bottle of rye. The rye was the only purchase made so far with the two dollars (he'd stolen a couple of sandwiches at a train depot on his way to the freight yards) and the warmth of the evening, the bottle and the free entertainment were all he needed to make him feel as though his luck were about to change. He'd worry tomorrow about money.

"What the hell you doing up on this here roof?" Ezra took him at first for a policeman. But as the man finished climbing the ladder and crunched his boots on the gravel covering the flat rooftop's tarpaper, the glow from the skylight revealed the threadbare gray flannel of a humble watchman's uniform. When he was about ten feet from Ezra's position he unhooked the billy club from his belt, holding it by the leather strap, and spun it in a circle like a propeller. It struck Ezra that the guard thought this was quite a trick, and also that he didn't really know how to use the thing.

Ezra stood up and grinned. "Just looking at a boxing match," he said.

"That there's a paying event. You take off or go down and buy a ticket." He waved the club in a menacing but not convincing manner, and Ezra leaned forward in a quick and easy motion, snatching it. He hit the very surprised watchman in the right hand hard enough to break it. The watchman grabbed the hand with his left and yelled in pain and dismay.

"Now give me your money," Ezra said, waving the club in the vicinity of the man's face.

Blubbering, the man dug in his trouser for a billfold attached to his belt with a chain. "Here," he said, handing Ezra a five-dollar bill and two singles.

"Smart fellow," Ezra said. "I won't tell nobody about this and if you don't either I reckon you'll still have your job."

WHEN THE MATCHES were over he climbed back down to the street and, feeling lucky and prosperous, bought himself dinner in a restaurant on Main Street. He had a ham steak and mashed potatoes and roast carrots and, just to be classy, a glass of wine. The waiter looked at him sideways—Ezra suspected he knew from experience what a penitentiary release suit looked like—but served him and took his money without complaint, so there wasn't any cause to get sore. When he was done he walked into the lobby of a hotel he'd passed by earlier and inquired as to the nightly rate. Finding it reasonable, he checked in and went upstairs for a good night's sleep.

ON HIS THIRD day in Los Angeles he went to the movie house. There was a Krazy Kat—how the hell did they get those drawings to move like that, anyway?—followed by a comedy featuring a pair of kids, a sister and her younger brother, wreaking havoc in a movie theater. The feature was a Western with William S. Hart playing an outlaw by the indisputably dashing name of Ice Harding. By the end of the picture Ezra was considering reforming his wicked ways just like old Ice. The only problem with such a plan, Ezra thought as he stepped out of the auditorium and into the warm Los Angeles evening, was the accrual of money. Ice Harding acted as though there wasn't any trick to that.

33

Grady was sitting at the counter of his neighborhood Pig and Whistle eating his breakfast and looking at the mail from his post office box. It was the usual, cashier's checks and orders from around the country, the latter all in code to fool the postal inspectors. One was a fan letter from the head of an Elk's lodge in southern Illinois, wondering whether there was any chance he could pay for an in-person meeting with Trudy:

> *I am quite taken with her way of making ecstatic faces when she is at the height of her arousal and I consider her to be quite a handsome woman. It is plain she is not the kind of woman one typically espies in these sorts of entertainments. In case she was agreeable I would consider it an honor to travel to Los Angeles or any place she chose for a few days of camaraderie and luxury.*

Jesus, where did people get ideas like that? After a moment's deliberation he decided he'd have Irene Buntnagel write the reply (the return address was the lodge, and not a residence; still, the man had taken an unreasonable risk). The one he was mentally preparing might have lost him a customer.

Then he opened an envelope with no return address at all, postmarked Indianapolis.

Dear sirs,

It has come to my attention that you are sending out films around the country by way of the United States Postal Service, in whose employ I work as an inspector. I am reliably informed that said films are of a disgusting and obscene nature, including but not limited to scenes of sodomistic homosexuality. This is of course a violation of the laws of man and God and the United States government. Please be assured that it is not my intention to put you into Leavenworth or out of business. I merely wish you to know that you have an ally in the United States Post Office and that instructions will be forthcoming.

A Friend

Irene phoned George as soon as she was off the phone with Grady. "What are we going to do about this?"

"We'll see what he wants when he contacts us again."

"That's no good, George."

"What else can we do?"

"You don't seem very damned worried about it." Her office door was closed, and she still had to force herself to keep her voice down.

"If this really is from a postal inspector, he's putting himself at risk by not turning us in immediately. Grady's got this letter, which could get the man fired or worse, so I don't see what the danger is. The worst is we have to pay him something to make him go away."

"No. The worst thing is there could be a headline in *Variety* about Provident Studios director George Buntnagel getting caught making . . ." Outside her office she saw Bernice Appleby turn in her direction, startled by the tenor and volume of her voice, and she lowered it to a hiss. "Making pornographic pictures."

"I'M REAL SORRY, Mrs. Stang, you've been a real good landlady."

"I'm sorry to see you go, dear, but I'm happy for your new position."

"Thanks awfully."

Mrs. Stang was a plump, sweet, credulous woman from Canada who believed every story Victoria had ever told her. Most of these involved what she did for a living, but they included fictions about her childhood as well. In these she was the black sheep of a manufacturing family back east, makers of surveying tools, cut off after she went west looking for work in the pictures.

"You'll show them someday," Mrs. Stang was fond of predicting. "They'll go to the picture show and there you'll be, bigger than life."

The funny part was that Victoria hadn't really come out to be in show business. She'd heard the weather was nice. And she'd ended up in pictures anyway, of a sort.

34

"Cocksucker."

"And a merry Christmas to you as well, Mrs. Duggins," Bill said.

She spat on the dusty floor in response. Abner was back but not in the mood to discuss politics tonight, which suited Bill fine. The bartender was in the midst of telling the sad story of how he'd been thrown out of high school back in Bangor, Maine, for setting the chemistry lab on fire, condemning himself to a less richly intellectual life than he might otherwise have enjoyed.

"I was always expected to go on to college," he said.

"Surely there was another high school in Bangor that would have accepted you."

"No, sir, I was considered a miscuant."

"Do you mean a miscreant?"

"I do."

Henry came in the front door and made his way to the bar next to Bill. The bartender poured him a shot of rye and a steam beer chaser without needing to ask.

"So anyway, Bill, I was wanting to talk to you. Thought I might find you here."

"You could talk to me at the studio. Glad to have your company here, though."

"It's a hard subject to broach at the studio. It's got to do with Flavia. Miss Ogden."

"I see."

"You know that she and I've been keeping company for a little bit now."

"That's no secret."

"Well, we've been up to more than that." He looked down at the sawdust on the floor, then back up at Bill. "Mrs. Chen's made it real clear she's on to us, you see, and I was afraid she might let you know before she or I did."

"Oh, she already has, my lad. But I already knew."

"You knew?"

"For God's sake, she's a widow woman, not some virgin schoolmarm. And you're a red-blooded American boy. No reason at all for her to keep you out of her bed."

Henry's face got hot fast and he swigged his shot and took a drink of his beer. "You don't mind?"

"I believe I just said that."

"But she's your granddaughter and all."

"And you're a young suitor with fine prospects."

"Prospects, hell, I still say you ought to be in the army," Abner said to Henry.

"Cocksucker," Mrs. Duggins said, and she turned toward Abner with cold fury in her eyes, one of them squinting so hard it looked like it must hurt. She pointed a gnarly finger at him and spat. "Vile thing, a slave to your vices and a spreader of disease."

Abner, who had only been a habitué since a week before Thanksgiving, had never heard her speak a word other than cocksucker, and he was crestfallen. "Ma'am, I don't believe you even know me."

Bill had heard versions of this before, directed on one

occasion at himself. Every man she had addressed it to seemed to consider it just, even as they stammered and tried to defend their characters. Henry had gone pale, as though she were addressing him and not big, dumb Abner.

"Any animal with balls twixt its legs is guilty of it. Lust and sin and plagues and who pays for it all?" She spat on the floor and returned her attention to her beer.

"A word of advice from an old man with several wives," Bill said to Henry. "Give her something nice for Christmas. That'll go a long way."

35

It was Christmastime and Ezra finally had his hands on a gun. He had burglarized a house in Santa Monica on a quiet street near the ocean, having taken the streetcar down to see the pier. It had been a balmy evening for December, even by the standards of Los Angeles, and he reckoned he might as well get some sea air in his lungs. The pier was crowded for a Thursday, the weather having lured a goodly number of his fellow Angelenos out for the evening, and among the throng he had noticed a big, drunken, red-headed lout in a fancy wool suit with a pretty girl at his side and a loaded wallet, which he kept taking out and extracting money from for the benefit of the girl friend. He had a loud mouth, and when he passed Ezra by he jostled his elbow purposely and guffawed. The girl, a pretty blond thing, started laughing hysterically, a high, thin cutting sound, as though the jostling of a stranger in a crowd were the soul of wit. Normally Ezra would have done something then and there but the man's full wallet and state of inebriation told him to wait.

He kept them in his peripheral vision, watching the big oaf getting drunker as he pulled from a pocket flask, losing badly at the shooting gallery and heckling a roly-poly gent playing the accordion. It seemed to Ezra the musician was playing well enough, and so irked by the redhead was he that he uncharacteristically tossed a penny into the player's upturned hat. After an hour they headed away from the pier and Ezra followed at a distance of twenty yards. If they got into an automobile he was sunk, but if they took a streetcar he'd get on. Neither of them would remember him from the pier, and if they did, so what?

As it happened he walked her to an apartment building a few blocks northwest of the pier and argued playfully with her outside about whether or not he could go upstairs with her. Ezra made his way to a bench on the sidewalk, the palisades to his back, and pretended to be otherwise engaged, though they'd taken no notice of him. He wasn't in earshot when she said it, but it was plain she was telling him he could come up but for just a second. Something made him think that the girl really might manage to get rid of him in a minute or two.

The evening was balmy and people walked past him, talking about this and that and laughing, all of them having a better time than Ezra was. It took about fifteen minutes for the big dolt to storm out the front door of the building, looking as though a great wrong had been done him. No doubt he subscribed to the notion that if a gal invited you into her living quarters she was inviting you into her bloomers. He lurched down the sidewalk, unsteady on his big feet, and headed northeast toward a neighborhood of neat bungalows with nicely trimmed lawns and a surprising number of automobiles parked on the streets. He turned onto one of the streets and walked up the path to the door, which he opened without unlocking it. Perfect. It was dark already, but early enough that people were still out and neighbors still looking out their kitchen windows.

Ezra went back to the pier, content and determined to

spend the rest of the seventy cents in his pocket. He might even tip the accordionist again if he'd play a request.

He had himself a good time. He ate a frankfurter with extra sauerkraut and mustard and had a couple of beers and tipped the accordionist a nickel for knowing "The Convict and the Bird." Then he wandered around Santa Monica humming to himself until he heard the bells of a church in the distance tolling midnight.

Out of caution he tried the back door first, and found it unlocked. He found himself in a dark kitchen, and in another room someone was snoring as only a big, fat drunk can snore, horrible long heaving mucousy sounds followed by breathless wheezing. He peeked into the room from which the sounds emitted and saw the ape sprawled across a bed intended for two, reeking of gin and vomit. A cursory check of the rest of the house revealed no other inhabitants, and Ezra began ransacking the place.

In the lid of the sugar jar were twenty ten-dollar bills, and on another night he might have declared victory and left in a state of elation. Tonight he went back into the bedroom and looked around. There was a dim light from a streetlamp streaming through the window and he started pulling drawers open. One contained a woman's clothing and effects, and he noted that there were several pictures on the dresser of a rather pretty, sweet-faced woman as well as a wedding photo of the same woman with the red-headed brute. Examining one of them in the faint light of the window he decided he would like her if he knew her, and this made him hate old Red even more. Had he driven her away, back to her parents, or into the arms of another man? Or was she off somewhere taking care of an ailing relative, with him taking advantage of her absence to dally with the blond hussy from the pier? Perhaps she'd died. The thought made Ezra strangely melancholy.

Beneath her delicate undergarments Ezra touched something hard and cold. Without shutting the drawer he brought it into the light. It was a revolver, a big one, and loaded. He considered waking Red up and getting the woman's story from him. But if it was sad he might take pity on the galoot and that could lead to complications. Also, if he didn't wake him, he could use the pillow to muffle the sound of the gunshot, and he was eager to assess the trigger's action.

Red made a gurgling noise when the pillow went over his face, but he didn't wake. Even pressed into the pillow the gun made more noise than Ezra had expected, and there was a hell of a mess, with blood and brains all over the head of the bed. After waiting a minute to see whether any of the neighbors' lights came on he left out the back door and crossed a back lawn to reach the next street over. Then he started the long trip back to his flop.

AND NOW THE lovely gun was his. The murder had made the papers, from which Ezra learned that the man he'd killed was an employee of one of the motion picture studios—he wondered if he'd seen any of the man's pictures—and that he had in fact been a widower.

It was a few days before Christmas when he thought about using the gun again. He'd been careful not to spend too much, as it would be nice to have some time to plan before he absolutely needed to rob someone or someplace. He'd moved into another residential hotel, the

Strathmore, and so far hadn't been importuned by any thieving neighbors. Despite its considerable cost the hotel had a clientele that was on the seedy side. There were actors and musicians, of a higher caliber and status than those of the Crosley, but actors and musicians nonetheless, and Ezra was far from the only ex-convict there. The night before he'd spent thirty-five dollars on a tear with an Irish tenor named Maloney, an amount he'd never dreamt of spending in a single night, and after that they'd rolled a drunk on Sunset Boulevard, only to find him penniless.

He had money left, but the omnipresence of the holiday decorations around town and the absence of his lost little family had put him into a deep funk and he needed something to revive his spirits. He decided to rob a pharmacy and take some medicine as well as cash. He could sell the medicine to some of his new friends at the Strathmore.

It was the twenty-third of December when he boarded a bus headed for downtown, gun in his coat.

THE WOMAN BEHIND the counter was stupefied by the stranger's demand for all the cash in the till. "It's a quarter to six in the afternoon, mister."

"What the hell's that got to do with it?"

"Well, you see, we close at six."

He waved the barrel of the gun in her face. He had a bandana over his nose and mouth and despite the cool weather he was sweating through it pretty good in spots. He'd turned the bolt shut on the front door on entry. "Give me all the goddamn money in the cash register right now or I'll shoot you in the goddamn eye."

She opened the cash register, with its little ringing bell, and gave him the two silver dollars, ten quarters, eight dimes, six nickels and twelve pennies in the drawer.

"That can't be all of it."

"But it is. See, mister, once the owner's done for the day he closes out the register and goes to the bank to make the deposit and just leaves me enough to make change for the rest of the day."

"But you're not closed yet. Don't he still have to fill prescriptions?"

"Not after five-thirty."

"All right." He pulled down the shade and turned around the CLOSED sign. "You get back there and get me some cocaine. And some heroin."

Where had this fellow been? "That stuff's against the law now. We don't have it any more."

"Get me some goddamn morphine then."

"It's all locked up after five-thirty, mister."

The stick-up man was distraught, but he seemed to believe her. "Damned little for a man to risk his neck for," he said as he left.

She watched him take his bandana off out on the sidewalk and wipe his face with it. She wondered if maybe that had been his first attempt at a robbery, and she felt a little sorry for him as she picked up the phone and asked the operator to connect her with the boss's house.

IT WAS A good thing he hadn't, for once, needed the money. Maybe that had been the problem; his ability to eat hadn't been at stake. His latest crime had made the *Examiner* as well, but in a very different tone than his previous appearance there. This time the article belittled the pathetic armed robber who'd made off with less than six dollars and, according to the woman he'd held at gunpoint, seemed "awful anxious and even a little sad." Furious, he considered going back and shooting her after all, but after he thought about it he realized it was an over-reaction; besides, that would have been a good way to get himself caught again. He still had over a hundred and twenty dollars left of big Red's money. Once it was nearly gone he'd get to stealing again.

36

It was a more opulent holiday than any of them had ever known. Trudy scarcely knew where to put all the gaudily wrapped packages the studio had sent over, so she covered them with a canvas tarpaulin. One afternoon Victoria had brought home a fir tree with a cunning metal stand that had a dish underneath it to hold water and keep the tree from dying too soon. On the morning of Christmas Eve she went to a department store in Glendale and returned in a taxi with several boxes full of multicolored ornaments, variously gilded or crystalline. A little ceramic baby Jesus with bright red cheeks and lips smiling from within his robin egg blue swaddling blanket, a dove with its outstretched wings covered in glitter and a beehive made of glass were the favorites of the children. "Don't worry, I spent my own money," Victoria had said, seeing the expression on Trudy's face.

"I didn't say anything."

"I just don't want you to think I'm wasting the kids' earnings."

When the studio car brought the children home that evening they found the tree completely trimmed and some of the gifts piled upon the red blanket underneath it. Four stockings hung by the chimney, with their names embroidered thereupon.

"Aunt Vickie did the needlework herself," Trudy said.

This talent had come as a surprise to her, as she hadn't thought of Victoria as domestic in any way.

ON CHRISTMAS MORNING Tommy Gill was goddamned sad to spend it alone. Whatever else she'd done to him, Beatrice had always provided him with a decent breakfast on the twenty-fifth, whether she made it with her own hands or not, and even when they were broke she'd made the day a jolly one, exchanging gifts silly and not. And even in their touring days he hadn't spent the day alone.

It had been nearly eleven when he woke up, his sheets rancid and slightly damp from sweat. Immediately upon her departure Beatrice had notified the servants and all of the outside household services of her change of address, and Tommy hadn't any of their information. He had no idea how to arrange such things, and no inclination to learn. When he got around to it he'd hire a household manager and have her supervise such things. A stern old termagant with white hair in a bun, or maybe a younger lady he might occasionally lure into an illicit embrace.

Thinking about it made him horny. Christmas morning was a hell of a time to be randy and alone, but he didn't fancy a trip to a brothel and he had no desire to risk a venereal infection from a streetwalker. And as a popular motion picture star he certainly had no intention of committing the sin of Onan; that was beneath his dignity. He recalled Chalky Fagin telling him how when his family went back east for a month one summer to visit his wife's relations he'd taken advantage of a service that provided high class girls who made house calls. He found Chalky's number in his address book and telephoned him. He was certain the operator could hear the near-panic in his voice, and he wondered if she knew who he was.

It was Mrs. Fagin who picked up the phone. He wished her a very merry Christmas and could hear the children laughing in the background. She reported on their holiday in far greater detail than Tommy cared to hear, and finally he asked for Chalky.

"Merry Christmas, Tommy," Chalky said.

"And the same to you, old pal. Say, can you give me the telephone number for that service you were using a couple summers back?"

"What service is that?"

"You know. The girls who come straight to your house."

"Why you son of a bitch, you've got a hell of a nerve calling up my house on Christmas morning and asking a question like that."

Tommy could hear Mrs. Fagin in the background, remonstrating him for using such language in front of the children, and on a holiday yet! Then there was silence, and he jiggled the hook a few times before accepting the fact that he'd been hung up on.

He got dressed and went out to the garage. He didn't feel like driving but he didn't suppose there'd be many taxis out and about, and when he pulled out of the alley and onto the street his was the only vehicle in sight. The day was beautiful, the sky an intense, pale winter's blue, the slightest breeze rustling the palm trees and the temperature neither hot nor cold but perfectly suited to the lightweight suit he had on.

Just for fun he drove into the unoccupied left-hand lane and zigzagged, drove in a circle then began driving in wide curves, going from lane to lane and having a pretty good time for about five blocks until he heard the screech of a whistle and noted for the first time an angry policeman, whistle in his mouth, pointing an accusatory finger at him. He pulled on the brake, cut the ignition and stepped out of the car.

"I'm awful sorry, officer, you see there weren't any other cars on the street."

"You sit back down, pal. I suppose you're licensed to drive."

The copper approached, hand on the billy club dangling from his belt. His helmet was slightly askew and his scowl looked habitual.

"I am, officer, and by the way, merry Christmas."

"Show me."

He pulled his wallet from his back pocket and leafed through it. "It's here somewhere . . ."

"Just because you don't see anyone else on the road doesn't mean there isn't anybody. You didn't see me 'til I blew my whistle."

"That's true, officer, and I'm awful sorry about it. Just caught up in the joy of the holiday . . . this is embarrassing, I seem to have left the driver's license at home someplace."

"How drunk are you, anyhow?"

"Sober as a judge."

"What's your name?"

"Tommy Gill."

"Just like the picture clown."

"Exactly the same, officer, in fact I'm he."

The policeman looked him up and down, unconvinced. "So you say."

"I look a bit different without my signature whiskers and makeup."

"Do your funny walk, then."

Tommy got out of the car and did the walk, goofy face and all.

"All right, Mr. Gill. I ought to run you in for driving without your license, but seeing as it's Christmas I can let you off with a warning. It'll just be a twenty-dollar fine, payable in cash."

"Aren't these things usually dealt with via some sort of citation? A traffic ticket, as they say?"

"Well, Mr. Gill, I see it like this. Someone has to guard the streets, even on Christmas morning. I'd rather be home with the wife and kids, but I have a duty to perform. And tonight, when I get home, my wife and kids and I are going to have a late celebration. And what would put me in a mood for celebrating would be an extra twenty-dollar bill to hand my wife, sort of a way to make up for my being gone on the morning of, you get me?"

Tommy already had his hand in the wallet. He handed the officer a twenty and then, on some impulse he couldn't quite define, took a second and handed him that, too. "Of course I understand. Have a wonderful holiday with the family."

"You're a real gent, Mr. Gill. The kids'll be thrilled to hear I met you." The scowl was gone, replaced by a genuinely good-natured smile on the man's red face. "You drive carefully from now on, and have a merry Christmas yourself." The officer gave him a contented, casual salute and walked back to the corner.

THE STUDIO PHOTOGRAPHER and publicity man showed up at nine in the morning, and the children were ecstatic because that meant they'd soon be unwrapping the gifts scattered beneath the tree.

"Mrs. Crombie, you remember me, studio publicity, and this fellow here holding the camera's Asa. We sure are sorry to be interrupting your holiday for this, but Mr. Kaplan is awful keen to get these kids in the newspapers and picture magazines."

"It's all right," Trudy said, showing the men into the parlor. "Mr. Kaplan was very kind sending over all these gifts."

"And these are the tots themselves," the publicist said. "Acey, why don't you get your lights set up."

The photographer set about removing his lights from his case, and the publicist pulled out a pad and pencil. "Tell me a little bit about last Christmas."

"Last Christmas?"

"Sure. Just a little bit about how much better things are since the kiddies got big in pictures."

"Well. We were living in a tiny little apartment. And of course their father's dead."

"Can you tell us how he passed?"

She hadn't considered this. "Well, you see, it's like this, he was run over by a locomotive."

"Oh, boy, that's tough, all right. Railroad man?"

"Yes. He was a railroad man."

"Railroad make it right by you?"

"Well, no, they didn't."

"That's rotten."

She regretted it already. As lies went it was easy to disprove. "Please don't put that in your story."

"That's right, we don't want it to seem too tragic, do we? All right. But you're a widow woman, and last Christmas was bleak."

"Oh, it was. Pearl got an orange and a little cloth doll no bigger than your thumb, and little Ezra got a little clown the same size, and I counted myself lucky to be able to offer that."

"No orange for Ezra?"

"Pearl shared hers with him."

"Now that's what I'm talking about. That's pure gold right there, Mrs. Crombie."

"Please call me Trudy."

At that moment Victoria came out of the kitchen carrying a tray with a pot of hot chocolate and six demitasse cups on matching saucers. "Allow me to introduce myself," she said, placing the tray down on the dining room table. "I'm Miss Tessart, Mrs. Crombie's sister."

"And you're visiting for the holidays?"

"I've just moved here to help with the children. It's just wonderful, seeing how they're getting on in the pictures."

Trudy watched as Victoria poured the hot chocolate, demure and charming and quite comfortable with the press people, as though she'd been doing it her whole life. They chatted for a minute and drank, and when they were done Victoria wetted a tea towel and wiped the children's mouths clean for the photos.

"I'm all ready," Asa said. "You want the kids by themselves on the canapé?"

"Yeah, get me two or three and then we'll do one with Mama and Auntie and then we'll get some with the tree and the presents."

TOMMY DROVE AROUND for a long while without seeing any restaurants that seemed to be open for business, and then on Colorado Boulevard he spotted a greasy spoon with lights on inside. He parked at an angle and went in. With the sole exception of a morose counterman the place was unoccupied.

"Come on in," the man said. "Grill's still hot."

Tommy took a stool at the counter and looked up at the clock above the grill. It was almost two forty-five already. "Little late for lunch, but too early for dinner."

"I haven't had anyone in since ten-thirty. Just didn't see the point in closing up." He had on a little paper hat, and a black bow tie, and at some point his nose had been broken and set wrong.

"What I'd really like is breakfast," he told the man. "I woke up late and I'm a little hung over."

The counterman considered it. "No law says I can't cook you breakfast past noon." He spoke without removing his cigarette from his mouth, and though it bobbed up and down with each syllable its ash did not drop. "I'll get you a glass of orange juice and you can top it off from your flask."

Tommy was a little startled that the man knew he carried a flask. Surely he wasn't that obvious a soak? But he was glad for the suggestion. "Eggs over easy and bacon. Home fries."

The man nodded and went to the icebox, from which he extracted a pitcher of juice. He poured Tommy a glass with a little room left for gin. "I squoze a whole dozen oranges this morning, don't know what I was thinking. Should have knowed there'd be no business on Christmas day."

Tommy unscrewed the top of the flask and poured a generous slug into the juice. "Why don't you pour yourself a glass?" he said, offering the man the flask.

"Don't mind if I do," the man said, taking it out of Tommy's hand with a grateful nod.

Half an hour later Tommy's plate was clean, the flask was empty and the two of them were plotting where to get more gin on Christmas day. "I know a Jew runs a liquor store downtown," the counterman said.

"Might be worth the trip. What if it's against the law to sell liquor on Christmas, though?"

"Then we will have tried."

Tommy nodded. "Let's go. Now I've got a meal in me I feel like a little drive."

The counterman, Marvin by name, asked if he could take a turn at the wheel.

"You know how to drive?"

"Sure I do. Before the Missus took off I used to drive her and the little ones around all over the place."

"She got the car?"

Marvin nodded. "And she don't even drive. Her pa come up from San Diego on the train and drove them all back down there. You got any kids?"

"None as I know of," Tommy said, elbowing his new friend.

Marvin took the driver's seat and started the engine. "If there is a law against opening a liquor store on Christmas day, it shouldn't ought to apply to a Jew anyway," he said, pulling out of the parking spot.

"Far as I'm concerned, everything closing on Christmas is a goddamned pain in the ass, Jew or not. You know how far I had to drive before I found a place open for a meal? Might have starved. Wife left and took the cook with her."

"You had a cook?"

"Sure did. Colored gal, really knew her way around a kitchen."

"This right here is a brand-new automobile, too. What do you do in the world, anyhow?"

"I'm in the picture business."

"YOU DON'T SUPPOSE your old man's going to see those photographs, do you?"

Trudy took a deep breath and found she needed to sit down. "Lordy, I never thought of that."

"Really? With the kids in the movies and all?"

"He's been gone so long he wouldn't know the kids, they've grown so much. But if my picture's up someplace . . ."

"Maybe better ask them to just use the ones of the kids. Or use the ones with me and say I'm their mama."

"Sure, that might work."

Pearl was playing with a new doll with a head of bisque, made in France and dressed in clothes nicer than any Trudy had ever had herself before this last year, and Ezra was running a tin fire wagon back and forth on the floor, making the sounds of the horses and the rumbling wheels and the klaxon one after the other. Victoria's hand was on Trudy's thigh, warm and strong, and they were both drinking toddies. Supper was in the oven heating up, and even the baleful prospect of Ezra Sr. finding them didn't seem likely enough to dispel the warm feeling the fire and the toddy and Victoria's hand brought. Still, she jumped at the knock on the front door.

"Lordy, who's that at five-thirty Christmas afternoon?" Victoria said, rising. The little ones hardly looked up as the door opened and George and Irene Buntnagel stood there on the stoop bearing gifts.

"Come in and have a seat," she said, gesturing toward the parlor.

Pearl jumped up from the floor and ran toward Irene, while little Ezra remained seated with his fireman's wagon. George took Irene's parcels and deposited the whole pile next to the other presents at the foot of the tree. "Looks like you haven't opened anything yet," he said.

Victoria smirked and gestured toward Trudy. "She won't let them. Just the dolly and the fire wagon."

Trudy could feel her mouth pinching up. "It just doesn't feel right, all those boxes from the studio. Spoiling them rotten, as though I had no say in the matter."

"It's for publicity's sake," George said.

"Still. That's too many. I never got more than one gift in my life, if I even got that."

He gestured toward the kids. "They don't mind?"

"They don't know what's in there. They're awful pleased with what they've got right there."

"Mama?" Pearl spoke up, still clutching Irene's skirt.

"Yes?"

"Is he talking about those packages Irene and him brought?"

She hesitated. "They're for other people."

"They're for you and Ezra. And one for your mama and one for Auntie Vic."

Trudy addressed the children while glaring at George. "You may open the presents the Buntnagels brought."

Victoria selected one gift for Pearl and one for Ezra and handed them out. As the kids demolished the intricately wrapped boxes, Irene put a hand on Victoria's shoulder.

"While they're busy with that, let's adjourn to the kitchen. Something's come up in regards to our little enterprise you should be aware of."

37

1917

Clyde had taken to avoiding the Gower property during the workday except when doing the book-work and editing. He hadn't shot a frame of film since before Thanksgiving and was preparing for a new picture for the second week of January, albeit with a reluctance bordering on dread. There had been two more letters from the blackmailer in Indianapolis, about whom he still knew nothing other than his supposed employment as a postal inspector. It wouldn't have been so bad if he'd just ask for something specific. The last one had ended with an offer to take part in the business himself:

> *I have some pretty good ideas for 'plots.' Perhaps you can use them. One is of the 'farmer's daughter' variety and another is a comic-type tale about a cock-sucking countess with a taste for her 'inferiors,' i.e., her husband's valet, the frenchie chef, the stable boys et ca., and the whole thing finishes in a sort of orgie in which her husband the count reluctantly joins in. As you will see I have quite an imagination and once we have settled our business deal-ings you may wish to include me as a participant in your enterprise. I would be quite willing to relocate.*

Magnificat Educational Distribution Company, Incor-porated had four customers in Indianapolis as well as one in Fort Wayne. There had to be some way of ascertaining which one had allowed a punter to get the name and address of the company. He doubted the letter writer could be the same person responsible for the ordering and exhibition of the pictures, because that person was taking almost as big a risk as he and the Buntnagels were. There were three fraternal orders that ordered three or four times a year and a whorehouse that ordered on the regular. That one seemed the least likely; it was owned and operated by a madam, and he doubted any men ever got anywhere near the business office.

Grady's daughter was fifteen, his son twelve, and over their Christmas holiday they hadn't failed to notice their dad's ill humor. "It's just business worries," he told them on New Year's morning. "Things will work themselves out before long."

"I thought business was going so well lately," his daughter said. She was seated across from him at the breakfast table, next to her brother, and their mother was still in bed at almost eleven in the morning nursing a hangover. They'd been to a party at her brother's house the night before that had got out of hand in ways no one had anticipated, and he'd walked in on her and some cousin of her brother's wife *in flagrante delicto*. It had been something of a blow but he figured turnabout was fair play and all, and in the end he'd enjoyed watching.

"Oh, it is, just a few little snags that are giving old Dad some headaches. No reason at all for you to fret."

"Dad?"

"Son?"

"What is the business, anyway?"

"You know what it is."

"Educational films, I know that. But what sort of educational films?"

"Oh, films for churches and schools and such like."

"I've never seen a moving picture in school."

"Oh. Fortunately for me—and for you—not every school district is as backwards and benighted as in Los Angeles."

"Or church, either."

"When's the last time you were at church?"

"Mama took us on Christmas Eve," his daughter said.

"Ah, well, they're not going to screen a movie on the most sacred day of the Christian calendar, are they?"

"I don't think Christmas Eve is the most sacred."

He inhaled through clenched teeth. "All right. But there are lots of churches out across the country who like to spice things up with a motion picture about the life of Christ or Moses or what-have-you."

"I'd like to see those," his son said.

"I would too," said his daughter. "Can we have a show?"

"We don't keep them around to screen for ourselves. They're always out on rental."

"Maybe one day when one comes back in you could show us."

"Sure, one day."

"I'd like to come see one being made," his daughter said.

"So would I."

"We operate on what they call a closed set. No visitors. That allows the actors to concentrate and do their best work without a whole lot of delays."

"But shouldn't we learn the business?" his son said. "Someday we can come in and help you out, and when you retire you'll need someone to take over."

Jesus Christ, it was as though they could read his mind and were trying to drive him crazy just like the phantom postal inspector. "We'll see about it, kids. In the meantime you just take school as seriously as you can."

On his way to the office that day he found his thoughts drifting to the story idea about the countess, and it occurred to him that he should run it past George. If the costume rentals weren't too expensive it might make a good dirty picture.

MELVIN VAN DE Kamp was getting to be the most regular client of all at Mrs. Spencer's, though he rarely bothered with a girl any more. Mostly he just wanted to watch the picture shows. Mrs. Spencer was just fine with that, because what she lost in per-transaction payment she made up for with the frequency of his visits. The poor squirrelly fellow could get his rocks off watching the same picture three or four times, and he didn't care what kind of picture it was, girl on girl, gang bang, boy girl, he even watched the one with the masks and whips she'd almost regretted booking a whopping five times. And every third or fourth visit he'd retreat to a boudoir with one of the girls.

His personality was different now, more confident, it seemed to her, less embarrassed. It was something she saw in a lot of men, embarrassment, especially the ones from small towns and the ones who hadn't ever had any experience before they got married. Some of them lost it after a while, and others didn't. Some of them enjoyed it, she suspected, secretly enjoyed the shame of sneaking around with women of low character, at least the way they saw things. Melvin used to be one of those, and now he acted like a man of the world instead of a mousy little postal worker from New Albany, Indiana.

"You ought to make some of those pictures right here," he'd said to her not long before. "These gals are as good looking as the ones in the movies, some of them are at least."

"I don't want to do that, Melvin, that's just a lot of headaches for me and more cops to pay off. Besides, who do you know who's got a motion picture camera? Or who knows how to operate one?"

"I'm sure I could learn. How hard could it be? You know how to operate the projector yourself, it can't be much harder than that."

MIRIAM VAN DE Kamp was at her physician's cabinet, dressed again and seated on the examining table, not a little flustered by the pelvic examination Dr. Fletcher had just administered. He'd left the room shaking his head and muttering, told her to leave a urine sample in a bedpan and then get dressed. A nurse came in to collect the sample, and after nearly an hour's wait the nurse returned, red-faced and avoiding her gaze.

"Dr. Fletcher wanted me to come in and have a little talk with you about your condition."

"My condition."

"Your complaint. What brought you in. The case . . ." She stopped, looked up into Miriam's eyes for a brief moment and then cast them downward again. "The inflammation in your pelvic area."

"Yes?"

"The urine test."

"Yes?" she said again, impatience starting to rise.

"I'm afraid it's gonorrhea, ma'am."

Miriam realized that her mouth was hanging open. "It's what, now?"

"Gonorrhea. It's a type of social disease."

"I know what it is . . . but how? I've been intimate with no one but my husband Melvin."

"Well, then . . ." The nurse stopped herself.

"But that's ridiculous! When would he have the time? He does that to me every single night regardless of my opinion on the matter, even when I was expecting a baby. He can't possibly have the energy or desire to do it to others in my absence."

"Nonetheless, ma'am, it's gonorrhea. We treat it with what's called a silver proteinate. I'd recommend you have your husband come in as well."

"I won't have to. That two-timing son of a bitch. I'll kill him, that's what I'll do, I'll cut his lying throat while he sleeps."

"THAT'S IMPOSSIBLE," HE said without looking up from the sports page. "You can go back there and tell that quack he's out of his goddamn mind." He was sitting in his favorite stuffed chair with the floor lamp on, trying to read the evening paper. He was engrossed in an article about an upcoming three-cushion billiards tournament and was not going to allow her hysterical fantasies to intrude upon his hour of reverie.

"I didn't talk to the doctor, I talked to the nurse, who

could barely stand talking to the likes of me. Believe me when I say you gave me a dose." Miriam's face was drained white in the light from the floor lamp, her mouth pinched tight, her hands in useless little fists at her side.

He put the paper down and dug his fingers into the doilies on the arms of his stuffed chair. "Then it must have been somebody else give it to you."

"I haven't done it with anybody else. I don't especially like it lately, as you might have noticed if you ever paid attention."

Shit. Melvin was certain none of the girls at the whorehouse had it, they all had regular checkups. Maybe it was that streetwalker back in the summer, the one with one leg shorter than the other. He knew he shouldn't have, but she was so pretty, and he felt bad for her, having to ply the sidewalk because of her infirmity. "Well I guess they've got treatments, don't they?"

"They do, and you'll be going in yourself. Along with anybody else you've . . ." Her face contorted, she was so mad. He was actually scared of her, to his own astonishment.

"All right, honey bear, you win, I admit I had a little mistaken adventure last year, I should have admitted it to you . . ."

"You lying bastard. I want you out of this house. Pack yourself a bag and make yourself scarce."

"All right, now, sweetie, you just calm down and I'll do just that, spend a few days in a hotel and then when you're all cooled down we'll sort this all out."

"Nothing to sort, Melvin. I'm filing for divorce. If you contest it I'll make the grounds public. If you want the

United States Postal Service knowing about your unclean habits, go right ahead, then."

"Aw, but sugar, what about the kiddies?"

"They never see you anyway except at supper, when you bother coming home for it. You're gone before they are in the morning and after supper you go out God knows where, and you don't come in until God knows when and after you bother me you pass out."

"I'll just go pack then, and we'll talk again in a few days when your head's a bit calmer."

He set about packing a bag, just enough for two or three nights. Truth to tell he'd enjoy a little time in a hotel, taking his meals in his room and having girls come up via the intervention of the bellboy. He was just about done when he reached in the top drawer of the dresser and felt around on its inside top plank, and when his fingertips touched only the smooth wood he felt his stomach tighten.

"Miriam, sweetie. You moved my little bankroll."

"That's just what I did all right."

"I'll need that if I'm to leave home for a bit."

She handed him a ten-dollar bill, neatly folded into fourths. "There. Have yourself a ball."

38

Ezra had pulled off a pretty good one, in his estima-
tion. He wore a deliveryman's uniform, obtained
by securing such a job for the Innes Shoe Company.
Having scrubbed himself and wearing his neatest suit of
clothes, he had lied on his application, saying that he had
a license to drive a truck, when in fact he had no idea
how an automobile operated other than it had a wheel
you turned to make the wheels change direction. But he
had the uniform, which made it possible to go around in
back of people's houses and inside apartment buildings,
and as long as he was reasonably inconspicuous he could
go places where normally the sight of him would set off
considerable alarm.

Today he was walking along Las Palmas holding an
empty parcel wrapped in butcher paper, which he held by
a knot in the twine that held it together. In the other hand
he held a clipboard he'd stolen from the shoe store along
with some blank invoices. He walked to the front porch of
a neat-looking bungalow and knocked. When no answer
came he pretended to consult the clipboard, then went
around back.

Having ascertained that the back door wasn't visible
from the surrounding backyards he crashed in a pane in
the door next to the handle and opened it. A small tabby
cat rubbed against his shins and he considered kicking it

away, but some instinct told him that would be bad luck. He carefully shut the door, noting that the cat didn't seem to want to go out. That struck him as odd.

It was a show person's house, an actress or a singer. There were portraits of her and photographs all over the place, and she was quite a handsome woman. On the walls of a front room, which contained the biggest piano Ezra had ever seen, were pictures of the woman with various swells, motion picture and theatrical stars by the look of them, and in the boudoir were several of the lady in the company of men older than she who looked like tycoons of some sort or another. One of them had a familiar face, Ezra knew it from the papers but couldn't put a name to it.

And so he began searching for a jewelry box. He hadn't been at burglary long himself, but he'd known lots of burglars and he'd always liked listening to them talk. He'd found lately that he liked some of the same things they did, for example that feeling of intimacy you got from being in someone else's house outside their presence. One strange old coot he'd known back in Maine had told Ezra he always liked looking at the bookcases in the houses he robbed. He couldn't imagine doing that himself but he supposed it was like looking through their photograph albums.

The house was neat, but her current correspondence was on the kitchen table. Her name was Mrs. Hamish Burlington, and her first name was Bridget. He didn't imagine that was her stage name, but that was how her bills were addressed. There was a postcard from someone named Irma, sent from Montreal, Canada, and an unopened letter with a handwritten return address in New York City. He fingered it and, having determined it didn't hold any banknotes, put it back in its place.

He found a stepladder in the utility closet and took it into the bedroom where he placed it next to the closet. He stood on it and fingered the upper shelf and found nothing that didn't belong there, some sweaters and silk scarves. He ran his fingers along the top of the doorsill and found no hidden keys.

Then came the sound of a key in the front door. He froze and considered his options. He had the gun, in a shoulder holster underneath the deliveryman's jacket, but firing it would make a hell of a noise by the standards of a nice quiet neighborhood like this. He could hit the lady—if that's who was coming in—on the head, or tie her to a chair, and then keep going through the house until he found something worth his time and trouble. He could just cut his losses and get out through the back door before anyone realized he'd been there in the first place, but he knew it was already too late for that. There were voices now, coming from the parlor, a man and a woman. Shit, that meant they'd be headed straight for the bedroom. He wished he was still carrying that old trusty hammer.

He had trouble making out the details of the conversation, but the woman called the man Professor. To his great surprise they didn't hightail it immediately to the bedroom, and their voices grew quieter as they headed for the other side of the house. Soon enough the piano started playing, and the lady started singing along. He didn't know much about music but he knew these were scales. As long as this professor was at the keyboard and the lady was singing he knew where they were, and he started searching again.

He found her jewel box before too long. They were done with scales now and the lady was singing something in a foreign language in a high-pitched voice, and as he went through the jewel box he had to allow as how that voice was one of the prettiest sounds he'd ever heard. He'd have liked to hear her tackle something more familiar, like "The Star-Spangled Banner" or "Amazing Grace," but despite the trickiness of the tune and the incomprehensible words, that voice was like nothing he'd ever heard in his life.

There was a brooch with a big diamond surrounded by smaller ones that looked real to Ezra, but he was no judge of such things and at a dime a dollar it wouldn't bring much even if it was. The rest of it looked chintzy and fake even to Ezra. None of it was worth getting busted over, he decided, and returned the box back to its spot, brooch intact.

They were still going at it hammer and tongs over in the music room when he found himself looking at a bookcase in the parlor. If either of them were standing in the doorway they could have seen him. He was quite impressed at the volume of the woman's voice; the piano player was hitting the keys pretty damned hard, and she was still clear and steady above it. Come to think of it this professor character wasn't half bad either. He'd just about given up on getting out of there with anything, was just enjoying the music and the fact that they didn't know he was there eavesdropping, and thinking about his oddball buddy's comment about skimming the bookshelves.

There couldn't be much of value there, nothing you could fence anyway. There was a big old Bible and a dictionary that was so big Ezra wondered how the hell many words did a person need, anyway, that he didn't already know? There was a child's picture book and what looked like some of the kind of bullshit stories Trudy used to read, what she called her rosewater stories. And then there was one that looked funny.

It said *Principia Mathematica* on the spine, whatever the fuck that meant, and it was considerably older than the others. It was also a very large book, with a fancy leather binding. Maybe this was a book that could be sold after all.

Gingerly he pulled it away from the back of the bookcase. It was heavier than any book he'd ever handled, not that he'd had occasion to handle many, and there was something off about the way its weight shifted when he moved it. He unclasped the front cover and discovered to his delight that the book's ancient pages had been first glued together and then hollowed out, forming a sort of safe. Therein were two packages, the first a brown manilla envelope containing cash in the form of silver certificates. The second was a drawstring bag of crushed red velvet, and pulling the string he saw at a glance that it contained pearl pendant earrings, another brooch and a gold bracelet, all of them encrusted with what Ezra felt certain were real gems. There was more beneath them, and the sachet easily weighed over a pound. He stuck the envelope in his vest pocket and dropped the velvet bag into the inside of his jacket. He closed the clasps and returned the book to its spot, his chest warm with the feeling of good luck, of having been smiled upon by the fates. He eased out the back door, the cat slipping through his legs, once again uninterested in the outdoors. Strangest cat he'd ever met. The lady's singing could still be heard out to the sidewalk and it occurred to him that he was relieved that he hadn't had to resort to violence. Maybe this was a better way of getting what he needed.

HENRY WAS WALKING along La Brea heading back to the van, having dropped off a set of proofs to an architectural firm of a house Bill had photographed the day before. There was a mild breeze cooling his face against the warmth of the afternoon, and once again he found himself confounded by the oddness of winter in California. In the West Virginia mountains there would have been snow right then, and he could see some here on the peaks to the northeast of the city. Henry didn't suppose he minded missing the cold, but it was funny not to have the passage of time marked by the weather. He'd spent Christmas with the Ogdens and it had seemed much like any other holiday, albeit with a new and different family, but it had been damned odd trimming the tree in shirtsleeves with the windows open. He couldn't imagine leaving California after this, though. He hadn't ever had a steady girl back in West Virginia, not really, certainly hadn't ever expected to have one like Flavia, and he was carefully considering his next move. Since November they'd let him shoot no fewer than six portrait sessions on his own.

"Hey there," someone called out to him. He turned to a familiar face he couldn't quite put a situation to. "Remember me? Your old traveling companion?"

Now he recognized the crooked face. The fellow who'd stabbed the predatory old bastard in the railyard. He had on a deliveryman's uniform, and he was carrying a parcel by the string.

"There he is," he said, holding his hand out. "Say, I got what for to pay you back," he said. "Remember I owe you a buck twenty-five?"

"Sure."

"Would have done it before but I got busy with other things."

"Wouldn't have found me anyhow, I left the Y right quick after I got there."

The other man, whose name wouldn't come to Henry, laughed and slapped him on the back. "They gave me your forwarding. I went there thinking to pay you and a lady answered the door looked like she hadn't taken a shit in a week."

Henry's expression must have darkened, because his interlocutor was quick to backtrack. "I just mean she was a mite stern throwing me out. Didn't like the looks of me."

He didn't mention that he'd heard the meeting from Flavia's point of view. Looking at the man now he could understand her reaction. It hadn't been his condition she'd found offensive—in fact, at that moment he'd been as clean as and better dressed than Henry. It was the sinister look on his face and his insinuating tone of voice. She must have seen this leering creep on the stoop and by association questioned her decision to hire Henry.

"And how are the wife and kids?"

"They're fine, just fine. And I'm working for a shoe company."

He couldn't say what it was that told him this was a lie, even given the uniform, but he felt sure of it. "That must be interesting."

"It's all right. Making a damn good living and back in the bosom of the family. Life couldn't be better. Maybe you could come pay us a visit some time. Or better yet I'll come see you." He leered and grinned, and looked more sinister than Henry had yet seen him. "Long as I manage to steer clear of that bitch with the stick up her ass."

They were standing close to one another, and without giving it much thought Henry got him in the chin with a nice clean uppercut. He heard the man's teeth clicking together as he fell backwards and onto the sidewalk. People stopped to look, hoping for more mayhem.

"You watch your words, mister. Far as I'm concerned we're square, and you can stay away from me and mine."

"You son of a bitch, I won't forget that." But he didn't get up to continue the scrap, and when Henry walked away people started moving again.

BILL HAD SPENT his afternoon working on a years-long project, expanding upon the diaries and notebooks he'd been keeping more or less faithfully since the war. He included everything he'd written down at the time, details of conversations and business transactions and even the contents of his meals and with whom he'd partaken them. Not every single meal, but about one in ten, whenever it seemed worth noting for posterity. Posterity was perhaps the wrong word, for he had also written down the details of many an intimate encounter, rendering them unpublishable, at least by any above-ground outfit.

He had been delighted a few days before to discover a passage referring to a woman he remembered well, but who hadn't come to his mind in years. She'd owned a rooming house in Portland, Oregon, and when he'd presented himself as a widower she called him a liar. There was no venom in it, just a statement of fact.

"What makes you say that?" I said. I was seated on a small sofa in her parlor, and the boarders were all out. The wallpaper was a dark green velvet, framed lithographs depicting scenes of the Napoleonic wars tastefully displayed next to the heads of several antlered ungulates; this had once been a man's study.

"I know a widower when I see one. You're neither sad nor relieved. I'd say you walked out on her, if I were to guess, or she on you." Her nose was aquiline and her face long, and she had the sort of cheekbones that make it difficult to take an unflattering photograph, a look that young women regretted having but that often made for great beauty in middle age; I suspected that she was a better-looking woman now than she'd been in her youth.

"The latter," I replied, impressed with her intuitive skills. "You ought to volunteer for the Police Bureau."

She smiled faintly and showed no displeasure or disapproval at my attempt to deceive. "I suppose I've been sizing up boarders long enough I can spot a prevaricator."

"It's merely that widowers aren't looked down on as divorced men are."

"I don't believe you're divorced either."

"No," I said, flustered but impressed once again. "She just took off and went back to Kansas."

"You see? Kansas, I believe that. And don't think for a minute that I've anything against divorced people, I'm one myself."

I didn't know why, exactly, but I felt like telling her something true that I normally kept to myself. "To be quite honest I'm a bigamist."

"My, but you lead a complicated life." That enigmatic smile again, as she put her pursed lips to the cup and tipped it.

"I did once. Now I just move around from place to place taking photographs."

"And how long do you propose to stay in Portland?"

"That all depends on whether I find it to my liking. A month or so at the least."

"Mr. Ogden, would you like to know how I came to be divorced and the owner of as fine a house as this?"

"I didn't dare be so bold as to ask." I wondered whether the frank and friendly look she gave me was one she habitually gave prospective tenants or whether she was showing me special favor. I hoped it was the latter.

"My husband came from a prominent family in the other Portland, back East. He wasn't a favored son. His mother and father were quite blatant in their preference for his brother and two sisters, and instead of setting him up in the family firm they staked him to a business here. An ironworks. He did well, ended up owning that plus three livery stables and a restaurant. When we married no one from Maine came out, which was fine with both of us. When our children were born we didn't even inform them."

She spoke as casually as if she were telling me about a trip to the hardware store.

"He must have done quite well in business to have built a house like this."

"He did. He was also quite cruel, and a little stupid. I suspect that's why the family sent him West."

"Why did you marry him?"

"He was a successful man, and he wooed me with gifts and high times. I was only twenty and he nearly forty."

"He'd never married before?"

"No. I was too naïve to ask why. After a while I realized he was accustomed to women succumbing to his charms, or to his willingness to pay for intimate congress."

Here I will confess I found myself shocked, not in an unpleasant way, at her frankness.

"From me he wanted an heir, and I provided him with three healthy children. And he continued to lay with every sort of strumpet imaginable. I didn't mind, because he was a brute and a swine, and as long as he wasn't bringing home any diseases—and he'd long since stopped bothering me—it wasn't my problem. And then one night he was caught in a room at the Portland Hotel with a married woman, the wife of a well-known physician. He could have kept it quiet except that he'd beaten her half to death. It was the very devil of a scandal that year.

"So I sued him for divorce. The poor woman he'd beaten sued him too, as did her husband, who'd immediately divorced her, and once he'd gone to prison the house was all that was left to me. I could afford to keep it if I took in boarders. It cost me my social standing among the city's supposed blue bloods, but I didn't care. My children were grown by then and had all left Portland for places where their name wasn't associated with felonious battery."

He stopped there. He'd moved in that evening and within weeks he and Mrs. Sault were engaged in frenetic grappling every time the house was empty. She had an almost supernatural ability to know when her tenants would be in or out, and for a time Bill had thought he might make the situation permanent. He smiled at the memory and unbuttoned his trousers.

IT WASN'T TIME for supper yet, and Flavia sat knitting in the parlor. Henry came in and sat across from her on the sofa. "Remember that character who come by looking for me right when I first got hired?"

"Came by," Flavia said, and it conjured up so perfectly

the image the man had cast of her that Henry couldn't help but laugh.

"Saw him today over on La Brea."

"Speak to him?"

He was finding it difficult to look her in the eye. He held his cap in his hand and flipped it over a couple of times. "He called out to me. Said something untowards about you so I knocked him down."

"Henry. You didn't."

"Said the lady who'd opened the door here had a stick up her ass."

Flavia let out a loud, surprised bray of a laugh. "My hero. I suppose my normal way of dealing with strangers might seem a bit stiff and formal. Did he hit you back?"

"No, because I didn't turn my back to him. He swore he'd get me, though, so if you see him don't open the door."

She set down her knitting. "How seriously should I be considering the prospect?"

"I don't know. Maybe he's full of beans but I saw him hurt someone pretty bad when we first got to California."

MRS. CHEN HAD sautéed large pork chops for dinner, served up with mashed potatoes and gravy, and the four of them ate for the most part in silence, until she asked whether anyone wanted dessert. No one did, but Bill took a bottle of Calvados out of the cupboard and three glasses.

"Surely you can finish a meal without having to consume alcohol afterward," Mrs. Chen said.

He took out a fourth glass and shook it side to side,

raising an eyebrow. "May I assume, Mrs. Chen, that you will not be imbibing with us?"

She fairly snarled her response. "The number and sort of sins practiced on a daily basis in this household would have long ago driven me away if it were not for my Christian duty to stay and fight the devil's influence." She removed her apron and hung it on the inside of the kitchen door as she took her leave.

"What's gotten into you, Gramps?"

He poured her a glass, then another for Henry, and then one for himself. "If I feel like a drop after supper, I'll have one. Some nights I don't want to be preached to in my own house."

"The other day she called me a soiled dove," Flavia said. Bill snorted, and had to purse his lips to keep from spitting out the Calvados. "I believe she was trying to insult me in the politest way possible."

"In what context?" he said, once he'd managed to swallow.

"I'd asked if the sheets had been laundered, that was all, and she took it to mean that mine were in need of extra cleaning because of my character."

Henry looked back and forth between them. He still found it difficult to understand how people could talk that way with their own families.

"Did you get much transcribed today?"

"Not much, but it was wonderful stuff. Found my notes about a landlady of mine in Oregon a few years back. Got distracted but tomorrow I'll start again and reconstruct the dirty parts."

He'd offered parts of the ongoing manuscript for Henry

to read a few months back. It was entertaining enough but too filthy to be published. He understood why the old man did it, though. There was something about getting it down on paper that kept it from dying away.

Bill stood and began collecting plates.

"What are you doing?" Flavia asked.

"Well, I was a little mean to Mrs. Chen just now, thought I'd do the dishes to make up for it."

39

"You want to stay here?" Mrs. Spencer couldn't help laughing in Melvin's face. "This look like any hotel you ever saw?"

He knew better than to allow himself to take offense. It would show on his face and he'd be dead. "Hah, no, just, I need a place to stay for a night or two."

"Wifey kicked you out, is that right?"

"She did." He almost wanted to tell her about the gonorrhea, insinuate maybe that this was partly her fault, but he sensed it wouldn't help him in making his case.

"There's hotels all over downtown, honey."

"That's true, but you see, I got another problem to sort out, which is the post office is looking for me."

"Uh-huh."

"You see, there's been a misunderstanding about some cash and checks being taken from a post office branch in Cumberland."

"Oh, boy, Melvin. You better be headed out of town's what I think."

"I was hoping I could stay here. Take sanctuary, so to speak."

"Pal, this here is about as far from a goddamn church as you're going to find. Good luck, I'm sure the girls all wish you the same."

• • •

THE CUMBERLAND BRANCH had one of the hidey holes the inspectors entered quietly from the exterior, from which they could spy on the postal workers and make sure they weren't pilfering cash, checks, money orders and the like from the United States mail. The thing was, since in principle no one knew whether an inspector was in the hidey hole at any given time, no one knew if an inspector was still in there when the branch closed and everybody went home. The day after Miriam had kicked him out he'd gone out to Cumberland and, late in the afternoon, had ensconced himself inside the dark shaft and waited and watched. When the staff had locked up and gone home he'd stepped into the sorting room and, using an electric torch, examined the pickings. He'd never violated so many envelopes and packages at one time or branch before, but this was a desperate situation and called for desperate measures. Normally he would have taken the wrappings and detritus with him, but there was too much of it, and he left it lying on the sorting room floor where it landed. He left through the hidey hole, as he had before, careful to remove any sign that he'd been there, and went straight to his hotel to count it out.

The next morning, when the police and several of Melvin's fellow inspectors were at the branch examining the scene, a woman who lived across the street, having seen the commotion, came over to tell them something she'd noticed the night before.

"It was about an hour after they close up. Man came out of that funny little door on the side of the building. Saw him lock it up with a key. Walked down the street carrying a carpet bag. Wouldn't have thought much of it except the lot of you over there making a fuss this morning."

40

Magnolia Sweetspire was in the most expensive suite of the Huntington Hotel in Pasadena, regaling the correspondent from *Photoplay* magazine with tales of her adventurous youth in Tennessee. A tray of canapés sat untouched on a table in the parlor and a photographer lounged in the corner smoking with the studio's new publicity man.

"You sure you want to make her out to be such a country gal?" the photographer asked.

"We thought about making her minor European royalty, deposed," the publicity man said. "But she wouldn't go along. And the more I thought about it the more I liked the idea of her being a sophisticated hillbilly, if you see what I mean."

"Well, Mary Pickford used to sell bananas in Montreal," the photographer said.

The reporter was a former drama critic for the *Examiner* and well-versed in the ways of actors and publicity. "And once you were crowned queen of the Knoxville County fair . . ."

"McMinn County fair, ma'am," Magnolia said.

"Right. What then?"

"Well, about then I thought maybe I ought to come out and see about the pictures. And my fellow, he was known as the handsomest in our part of the state. And he'd been a track and field star, so we thought he might do well in pictures as well as me."

The reporter drew a deep, resigned breath and looked over at the publicity man. Without taking her eyes off him she once again addressed Magnolia. "And this young man came out west with you without benefit of matrimony?"

The publicist leapt to his feet and strode the length of the parlor. "Of course that was the plan, they were to marry and only then would they travel to California to try their luck in filmland."

"Right," Magnolia said, nodding. It was difficult for her to remember that there was a story other than the true one that she needed to stick to.

"Tragically, days before their nuptials, her fiancé was fishing along the banks of Judd lake . . ."

"Judd Slough lake," Magnolia said.

"Right. That's the one. He was fishing, and he heard an outcry from a family picnicking nearby, their baby had fallen into the lake. Well, this brave young man leapt straight in there and saved that baby, tragically drowning in the process."

"Wait," the photographer said. "He managed to save the baby, get it onto dry land, but he still drowned?"

"Jerry," the reporter said. She was known for her basilisk stare and her ability to shut people up with it.

"I just don't get it."

"You don't need to, Jerry, because I get it. Now shut your spinach box."

"That's right," Magnolia said. She continued, with more confidence than she'd felt rehearsing it, "He drowned tragically and heroically saving a little baby. And I knew he'd want me to come out here by myself anyway."

"YOUR PICTURES WITH Provident are all right, George. As good as any coming out of there or better."

He didn't like the sound of that, but he gave a tight smile and nodded. "Thank you." He'd ordered the quail, since he'd never seen it on a menu before. It was a busy lunchtime and the customers were well-heeled, businessmen taking clients or mistresses out for a fancy meal and upper-class women entertaining their peers. His interlocutor was a stranger whose name he knew well and whose telegram requesting an in-person meeting had puzzled him.

"Come now. You know what I mean. You're not given much to work with." The man was neither young nor old, one of those people who seem the same at fifty as at twenty. His head was shaven almost completely bald, other than a thin carpeting on the top of his skull.

"They're better now that we've learned how to use Tommy Gill properly."

"Yes, very true, and those children are funnier than most movie brats." He picked away a flaky chunk of sole meunière and speared a green bean, then gestured with the fork. "They have some life to them."

"That's because they're not acting. They're just doing more or less what they've been told to do. 'Kick the drunk when he falls down. Steal his wallet.' They love that."

"That's not why I wanted to meet you, though. It's the sex pictures. There's real art in those."

George stopped chewing and tried not to look horrified. "Sex pictures?"

"I know they're yours, a young protégé of mine was in one of them and I managed to catch it at a private party."

"All right."

"The shot of the majordomo ejaculating in his matronly employer's face is comic and erotic genius." His eyes were wide, his palms upraised. "A hundred times funnier and truer to life than anything in your commercial pictures."

That had been one of George's, all right. "That was a happy accident, that one. Tell me about this party." Magnificat Educational Distribution Company, Incorporated didn't have many clients around Los Angeles, and he worried about bootleg prints making their way into circulation.

"It was at a smoker in San Francisco. I recognized my young friend as the footman and telephoned him."

"He shouldn't have told you anything. I explain that to everyone involved, and usually it's not a problem because no one wants to be associated with that sort of thing."

"Don't be cross with him. I told him I wanted to help you."

"Help me in what sense?"

"I'm going back to New York in a week. I'd like to buy out your contract with Provident and bring you back there."

"That contract is about done anyway."

"Perfect. And I'll give you bigger budgets and better resources."

"I don't know how I feel about leaving California."

"It's different back east now. The trusts aren't a problem any more, no more running around hiding from goons. And we still have the real artists, the theater actors and crews. These people out here don't know what they're doing."

"In my experience they do."

"You strike me as a sophisticate, Mr. Buntnagel. I understand you're a Princeton man."

"True."

"How happy can you be in the company of tree farmers and rubes out of the Midwest?"

"I don't spend any time in such company. You've got the wrong idea about the place."

AFTER THE INTERVIEW they checked out of the suite and the publicist drove Magnolia back to the studio. "What if they find me out?"

"How do you mean?" The publicist was quite intent on his driving, a skill he had only recently acquired and at which he was not yet confident.

"About my fiancé."

"What about him?" His gloves tightened on the wheel and he could feel the tendons in his neck contracting.

"What if they find out he was a drug fiend and in the penitentiary for molesting a woman on the trolley?"

"He what?" He didn't dare take his eyes from the street, but they widened and his voice rose half an octave as he swerved into the next lane and back.

"They didn't tell you that?"

"They told me there'd been a fiancé and they needed a sob story involving a tragic demise. Wait, this wasn't Jack Strong, was it?"

"It was. You read about it?"

"Lady, every movie publicist on both coasts lapped

that story up. Part out of a sense of 'there but for the grace of God goes one of my actors,' because Jesus Mary and Joseph there's a publicist's nightmare. And partly because it was a hell of a story. He wasn't ever going to be a star, don't get me wrong, but that was a hell of a fall."

"He was real nice before he went crazy," Magnolia said. She seemed not in the least fazed by the publicist's driving, though it had become noticeably more erratic. Klaxons had begun sounding at their passing.

"Let's just be sure nobody else hears about this, all right? Nobody who doesn't already know." He shook his head and gripped the steering wheel harder. "You have any idea when he's getting out?"

"Oh, he's not. I found out he got stabbed."

"Stabbed? Jesus. How'd you find that out?"

"I wrote the warden to ask that very question. I wanted to know just out of concern for him and also because I was afraid he'd find me. But guess what? He made somebody sore and they stabbed him in the throat. Oh, well."

"It didn't make the papers, not that I saw anyway."

"No, he was in under his real name. Barney J. Sykes."

"Good. Don't worry, he'll be known but to God soon enough."

41

It was well into spring when Flavia began to suspect that her attempts at preventing pregnancy had failed. A visit to her grandfather's friend and physician Dr. Hiram McCallister set her mind at rest, and she'd scarcely thought about it again until a few days later when the doctor telephoned to let her know that the test results had arrived.

"*Le lapin est mort*, I'm afraid, my dear."

She spent a few days stewing over what, if anything, to tell Henry. She thought about asking Bill, but it seemed wrong for him to know before Henry did. Back in Wichita she'd have known whom to see about ending it, if that was what she decided, but she knew very few people in Los Angeles besides the household and their professional contacts and clientele. Jesus, she thought, at least in Kansas she'd had a few female friends amongst the teaching staff.

If she were indeed pregnant it might be prudent to have someone else dealing with the darkroom and its foul potions; she knew that a doctor would laugh at her fastidiousness in that regard but she nonetheless sensed that there was a biological reason the pungent aroma of the stop bath had made her nauseous that morning, when it never had before.

THE SITUATION SORTED itself out the following Friday, Good Friday as it happened, when the doctor entered the Flying Scotsman early in the evening, and finding Bill at the bar deep in conversation with the barkeep, slapped him on the shoulder. Already in his cups, McAllister cried out for a round for himself and his friend. The date was April sixth, and the talk in the bar was once again of war, for the President and Congress of the United States of America had on that day declared it against Germany. "We're for certain in the shit now, Hiram," Bill said.

"Couple of decrepit old shitbirds like us?" McAllister shouted, roaring with laughter afterwards and sending a waft of boozy miasma Bill's way.

"Not everyone's a codger. Before I left the studio this evening my young assistant announced his intention to sign up for some branch of the service posthaste."

"Nonsense. He can't."

"Can and will, I fear. The lad's from the hills and stubborn."

McAllister shook his head as though something painful were attached to it. "I mean he's going to be a father."

"I beg your pardon?"

"And you a great-grandpa."

Bill had not failed to note the look of discomfort—he wondered now whether it had literally been nausea—on his granddaughter's face at Henry's announcement. "Again, I beg your pardon. Aren't you medical men supposed to be like priests?"

"In what sense?"

"In the sense of confidentiality."

The doctor blew a raspberry. "I can certainly tell a friend about the state of his own granddaughter, can't I?"

◆ ◆ ◆

UPON HIS RETURN to the studio shortly thereafter he found Mrs. Chen preparing to set the table for the evening meal, going on at length about the wonderful Good Friday service she'd attended, uncharacteristically upbeat and describing in detail the floral arrangements as well as the gist of the sermon. She said that Easter Sunday services would be even more edifying and spectacular, hinting that anyone in the house would be welcome to join her then. The young people were both quiet, and during the meal he paid careful attention to their faces. He determined that Henry was as yet unawares, as he spoke excitedly about his upcoming adventures fighting the Hun. Mrs. Chen, however, seemed to sense that something was amiss—probably had guessed it days before—and when Flavia snapped an uncharacteristic demand for a clean fork after her own dropped to the floor, the older woman fetched one quickly without a rejoinder and, upon setting it down, patted Flavia on the shoulder and said, "There you are, dear."

Flavia then noted the look of concern on her grandfather's face, and the lack of all awareness on Henry's, and then excused herself from the table.

"I think she's upset because of the declaration of war," Henry said with a mouthful of Hoppin' John. Mrs. Chen gave Bill a look full of empathy, like nothing he'd seen on her face before. He excused himself in his turn and went outside for a stroll.

THEY WERE A fake sister act on the Empire circuit, their specialty being ever-so-slightly suggestive novelty songs with blond Marceline on banjo and brunette Cressida on the ukulele. They sang well enough to overcome the incongruity of the pairing of the two instruments, but what sold the act was their charm and easy camaraderie. The songs were either popular hits or bits and pieces of originals they'd picked up in their travels, and they knew that the act in its present form was on its way out.

After tonight's show they'd found a well-dressed, drunken man outside their dressing room who introduced himself as Tommy Gill, the picture comedian. "Prove it," Cressida had said, and presently he'd gone into one of his funny walks, and they'd invited him into the tiny, cramped dressing room, with drying laundry hanging from the doors and rods.

"Aw, this is terrible," he'd said after a brief look around. "Way too small for the two of you, let alone me. Let's go someplace and talk."

And so now they were in Tommy's parlor listening to gramophone records, hoping to gain themselves entry into the world of motion pictures through his kind intervention. Marceline had let down her cascades of luxuriant blond hair and was now allowing Tommy to play with the hanging tresses, teasing apart the strands and sniffing them as she leaned over the flocked red velvet upholstery of the divan. Cressida was operating the Victrola, turning the records over and replacing them and cranking the mechanism up when the time came. Her black hair was pinned up in a chignon held in place by a thin ribbon of white silk. Like her friend, she was only partially clothed and tipsy, and she was getting giggly as Tommy went on and on about their hair and how he'd be running his hands through hers next, so she'd better get ready to undo that ribbon. It sounded dirty coming out of his mouth, but she had a notion that he wasn't trying to be funny. He'd complained earlier in the evening, when they were on the way to his house, that as a comedian people expected him to be funny all the damn time, and they didn't understand that it was work, goddamnit. Now he was humming badly along with "For Me and My Gal."

"I imagine we'll be making service comedies next," he said, mostly to himself. "Course there'll be melodramas about the rape of Belgium. You don't suppose people might think times are too grave to want a laugh? There's never been a war since they started making pictures. Jesus Christ, it's uncharted waters we're in. Who knows if funny pictures will look like bad taste once they start burying American boys over there."

"Tommy, sweetie, you're going to get it all wet," Marceline said, as he had just put a long strand of hair into his mouth. He replied with an evil-sounding chuckle that made both girls laugh, and this time he didn't seem to mind them thinking he was funny. He unbuttoned his fly, extracted his male member and wrapped several golden tendrils around its base. As the thing swelled Marceline looked over at Cressida, who smirked, and she allowed Tommy to pull himself for several minutes to a messy climax, after which the blonde excused herself, asking after the bathing facilities and disappearing with her hair in her hands, the soiled portion held carefully away from her filmy peignoir. The brunette sat down on the divan next to Tommy, who was very amused with himself.

"I always wanted to do that, ever since I was a lad. I

never dared try it, or even ask. Not with the girls in the road, not with the wife. And now I'm a star and I can do it. She liked it, even. Didn't she?"

"Oh, Tommy, you bet she did. Every girl dreams of the day a handsome man shoots a great big load in her hair. That's half the reason we fuss with it so."

He looked at her sidelong, suspicious that he was being mocked. But she was a good enough actress to deadpan it, and he was high enough to believe her. "I guess I should think about getting you gals home. Whyn't I call you a taxi cab."

"Aw, Tommy, baby, Marcy had her turn, you can't deny me mine. Time she's done washing her hair you'll be all ready for another go."

Tommy nodded. This was probably true, and from the looks of her this one's hair might reach down all the way to her ass once it was undone.

WHEN BILL RETURNED to the studio no one was about. He heard no noise from the hallway where the bedrooms were and he retired to the parlor to read the day's newspapers. It was a busy and unhappy day for news. A draft looked inevitable if volunteer enlistment didn't meet expectations, and dissent was already being treated, at least in the *Examiner*, as something close to treasonous. *Faits divers* reporting on the change were already filling the front sections of the paper.

TEARS OLD GLORY; IS STONED AND EXILED
Adolph Bergonhoft, of Russian and German
descent, said to have torn an American flag

from a motion picture submarine at the Long wharf at Santa Monica today, ripped it and trampled it in the dust, was seized by a crowd of men who took him to his home and after throwing out his household goods, stoned him. He was last seen on the coast road closely pursued by a crowd of boys.

Wilson was making noises about resident aliens and hinted at a fifth column. Bill had disliked the man from the first time he'd seen a picture of that schoolmarmish, grimacing face, a man with no experience of war but hearsay, a perfect example of his type, so in love with the fruits of his own fertile brain as to be thoroughly disconnected from the experience of his fellows. American boys would go to the slaughter to protect the interests of British bankers and aristocrats, and Wilson would sit there in the Executive Mansion with his thumb up his rectum, thinking what a big jolly adventure it was. He went to his desk and took out a sheet of stationery and a fountain pen.

Dear sirs,

Our nation finds herself embroiled in an overseas catastrophe in which we have no interest, none whatsoever. Our feckless popinjay of a president has embarked on a folly, sending our American lads to fight a mysterious foe whom you and others have painted as bloodthirsty monsters. Unless I am greatly mistaken, Mr. Wilson, with his pince-nez spectacles and pinched mouth to match, has never spent a day in uniform, having spent them

*all thinking sublime thoughts in the groves of academe.
Were it in my power I would issue the son of a bitch a
rifle and some basic training and send him over to fight
the Kaiser's men himself.*

*In case the reader thinks I am a pacifist or shrinking
violet eager to avoid the draft that will surely come, I am
seventy-two years old and a battle veteran of the GAR.
I would gladly and proudly fight that war again. The
current one is not worth the life of a single American boy,
be he descended from Yankee or Reb.*

Signed,
Wm. Ogden
Los Angeles

IRENE WAS REWORKING a drawing of a neigh-
bor's cat, a big female tortoiseshell sunning herself in a
bright spot on the G's Persian rug in the parlor. The cat let
itself in regularly, slipping through the back door when she
stepped onto the porch to fetch the milk and eggs or when
George came in late from one of his excursions. They
never fed or watered her and there was no sandbox, but
the animal seemed to appreciate their company and they
were fond enough of her. She was pleased with the draped
form of the cat and her face but the chiaroscuro effect of
the sun-dappled fur and carpet and the darker patches of
fur and weave had yet to satisfy her.

She had, as it happened, been thinking about New
York. She'd received a letter from a friend, detailing the
social and sexual liberties to be enjoyed amongst a bohe-
mian crowd in certain parts of Manhattan, and she was
exhausted by the West Coast Art Company. The stag

pictures had been fun at first, and they were still making good money, but the novelty of the situation had worn off and with the retirement of Victoria and Trudy she found she didn't care much about the quality of the product any more. And then there was the question of the strange man in Indiana and his persistent yet vague threats, if threats they were.

"What do you say?" George had said the evening he'd got the offer. "Would you come with me?"

"I don't know. I'd have to think on it."

"What's keeping you here? The weather?"

"I suppose not. It's a lot of trouble, moving, though."

42

In the morning he arose and went down to the breakfast table where he found Flavia and Henry eating in silence, his out of cheerful ignorance and hers out of anxiety and malaise. She gave him a sharp glance and handed him a sheet of folded paper. "You can't be serious."

It was his letter to the *Examiner*. He reread it and, in the light of day, thought it a bit mild. He hadn't quite captured the depth of his loathing for Wilson, whose persnickety visage peered, disapproving, off the front page of the morning's *Times*. He picked the paper up and pointed at the photo. "Doesn't he look like he'd be a whole lot gayer if someone would just feed him some prunes followed by a double dose of Fletcher's Castoria?"

Henry laughed at that and even Mrs. Chen smiled, but Flavia scowled. "You find that funny? Suppose they published it? You could get in a lot of trouble for that kind of talk."

He pointed at Wilson's photograph. "Look at that mouth. Looks like the penny slot in a chewing gum dispenser."

Flavia passed Henry the letter. "I'm quite serious. They're not going to be tolerating that kind of sentiment expressed openly from here on out. And you went and signed it 'William Ogden, photographer.' Good grief, there goes business."

"You can't call the President of the United States a son of a bitch," Henry said.

"They can censor that part. Call him a eunuch, maybe."

"What's that mean?"

"It means someone whose balls have been cut off," Flavia said in a louder and angrier tone than was her habit.

Mrs. Chen stiffened, closed her eyes and shook her head.

Henry seemed genuinely baffled by his thinking. "Bill, this country's at war now and it's just wrong talking like that. What makes you think it's all right to put this in a letter?"

"It's the truth. That sanctimonious, un-de-hemorrhoided corner preacher's gone and led this country into a foreign adventure we've no stake in."

"So you think I'm a fool for shipping out?"

"I think like a lot of people you're being led around by your nose. Tell me what you're going over to fight for."

"Liberty and democracy."

"I don't see how the Kaiser threatens either one in the USA."

"They're raping Belgian women, the krauts."

"Probably eating little kittens and beagle puppies too. I say that's bunkum."

"And once they take England and France they'll be on their way over here."

Bill let out a guffaw. "And how are they going to

bring us an invasion force big enough? There are a hundred million people in this country. Going to have them come over in ten thousand hot air balloons? Cross over the arctic with sled dogs? Build the world's biggest troop transport ship? Use your bean, lad."

"Oh, hell. I'm not going to sit here and listen to this pro-kraut bullshit." Mrs. Chen drew in a loud gasp as Henry shoved his chair back and stood. "You'd better watch that kind of talk, Bill. They're looking out for kraut sympathizers." He left the room and went downstairs, and the door slammed.

"Seems no one ever leaves a meal in this house any more without making some sort of dramatic pronouncement," Bill said.

Flavia took the letter back from where Henry had set it down. "Think about the business, Gramps. Think about what's best for all of us."

"What I think is you'd better have a serious talk with that young man before he goes off and leaves to be cannon fodder."

She took it as a rebuke. "I wouldn't do that to him."

Bill drank his orange juice and got up. Mrs. Chen had not yet placed his eggs and bacon before him. "Oh, balls. I'm going to the Pig and Whistle."

THE COUNTERMAN WITH the goiter was there, beside himself with glee at the prospect of America's participation in the mayhem across the Atlantic. Though it was a busy day he managed to stop by Bill's spot at the counter every few minutes and gloat. "We're going to show that German scum what we're made of, by gosh.

Going to slaughter 'em in the trenches by the millions." He took Bill's empty coffee cup over to the big silver urn and refilled it.

"You decide yet whether you're army or navy?" he said as the young man set the cup on its saucer.

"It's a damned shame but I can't join either. Got this thing on my neck."

"That's just a goiter."

"It's an enlargement of the thyroid gland is what it is, and if I didn't have a medical condition I'd be in line right now, believe you me."

"I've got excellent news for you. I served in the Grand Army of the Republic with a fellow from the town of Benton Harbor, Michigan, and he had a goiter quite as large as yours, if not so fine. He was a hell of a soldier and that thing never affected his performance thereas in the slightest."

The counterman showed himself slightly abashed. "Times were different."

"No, I read in the evening edition of the *Herald* yesterday. Goiters are no barrier to enlistment, and they won't be an excuse to evade the draft either."

The counterman's face had taken on an ashier tone. "Your comrade ever succeed in making his go away?"

"He did not. One fine afternoon he was torn in half by rebel artillery, right at his midsection. It was as painful and bloody a death as I witnessed in those years."

The counterman walked away, dazed, to take an order, and a man his own age a couple of stools over spoke without looking up from his paper. "You're a mean old man."

"That I am. Maybe it'll change his way of thinking, though."

"Doubt it," said the other old man.

"So do I."

"YOU RECKON YOU'LL enlist, Ez?" The girl was on her belly on top of the bedclothes, with her head held up, her hands clasped under her chin, and she smelled of lilac, though Ezra couldn't have named what flower it was.

"Nah, they wouldn't take the likes of me."

"How's that?"

"I been to prison and I'm missing a chunk of my ear if you didn't happen to notice."

"I don't know if they care about either one of those things," she said. "I don't want you to go, is all."

They'd been together for three weeks now, a long time by Ezra's way of thinking. This one made him happy in a way most didn't. It wasn't a question of how she was in the sack, either, though she was fine as far as that went. She wanted him to be happy, that was the thing that surprised him. Trudy had been that way, too, before they'd had the kids anyway, after that it was all about them and what they needed.

"Don't worry about it," he said. "I ain't about to go offer myself up."

He was thinking about money. He wasn't running low yet, and that was another funny thing. Normally he was only worried about his next infusion of cash when he was out or nearly out. The place they were in wasn't luxurious or shabby, and at the rate they were going through it they had enough to go for another three months or more.

"Ezra, baby, what you think about you and me getting married?"

He regarded her in shock. "Married?" She had some gall.

"Sorry, honey, I got carried away with myself. I'm just crazy about you and it slipped out."

The stricken look on her face was enough to win him over. "Aw, don't feel bad, sugar, course we could get married, but I got a wife already."

She started making a sound that was like hiccoughing but got louder and longer and she curled into a ball on her side. She wasn't crying but she couldn't control the intake of her breath.

"Aw, honey, don't do that, she took off and left me and I don't know where she's at is all. You're the only gal for me." The funny thing was that he meant it when he was saying it. She calmed a little and her breaths slowed and became more or less regular. When she turned over to face him she stretched her arm behind her head, the hair under her arms as red as that on her head and down below.

"You mean it, Ezzie?"

"I sure do. That bitch took off a long time ago."

"You could sue for desertion and get a divorce that way," she said.

He thought about it. He understood finally that he wasn't likely to ever find Trudy and the kids ever again, and he also understood that it didn't matter that much to him one way or another.

"Yeah, I guess maybe I could."

◆ ◆ ◆

VICTORIA CAME IN the front door accompanied by the children, the studio car having just dropped them off in front. Trudy was reading an advance courtesy copy of the *Photoplay* number in which the kids appeared. She found she wasn't comfortable with the exposure, neither of her or of the children, even if their real names weren't used. Someone back home might recognize her. And if Ezra ever saw it they'd all be at risk. Especially, even, if he caught on to the nature of her relationship to Victoria.

The children kissed their mother and ran off into the kitchen, and Victoria sat down in the armchair opposite the divan where Trudy was. "So something's come up I need to mention," she said, unpinning her hat.

"What?"

"Well, one of the directors, Mr. Chippen or Chipney or something, saw me with the kids and wanted to know if I'd ever acted in pictures."

"Good Lord," Trudy said.

"He didn't know anything. Anyhow I said no, I hadn't but I'd been on the stage. He said I was pretty and would I do a screen test."

Trudy could feel her stomach getting tight. "What did you say?"

"Well, I thought about it, and it's true that a lot of girls would give a lot to be in the pictures, the real ones, if you see what I mean, but I said I didn't think so, I thought I'd just keep helping manage my niece's and nephew's career."

"Oh, praise Jesus."

"So you think that was right? I'm sure I could change my mind if you thought it was a good idea."

"No, no, no. Please. It's bad enough the exposure the children are getting."

"Are you scared I'd get to be a big star and move on to somebody else?" she said, and she got up and sat down next to Trudy with her arm around her waist. She kissed her gently on the mouth. "You know better than that, sugar."

Trudy handed her the *Photoplay*, opened to the page showing the two of them sitting on the very same divan. "I'm just feeling a little more cautious than I have been."

THERE WAS A crowd at the recruiting station, which consisted of a bunch of big tents on a vacant lot, and it took Henry an hour before he could get inside one of them. He waited patiently in line until he reached the long table, where a dyspeptic man in a sergeant's uniform handed him a clipboard with a form attached, and a fountain pen. "Name, date of birth, religion. In the blank area below that, note any unclean personal habits such as self abuse, alcoholism, fraternization with women of low character, the sins of Sodom, narcotics use, et cetera. Also any physical defects such as flat feet, deviated septum, herniations et cetera."

Slowly he printed out his name. The prospective recruits were enthusiastic to a man, the recruiters mostly as sullen and hostile as the man in front of him. Maybe they were unhappy about being in the recruiting battalion instead of headed across the Atlantic to fight.

They didn't look like they were in the best of shape, though, most of them non-coms, heavier and softer-looking than he would have expected a combat soldier to be. Maybe they were just sore that their cushy recruitment job had gotten hard all of a sudden. He left the lower part of the page blank. "All right, step into that line over there and we'll have the doc take a look at you. Next."

43

Melvin hadn't ever taken such a long train ride before. He was now a fugitive from the federal authorities, but he wasn't especially worried. He had liquidated everything he owned of value and had converted the personal checks he'd stolen into cash at twenty cents on the dollar, which was a pretty good deal in his experience. He'd managed to redeem three money orders and two cashier's checks totaling five hundred and thirty-seven dollars at five separate banks in Chicago, and the cash from the post office had amounted to three hundred and seventeen dollars. He had over one thousand dollars in bills on his person, more than enough to get a new start in Los Angeles. He had a new suit of clothes and a diamond stick pin he'd removed from one of the parcels, and he felt for the first time in his life like a big shot. In the dining car he ordered French wine, and nearly ordered the lobster until he remembered that he had no knowledge of how to eat such a thing. He would not reveal his naiveté by asking.

He was well into his porterhouse and baked potato when a portly, mustachioed gentleman seated at the table across the aisle spoke to him. "You going all the way to California?"

"I certainly am."

"Been there before?"

"Sure," he said. It was a lie, but the man of the world he was presenting himself as would surely have been there.

"Don't suppose you own property there by any chance?"

"No. But I'm considering buying some."

"As it happens, sir, I am preparing to sell off several sweet parcels of farmland in the beautiful San Fernando Valley. Lemon groves as well as orange, even grapefruit. If you'd be interested I could let you have one of our prospectuses."

"Thank you, but the property I'm interested in would have to be suitable for motion picture production."

"Ah. Picture man. Getting in on the ground floor, are you? I believe you're making the right move. It won't be long before the whole business is either in California or Florida. As it happens I also represent several sellers in the very same neighborhood where Mr. Lasky has his operations."

"Is that right?" This had some appeal to Melvin, who was worried that mere blackmail wouldn't be enough to get him in good with Mr. Grady and his confederates, especially now that he was no longer employed by the United States Postal Service as a fully deputized officer of the law.

"Let's retreat after dinner to my compartment. I've got some good scotch and I can show you my maps and explain a bit about what makes each location suitable for the making of pictures."

FLAVIA'S MOOD WAS somber while Mrs. Chen cleaned the kitchen after breakfast. The latter sped around from task to task, muttering under her breath and occasionally slamming a cabinet shut.

When Bill entered she stuck her index finger out at him. "Breakfast is no longer being served, it's past nine-thirty in the morning."

"That's all right, Mrs. Chen, I slept in this morning. A cup of coffee will suffice until luncheon."

"And I suppose you expect me to brew it?"

"You are the cook. I don't dare invade your domain."

She snorted but started the process of brewing. He gave Flavia a questioning look; Mrs. Chen was often brusque but not usually so much so.

"I explained things to Henry," she said by way of explanation.

Mrs. Chen stopped in her tracks and pointed at Bill again. "Men."

"Anyway it's too late, he's already enlisted. Supposed to show up for a train to take him to basic training up north."

Mrs. Chen very nearly spat on the linoleum. "All's he could say was 'how would it look?'"

Glum Flavia shook her head. "Not as though he could back out at this point anyway, is it?"

"Aw, hell," Bill said. "Where is he now?"

"Up on the roof, printing out some proofs from yesterday. That skinny bug-eyed woman with the opera glasses and the fan." Her voice was quiet and resigned.

After drinking his coffee Bill went up to his room and went through some of his possessions. When he found what he was looking for he checked its condition and went to stand by the staircase leading to the roof, where he waited for Henry to descend.

When he did come down, a folder full of proofs under his arm, the younger man was subdued. Once he made it to the floor he kept his eyes on it, as though looking for patterns in the carpeting. "I suppose she told you."

"She did."

"Nothing to be done about it now. I'll make an honest woman of her and I'm glad to, and I'll come back to her when it's over and I won't be at all sorry about it, but I'm signed up now and that's all there is to it. Can't just say I changed my mind on account of I'm about to be a father. Which I'd point out to you is a fact I didn't know until this morning after I'd already signed the papers."

"Calm down, son, I'm not sore at you. Let me see those proofs."

Henry handed them over. "Not bad at all. You lit her right, she doesn't look so much like a toad."

"Thanks."

He was holding the Dragoon behind his back. "We haven't talked much about my own experience in the war, have we?"

"Not much."

"I regret that now, son, because I think I might have changed your thinking about such things. I want to show you something. An old friend."

He held the Dragoon out to Henry, holding it by the barrel. Henry took it and examined it from all angles, like a relic of a forgotten age.

"Carried her with me throughout the war and after. Not proud to say I fired her more than once at human beings, during and after the conflict, but never was ashamed either, and never did when I thought there was a better option."

Henry nodded and handed it back to Bill, who pressed it against Henry's left shin and squeezed the trigger. The report echoed throughout the room, and the smell of spent gunpowder reached Bill's nostrils just as the lad dropped to the floor and screamed in pain and high dudgeon.

"Jesus Christ, you shot me!"

He heard some commotion downstairs, and Henry was on the floor bleeding a fresh pattern into the carpet as Bill performed first aid. When Flavia appeared at the door with her mouth hanging open Bill called out over his shoulder. "Better have Mrs. Chen send for a doctor, a gun went off by accident."

DAISY HAD BROUGHT home a motion picture magazine and was reading it cross-legged in the stuffed chair. Something about the speed at which she turned the pages was getting on Ezra's nerves and finally he said so. "Ten cents for a picture magazine and you're not even reading the words."

She looked at him, not sure whether he was joking or not. "Course I'm reading the words."

"Oh, hell, no one can read that fast. You're just looking at the pictures."

"Oh, am I? I'll have you know I was just reading a comical article about Miss Mae Murray and her automobile. Says she's such a bad driver all of Southern California's terrified of her." She leafed back a couple of pages and read aloud. "'The Lasky star has a clever plan of keeping down on the upkeep—she only drives on two wheels at a time letting the other two tires spin around in the air and cool off. You can't imagine what a weekly saving in tires this is.'" She laughed out loud. "Isn't that a stitch? If I was just looking at the pictures I wouldn't know it was funny, now would I?"

Daisy was a swell girl but he could hardly stand her being smarter than he was. He'd suspected it since the beginning but now here was his proof. "I'm going out. You want anything?"

"I'd like a box of chocolates, but I can tell you're sore at me."

This irritated him even more. "Why the hell would I be sore?"

"I don't know, sweetie, but you'll get over it. Go have a nice walk and when you get back I'll rub your back."

ON THE STREET he felt better. The thing was, she didn't seem to know or care that she was smarter than him. If she did she wouldn't be with him, would she? He knew she'd graduated from high school up in Portland and so had her brother and sister, so probably she thought everybody did. She was awfully nice to him, nicer than any woman ever had been before, and really an enthusiastic good sport in the sack. He found it impossible to stay mad, and six or eight blocks away from their hotel he stepped into a shopfront to get her some chocolates.

SHE REALLY DID read too quickly for her own purposes. Magazines and newspapers were finished before she knew what she'd digested and she had to go fetch a new one. *Photoplay* was a good long one, with lots of different sorts of stories and pictures, and she liked learning about the real lives of the stars, even when it was just silliness like the Mae Murray driving article. Sometimes they were tragic, too, like the story of poor Magnolia Sweetspire's fiancé drowning before he could come out to Hollywood with her. It was a happy story in the end, though, because she'd come out here anyway and was going to be a star. Few pages further and there was a story about the pair of little ones who were always bedeviling poor Tommy Gill, about Christmas in the new house with their mother and auntie. That one was a little sad, too, because their father had been killed working for the railroad and their last few Christmases had been pretty bleak. The article suggested without really saying it out loud that Mr. Gill was very fond of the kids in real life and reading it Daisy got the idea that Tommy might just set his cap for their mother, Mrs. Crombie, and give those tots a new daddy. She heard the key in the door, set the magazine down and stood up to greet Ezra at the door.

44

"What the hell do you mean you're one recruit short from two days ago?"

The sergeant was emptying a goodly part of the contents of a salt shaker onto his scrambled eggs, covered now in a rime of crystals. "I mean I lost one."

His commanding officer watched the dusting of the eggs with distaste but kept his counsel. "You can't lose one when they haven't even reported for duty yet."

"This one got his leg shot off below the knee."

"In Los Angeles?"

"In Los Angeles."

"I think that's enough salt, sergeant."

The sergeant shook his head. "I can't taste 'em at all otherwise, sir. Any who, his own grandpa shot him in the shin. Docs amputated."

"I'll be a son of a bitch. Sure he didn't get yella and do it himself?"

"Who knows. The kid sure was keen on signing up when I took his paperwork."

"Plenty where he came from, sergeant. Carry on."

TOMMY GILL WAS seated across from Kaplan, and for once the latter wasn't tempted to throw the son of a bitch out on his ear. "That's not a bad idea, Gill."

"Good will, see? Show 'em the motion picture business is loyal and supports the war effort."

"Yeah, I understood that part." The urge to shove him out the door was there again, but less urgently than normal. "I'll talk to publicity, see how we get it set up with Uncle Sam."

"Magnolia Sweetspire can be with me."

"I suppose she can come on before or after. I don't want to see the two of you at the same time. The kids will be a big draw, though, maybe we can come up with some bits of business for you and them up on the dais. I'll have the writers cook something up."

The look of disappointment on Gill's face was worth having to admit that the man had had a good idea. "Did you see those gals I sent up?"

"I did. Sent them down to see Mrs. Perkins."

"Gonna sign them up?"

"Not on contract, no, but she's aware of them and when she's casting something she'll let them know. She knows who they are now."

"Aw, I all but promised them they'd be under contract."

"And what the hell made you think you had the power to do such a thing?"

He straightened up and looked down on Kaplan, and he imagined that had an effect on the man. "I'm Tommy Gill, and I make a lot of money for Provident Studios."

Kaplan shook his head in wonderment at the man's lack of perspective. "You met a couple of good looking girls on the make, with some show experience, and you did just what they asked you to do. I'm sure they'll still be willing and able to make you happy, Tommy, now fuck off."

"You can't talk that way to me."

"You just brought me a good idea about the bond rally, don't fuck it up by talking back to me. Out."

THE CONVERSATION WITH the real estate man had convinced Melvin of one thing: that vipers could smell it on you when you had money to spend. He'd listened to the spiel, which sounded like some pie-in-the-sky bullshit to his ears. Maybe this Clyde Grady would want to invest the money in a nicer studio outfit, or maybe he wouldn't. Still, it occurred to him upon reflection, it might behoove him to have a proposal when he arrived more substantial than ideas for scenarios based on his own orgiastic fantasies. Clearly Grady knew a thing or two about the making and distributing of motion pictures of a forbidden kind. He seemed even to have ideas about keeping one step ahead of the postal inspectors. But did he truly understand the workings of the federal government of the United States?

He'd bought a morning edition of the *Albuquerque Journal* from a porter that morning and read it in more detail than was his custom. His reading of the international news now led him to question how the nation's new war footing would affect the manufacture and distribution of obscene materials. As he pondered the question he was thrilled to find in the national section, on page five, an article about his recent adventures:

SEEK POSTAL INSPECTOR
GONE ROGUE
Took Advantage of His Knowledge to
Rob Indiana Post Office
He is Thought to be in Canada or Mexico

It was assumed that he had escaped the country in order to be outside the reach of federal authorities, which would have been a good idea if he hadn't felt the absolute need to go to California to establish himself in his new career.

When he finished the paper he obtained a pencil and some railroad stationery from the same porter, this time tipping him a dime, and began a letter.

TO Hon. Newton Baker, Secretary of War, United States of America

Dear Mr. Secretary,

Allow me to introduce myself. My name is Reginald Rostand and I am a motion picture producer here in Los Angeles California. I am writing you on a most serious matter, the health physical and moral of our troops just now preparing for their overseas duties. Our brave young men are of good character, to be sure, and yet they are young men and prey to the temptations that plague all males, particularly those without experience in turning aside women of an unwholesome nature!

How well I remember my father's uncle, a veteran of

the late civil war, regaling us with tales of the wretched camp followers who stained many an innocent farmer boy's innocence during that conflict! And in the case of the war in which we now find ourselves embroiled, the ladies in question will be foreigners as well as harlots! Think of the ruination this would bring to our fine young soldiers and, not least, to the sweethearts and wives to whom they will come home.

You may say, then, "What if we supplied our fighting men with prophylactic devices?" Though federal law forbids their distribution through the mails, surely the government itself could order their quiet manufacture for distribution to members of the army, navy and marines. But! You must understand that few, given the option of separating his own staff from the slippery insides of a lady with a lambskin sheath or allowing their comingling, will opt for the former. This, sadly, is human nature.

What I propose will surprise you, but I believe that if you take a moment to consider it you will see its merits. Portable motion picture outfits can be manufactured and distributed, the logistics of which will surely be but a small challenge to the personnel of the Department of War. Films can then be shown to groups in camp or even at the front, using portable electric generators. These films, which I can provide at a deeply discounted price, would be of a nature to first arouse the soldiers' erotic instincts and then douse them. I am speaking of the sin of Onan, of course, which is probably forbidden by the military code of justice, but perhaps this could be changed or overlooked, since the act of self-pollution—certainly loathsome, yes, oh yes!—does not allow for the spread of disease, and the consensus among modern men of medicine is that the practice does not, in fact, lead to imbecility or madness.

Please consider my proposal, Mr. Secretary, with open mind and heart. It is with the utmost concern for our nation and its fighting men that I make it.

Yours sincerely,
Reginald Rostand
Magnificat Educational Distribution Company, Incorporated

FLAVIA SAT AT Henry's hospital bedside, outraged at her grandfather's radically simple solution to her complex problem and relieved by it at the same time. Henry was reading one of the morning papers and occasionally wincing in pain. A large-headed man in the next bed was having a heated, whispered discussion with a woman Flavia took to be his wife, and occasionally the whispers got loud enough that she could make out individual words coming from between the man's clenched yellow teeth: "son of a bitch," "cheating," "bulletproof." The woman appeared distraught and her whispers were inaudible. Then another hissed phrase from the husband: "Grave they'll never find."

Henry pointed at a headline. "Says the congress is going to send the allies two and a half billion dollars aid. I don't even know how much a billion is."

"It's a thousand times a million," Flavia said.

"I can't even picture that big a number." He unfolded the paper, turned the page and folded it into quarters again. "You ever think about how much more education you got than I do?"

"No."

"Sure you have."

"It doesn't matter. You're as intelligent as any man I ever met. There are plenty of people with good educations who are regular ignoramuses."

"See, another big word."

"You knew just what it meant, though, didn't you?"

A red-faced nurse with strands of dishwater blond hair escaping her wimple came limping in to take the other patient's temperature, and the man's wife left the room, holding a handkerchief to her eyes. Henry went on reading for a while, his expression growing darker until finally he spoke. "You let the old man know I don't intend ever talking to him again."

"Never's a long time."

"Flavey, he shot me in the leg and they cut it off."

"All right, he's aware you're sore at him. I think he's waiting until you cool down a little bit before he comes around."

"I'll be damned if I cool down over a thing like this. If he comes around I'll have him chucked out."

OLD OGILVIE WAS at the Flying Scotsman that evening, as near sober as Bill had seen him. Like almost everyone he was eager to discuss the declaration of war, but Bill waved him off. "I've already committed all the violence I intend to do in this conflict."

"I've been thinking about it. Maybe I was dead for a few days after all." His rheumy red eyes widened. "The departed are certainly speaking to me of late."

At that Bill signaled the bartender. "Two shots of your best scotch for me and the landlord." Two shots appeared on the warped surface of the bar and were quickly downed. "So what have the spirits got to say?"

"They say the old woman's in service of the Beelzebub himself, that it's not really her but a replacement, brought here in the guise of the old virago for the sole purpose of tormenting me."

"And why do you suppose the Lord of the Flies himself has it out for you?"

"That's just it. If I were a man of God or even a reasonably virtuous one I'd understand his hatred of me, but I've never cared a jot for anyone but myself."

"And how come the spirits of the departed to be privy to this information? And why do they pass it along to you?"

Ogilvie looked abashed. "I'll tell you the truth, I don't know for certain that they're not . . ." He looked from side to side as though afraid he might be overheard, then lowered his voice. "I think they might be wee folk."

Bill didn't understand, and cocked his head to one side.

"Ye might call them fairies."

There it was, the source of the old Scot's discomfort. It was perfectly fine in his eyes to believe in dead wives being replaced by spiteful changelings, and in messages from the other side of the barrier between worlds, but to believe in the folklore of his native island was a disgraceful thing to reveal to a modern man.

The front door opened and a silence fell upon the room, akin to an arrested gasp, and all eyes were on the figure in its frame. There were often women in the saloon, but they were generally sots, as were their male counterparts. Sometimes women would enter in pairs or in the company of men. But it was extremely odd for a woman to enter on her own, a sober and attractive and well-groomed woman at that, poised and genteel and yet not at all uncomfortable. She made her way across the room to Bill.

"So this is the famous saloon you and Henry are always repairing to in my absence."

"Flavey. How'd you know I'd be here?"

"A wild guess."

"Mr. Ogilvie, this is my granddaughter, Flavia."

"Charmed," Ogilvie said, and he signaled the bartender for three shots of the same.

The shots arrived and the three of them knocked them back. Flavia then looked at her grandfather without blinking. "I've got a bone to pick with you, Gramps."

"I know you do."

"How could you do a thing like that without even consulting me first?"

"What would you have said?"

"I'd have thought you were joking."

"And I'd have done it anyway."

"You hadn't any right."

"I don't care."

"You don't, do you? You assume that you know best, and only you."

"Here's what I know. It's worse than my war, and mine was plenty bad enough. They're using mustard gas over there, boys on both sides are dropping like rain. You'd be lucky if he came home alive, let alone whole. One leg below the knee is something he can afford to lose, and he'll come to accept that if he's smart, once those other boys start coming home."

She was quiet. "Another shot?" Bill said.

"No, thanks. I don't think Henry will ever talk to you again, you know."

"Don't suppose I blame him. It's a wonder you do yourself."

She nodded. "That it is." Then she headed for the door.

THEY GOT BACK to their room after dinner and she pulled the chain on the lamp beside the sofa. On the sofa's arm was the motion picture magazine she'd been looking at, face down to mark the page she'd left off at when Ezra had come back from his walk with a nice big box of fancy chocolates and a garland of poppies he'd picked himself. She'd eaten a few of the bonbons and then he'd given her a real good screwing, after which they decided a couple nice bowls of chop suey down the street would be just the thing. Ezra talked all through supper about the things he wanted to do. Open a candy store was one idea, and when she asked him had he ever run a store before he said no. "But there can't be much to it." Another was a plumbing supply business, if he could just raise some more funds to make a down payment on a warehouse. "I didn't know you knew anything about plumbing," she said, to which he replied that you didn't need to be a plumber to sell them supplies.

He wouldn't tell her where he got his money and she could tell he wouldn't like it if she pressed him, so the whole business remained a puzzle. She didn't want to ask how soon it was going to run out, either, but Ezra didn't seem worried so she left it alone. He'd picked up a half pint of rye on the way home and he sat on the bed pulling on it as the sun went down outside, a look of dim satisfaction on his face.

Then he came over and sat next to her on the sofa and looked down at the magazine. "Hey, there's the kids who keep kicking the shit out of that baggy pants comic."

"Uh-huh. Says here in real life he's like another father to 'em, all that fighting's just a gag. Their real daddy got killed working for the railroad, isn't that sad?"

"Lots of people get killed doing all sorts of things."

Something made her turn back to the previous page, to the photograph of the poor widowed mother and her sister, and she noted again the melancholy look on her face, and the kindly expression on that of her sister. She was about to turn it again when Ezra's hand stayed hers.

"Hold on just a second there, that's the damnedest thing I ever saw."

"What is?"

"That gal looks just like my wife."

"She's a widow," she said. "Like I said, husband was a railroad man."

"Turn back to the kids." She did so, and he squinted at the photo of the brother and sister, sitting amid a pile of brand-new expensive Christmas presents. "Huh," he said.

"What?"

"I ain't sure, but I think those might be my own two babes."

"You can't tell?"

"They grow up, you know, they don't look just the same."

"She look like your wife's sister?"

"Doesn't have one, far as I know."

"Well there you go, then, that's her sister."

"Huh," Ezra said. "Read that to me, would you? You're a lot faster at it than me."

"The whole article?"

"From the start."

She sighed, but she didn't really mind. She liked reading aloud, and it was a good story anyway.

"WE CAN'T STAY here forever, Mister Gill," Cressida said.

"Goddamn it, don't call me that. Once I've done what I just did to you two we ought to at least be on a first name basis. I'm not asking you to stay forever. Just be my guests until I get something going for you over at Provident."

Marceline raised her head up. "It's real nice of you, don't get us wrong."

"I don't like being in this big place all by myself, see?"

They were all splayed over the big, canopied bed in the master bedroom, sheets wet and askew and the bed-spread, similarly defiled, rumpled on the big oriental rug on the floor. Clothes, his and theirs, were strewn about the room, and even Tommy had begun to notice that the bed had a sour milk smell to it of late.

"But we need work so we can get places of our own."

"One thing at a time, now. First thing, I don't see any need to rush into things. What if you gals were to stay here with me?"

"You mean live here?" Cressida said. "That's what you might call scandalous."

"Here's another thing. I'm going to get some new servants. Get this place cleaned up, get a cook and every-thing."

Marceline laughed. "That's a good way to get found out. You hire a cook and a housemaid pretty soon everybody's going to know you've got two girls shacked up here."

"I'll pay them enough they won't blab."

HAPPILY SETTLED IN a deluxe room—by far the nicest he'd ever seen—at the Nottingham Hotel on Sixth, which the mustachioed real estate man had recommended, he descended to the street in search of a newsstand. On the train a portly matron had tossed a novel aside onto her seat in the dining car, informing her nearly identical tablemate (floral hat, tiny spectacles, black dress with white lace at the throat, a potentially lethal concentration of rosewater) that it was immoral trash. When the ladies had finished their luncheon Melvin had picked the book up—*The Real Adventure*. It was a racy story and much to his liking and set in Chicago, a city he knew and liked. But he'd finished it the morning of the train's arrival in Los Angeles, and he lacked another book. In addition, he reasoned that if he was going to be an important producer of motion pictures, even those of a clandestine nature, he should learn at least the rudiments of the workings of the business.

There were a number of movie periodicals, however, and he was unsure of which titles would be of use to him. A tiny man in tattered coveralls who ran the booth, his face like a shrunken apple, was unhelpful.

"I don't know squat about what's inside the magazines, I just unload 'em, sell 'em, and return the ones I ain't sold."

"All right, but which ones do the picture people read?"

"How should I know? I don't know any picture people."

Browsing, he found that the magazines were geared not toward professional picture makers but to the viewers of those pictures, skewing female at that. Nonetheless he bought several and headed for a French restaurant nearby, recommended by the front desk clerk. "Make it an expensive one," Melvin had said when he asked.

Once seated he began perusing the magazines. The lights were dim, augmented by candlelight, but squinting Melvin managed to make out the titles of the articles. The waiter interrupted his skimming of the table of contents of *Motion Picture World* and handed him a wine list, at which he squinted for a few moments before handing it back to the waiter, a skinny, balding man with a tightly waxed black mustache and a distinct military bearing. "I'll be honest with you, I don't know diddly about wine. Why don't you just bring me a really good red, all right?"

He started in on an article about John Bunny, which he quickly decided he wouldn't finish, and momentarily the waiter returned and opened the bottle with great flourish and held out the cork for Melvin to sniff.

"You can skip all that stuff. It'll do fine." He picked up the menu and pointed. "I'll have the egg pie to start and the steak whatsis, medium well."

The waiter snapped his heels and nodded, then turned tail and headed for the kitchen. At one point Melvin looked up from his reading and noticed that an older man in formal evening attire was glaring at him, like he'd never seen anybody reading in a restaurant before. He swallowed the tiny slug of wine the waiter had dispensed into his giant balloon of a glass and poured himself a bigger slug of it. It was good, not as sweet as he'd expected, and he thought he'd better take it slow lest he get through the whole bottle before the appetizer came.

He was hoping one of the magazines might have some nice girly pictures, maybe some of Sennett's Bathing Beauties, just a little something to get his imagination going for when he got back to the hotel. It had been days since he'd had actual sexual intercourse with a real live woman, and he thought it might be wise to consult a doctor before trying again. The act of self-pollution would have to suffice for now, though recently even that poor substitute had become unusually messy, malodorous and rather painful.

There was nothing in *Motion Picture World* that caught his fancy in that way, though he did enjoy the articles, with their stories of genteel eastern writers engaged to concoct stories, of brash men lured from lives of adventure to become picture directors and finally of magnetic, attractive players brought into the field from the legitimate stage, or perhaps discovered by the movie men among the working populations of New York or Los Angeles.

He remained unaroused when his egg pie was set before him. The pie was delicious, with a flaky crust and some exotic combination of foreign herbs that he found delightful. Once he was finished with it he picked up the second magazine, *Photoplay*, still hopeful of finding a revealing picture of a pretty girl or two. It didn't take much to get him going, usually.

His steak arrived, a dollop of melting butter on top, with roast potatoes and white asparagus spears, and he leaned back in his seat, one of the spears in his left hand

and the magazine in the right. He glanced over at the tuxedoed man, who continued to scowl in his direction.

"Why'ntcha take a picture, bub, it'll last longer," Melvin said, and the attractive young lady across from the man put her napkin in front of her mouth to disguise a laugh. The man's face took on a shade of red visible even in the dim amber light of the dining room.

When he'd finished the asparagus he turned to his steak and began cutting it into pieces, the magazine open face down on the tablecloth. The steak was good, not chewy at all. When he had enough morsels cut to make one-handed feeding possible he picked the magazine back up and, impatient, flipped through looking for a pretty girl.

He stopped at the sight of two women sitting on a couch and holding hands. There was something in their demeanor that he liked, and he paged back to the start of the piece, a profile of two child comedians who'd made a splash tormenting Tommy Gill, a comic actor whose photograph Melvin found vaguely familiar. When he got to the picture of the two women a couple of pages hence he'd finished his steak and potatoes, and he learned that the women were the children's mother and her sister, their aunt. Just as the busboy took away his plate and the waiter arrived with the dessert menu it hit him: these were the women in the Magnificat pussy-eating pictures!

He looked up at the waiter with a delirious grin and pointed at the photo. "I saw these two in a stag picture!"

The waiter maintained his equanimity. "Would monsieur care for some dessert? We have a very nice tarte Tatin this evening."

"Nah, not now, thanks. I would but I gotta get back to my room. What's the damage?"

The waiter nodded his assent and produced a check on a silver tray. Despite Melvin's joy he was taken aback by the total. "Wait, this can't be right. Ten dollars and fifty cents for a bottle of wine?"

"It's a very fine Pessac-Léognan, monsieur, aged fifteen years."

"I guess I did ask for a good bottle, huh?" He pulled out his wallet and put a twenty-dollar bill on the tray, not without wincing, then he poured the remnants of the bottle—nearly a quarter of its original contents—into the glass and swallowed it in a long, happy swig. "Would have been a shame to waste."

The waiter gave him a kind smile and nodded. "It would."

When he stood he discovered that he had the beginnings of an erection, thanks to his thoughts of the two women from the cunt-lapping films, but he didn't bother to sit or cover his midsections with the magazines. He detoured on his way out the door to the table of the man who'd glared at him earlier, where he addressed the young woman opposite him. "You take good care of this old fossil tonight. He looks like he could use a giggle or two."

As the man got to his feet, speechless with indignation, Melvin arrived at the door and headed out into the night, back to his hotel and his project for the rest of the evening.

THE CORRIDORS OF the sanitorium were high-ceilinged and most of the light came from the tall windows. Nuns glid past him on the worn oak floor as he searched for someone who could tell him where Henry's room was; the sisters themselves wouldn't tell him, and he'd asked three of them. The first had glowered and shaken her head. Perhaps a vow of silence, Bill thought. The second, whom he'd found at the top of a flight of stairs, was younger and more cheerful, but claimed not to know. The third, grouchier and older than either, fairly snarled in reply. "I'm a Sister of the Blessed Virgin Mary and a skilled nurse, not an usher."

In time he figured out where the semi-private rooms were. He was in fact rather stricken by his conscience, if only for the pain the boy was suffering, and he'd insisted on paying out of his own pocket to keep Henry off the general ward. A fully private room, though, had struck Bill as more generous than strictly necessary, and in the third semi-private room he looked inside he found him.

The man in the next bed seemed to be unconscious. Gauze covered his whole head except for his swollen red face, and blood seeped through it in spots.

Bill took a seat at Henry's bedside. The lad gave him a sidelong look but said nothing. The silence lasted nearly ten minutes, neither in a particular hurry to start the dialogue, and finally Henry spoke, without looking at Bill.

"You're damn lucky I didn't have you arrested."

"That's true. I'm grateful you didn't," Bill said.

"I'd reckon you think I'm grateful you saved me from a big mistake."

"Not really. I'd have been mad as hell if someone did that to me in '62."

"You know a whole lot better than I do, don't you?"

Bill laughed and regretted it, as the lad's face got harder

than it already was. "I know I want my great-grandchild to grow up with his daddy."

"Nurse!" Henry shouted, face flushed, tears in his eyes, and Bill felt certain he was about to be ejected, but when the sister poked her head in the doorway Henry just asked if he might have some morphine.

"I'll ask the doctor," she said, and disappeared again. She didn't seem happy about being bothered by a patient over something as trivial as pain.

"I ever tell you about the time I got shot?"

Henry shook his head. "Hurts, don't it?"

"I'll say. Caught a Minié ball in my left ass cheek in Tennessee. It was a fairly chaotic situation and I suspect it might have come from a rifle on my own side, either by pure accident or from someone who'd taken a dislike to me. Kept me off duty for a whole week, then they put me on kitchen patrol and before I knew it they decided I was fit to march."

Henry nodded.

"Flavia give you the bad news?"

Now he looked at Bill with some alarm. "What?"

"The old woman's given her notice."

"Mrs. Chen? What for?"

"Says she's had enough. My crippling you was the fatal blow."

"You didn't cripple me. Sawbones says I'll get around just fine with a pegleg."

"In any case she says she prayed on it for a couple of nights and then the Lord told her to go and live with one of her sons, as her current household had moved from merely sinful to homicidal."

The bloody-headed man in the next bed stirred and cried out for the nurse. "It hurts," he yelled.

"He got knocked over by a horsecart crossing the street," Henry told Bill. "Hit his head and then it got hit by the edge of an automobile tire, would have been crushed flat if the driver hadn't seen him. Now he doesn't know how much a whole bunch of nines is, maybe won't ever again."

The sister reappeared in the doorway, arms akimbo, fists on her hips. "I haven't found the doctor yet, and I don't want to be called back here until I do. Yelling won't get you medicated any faster than staying still." She fondled her rosary with her thick pink fingers and hurried off.

"I suppose I'll be on my way," Bill said. He got no reaction from Henry. "I just wanted to say if you want to come back to the job I won't hold it against you if you don't address me. You can do all your working with Flavia and treat me as if I were a ghost, invisible and inaudible."

Henry picked up a newspaper from his nightstand and began reading it.

"But we're family now," the old man said. "Whether you like it or don't."

"FIND OUT WHERE that studio is," Ezra said. "I've got a mind to pay them a visit."

"Oh, Ezzie, those aren't your kids in the magazine. And that's not your wife either."

"That's what I mean to find out for sure. If it ain't them, fine. If it is, then I mean to get a share of what they're making down there. And as for that shit-heel clown, if he's 'like a daddy' to 'em, I mean to find out what he's like to my wife."

"Is that so," she said, turning her back to him. She was standing by the door to the room and he was sitting on the bed in his undershirt and BVDs. "I suppose you'd like to have her back."

That came as a surprise. "Aw, no, honey. It's just, if someone's putting it to your lawful wedded wife, a man's got a duty to do something about it, you see what I mean?"

"Sounds to me like you're jealous. Like maybe you're thinking what you've been missing these last few years."

He surely did like this gal, but oh, boy, right now she sounded just like a wife. He stood up and put on his good shirt and his trousers. "I'm going to go and get a plate of eggs and ham."

"I don't suppose it occurs to you that if we got an apartment with a kitchen in it I could fix that up for you at a fraction of the cost."

Jesus, what had gotten into her? She'd been all sweetness and light up until now, with hardly any guff at all. And yet even now he was going out instead of smacking her, the way he would have with any other woman he'd ever known. Maybe this is what love is, he thought as he headed down the stairs.

He gave the desk clerk a cheerful hello as he passed, and heading out into the morning sunshine he felt as good as though the previous clash hadn't happened at all. Most likely her monthly visitor was on its way; he could remember how cranky Trudy used to get when that happened.

He thought he might bring Daisy back a newspaper

as a peace offering. He might even glance at the head-lines while he ate his breakfast, the way he saw people do. Maybe he ought to make a habit of reading. He wasn't stupid, he knew that. Maybe it was just a question of applying himself. He knew he could read as well as any-body else, he just didn't have the practice.

He decided at that moment to improve his reading skills. He picked up a copy of the morning *Times* at a newsstand and on his way to the diner scanned the front pages. There was something about funding the war and recruitment and the draft, none of which interested him. Of more interest was a murder in Eagle Rock, complete with a photograph of the killer, a grandmotherly woman with a shawl. The victim was her husband, a prominent Glendale jeweler who she'd caught playing around with a chorus girl. This was the sort of thing that could make him a regular reader, he thought.

He was in the diner and nearly finished with his scram-bled eggs and ham steak when he got to the end of the article. He took a swig of his coffee and motioned the waitress for a refill, and that was when another headline caught his eye:

**STARS TO APPEAR IN RALLY FOR
LIBERTY BONDS**

45

"Are you quite certain you're not ashamed marrying a murderess? And a husband-killer at that?" The other bed in the room was empty for once, its occupant having expired during the night, and they spoke without inhibition.

"Reckon it adds a little spice to the whole business."

"In that case, my answer's yes."

"You sure you're not bothered marrying a fellow with a pegleg?"

"It'll make it harder for you to get away from me when I'm after you with the carving knife."

"Guess it's settled, then. Soon's I'm out of this monkey house we'll do it."

One of the sisters came into the room just then, which ordinarily would have stopped her from leaning down and kissing him, but they went right ahead, tongues and all, until she cleared her throat. She was one of the less combative ones, and after ten awkward seconds she spoke, her voice an octave higher than normal with ill ease.

"It's I, Sister Thomas Aquinas, here to check your vitals."

Without raising her mouth from Henry's, Flavia waved her off, and after another ten seconds of averting her gaze the sister left the room. "I'll be back in fifteen minutes."

◆ ◆ ◆

FEENEY WINCED. HIS big toe felt as though it had been transpierced with a dozen long, thin needles and with every step he grew more unbalanced. He knew he ought to have stayed home that morning but there was a two-reeler being cast at Provident that morning with a call for an old ragpicker, and he knew it was a good and noticeable role for him. So despite Sukie's protests he'd headed out with his gouty foot and, sure enough, he'd been cast as the ragpicker and made a good job of it, too, with the director singling him out for praise afterward. So, he thought, it had been the right thing to do, despite the pain, and his reward was a trip to the pub to see his boon companions and regale them with the tale of the day's tour de force. He knew Sukie would be intransigent on the question of his having a tipple under the circumstances—she still held to the notion that gout was caused by drink, an old wives' tale thoroughly rejected by modern science, but then she wasn't there to stop him, was she?

It had already grown dark, the dim orange light from the saloon's lamps glowing through the grime of the windows. Inside Lily sat on her usual barstool clutching her handbag to her wizened chest and muttering, facing the barroom and not the bar. This was unusual, since she habitually clutched her glass tightly pressed against the surface of the bar. "Eat shit, limey," she said as he crossed the threshold.

"That's not really necessary, Lily," he said. "In any case I'm as American as you, and of Irish origin to boot."

"Eat shit, you limey bastard."

"Evening, Feeney," Bill said as Feeney took the adjoining stool.

"Evening, Mr. Ogden."

"You seem to be in pain."

"It's gout, Bill. Should have kept off my feet, but there was work today and I've been on a bit of a roll. Have to take advantage when the muses are smiling down upon one."

"You sure a drink is what you want, gouty as you are?"

"I am quite certain it is."

"And how were Miss Connie Talmadge and Mr. Griffith this afternoon?"

He drew back and puffed his chest out, uncertain whether he was being mocked. "Today's work was of a somewhat lower profile. I played a lowly chiffonier."

"As in a chest of drawers or a rag-and-bone man?"

"The latter," Feeney said, unamused, as the bartender handed him his tipple. Lily, meanwhile, had begun eyeing him with something more baleful than her usual generalized malevolence.

"Well you sure have got yourself a lot of gall coming in here tonight of all nights and strutting right past like nothing's doing," Lily said, her lower jaw hanging open and revealing the yellowish gray stumps of her remaining teeth. She descended from her perch on the stool and advanced toward Feeney with a low animal growl. From a crouch she leapt at his throat, her stiff, gnarled fingers curved to scratch at his face. He went down to the dusty floor, screaming.

"You need a hand, Feeney?" Bill said, taking a sip from his mug.

The actor continued his caterwauling, his attacker's growl having mutated into something like a shriek. The bartender stood on tiptoe and hoisted himself so that his belly rested on the bar and watched for a few seconds, trying to determine how seriously to take what was happening.

"He's bleeding," Bill said. "No telling how clean those talons of hers might be." He stood up then bent down and lifted the old woman into the air and away from her victim. The barkeep came over and took hold of her by the waist as Bill helped Feeney to his feet, fine rivulets of blood trickling down his face.

"I never did a damned thing to her but buy her a drink once when I was flush!"

She struggled to get free, but she had no beef with anyone but Feeney. She pointed at him and yelled. "He left me with child!"

"Lily, I assure you," he said, daubing at the blood with his handkerchief, "I never met you before I set foot in this place, many years after you were last capable of conception."

She looked around the room at the assembled collection of sots. "He left me with child!"

The bartender looked at Bill. "You reckon I ought to call the nut wagon?"

The door at the rear of the barroom, the one that led to the living quarters upstairs, could be heard to unlock, and Mrs. Ogilvie, dreadful in her widow's weeds, appeared in its frame, her face still indecipherable behind the veil. Ogilvie, who until that moment had been half asleep at his pots at the end of the bar, made a loud, wet inhalation of terror, and as his wife advanced through the room he dove for the floor behind the bar.

At the sight of her Lily had calmed, and when Mrs.

Ogilvie beckoned she slid effortlessly from the barman's grasp and walked toward her, arms outstretched. "Come now, let's bring you upstairs and have something to nourish you," she said, and she put a black-clad arm around the deranged woman to lead her out and up the stairs.

At the sound of the door locking again from the other side, the women out of sight, the barroom was quite still for a minute or so, until Bill broke the silence. "Must be something in the air this evening."

MELVIN WAS WAITING outside what looked to him like a warehouse. He'd been there off and on since morning, hoping the fellow from Magnificat Distribution was going to show his face. He was about to give up for the evening when a man in a heavy overcoat approached the front door, extracted from his pocket a key ring and started fingering the keys, looking for the right one. Melvin crossed the street in a hurry and accosted him.

"Excuse me, sir, my name's van de Kamp, United States Postal Service Office of Instructions and Mail Depredations." He showed him his badge.

Outside of a moving picture comedy he didn't think he'd ever seen as scared a face as the one across from him right then. The man fumbled with the keys and dropped them.

"I don't know anything about it, I'm the night watchman and I'm just here to . . . this is a paper warehouse, you see that?" He gestured toward the words CARMICHAEL PAPER CO. WAREHOUSE NO. 2 carved over the doorway.

"Paper warehouse. I see." He held a notebook to his face and pretended to read in the feeble light of the streetlamp. "According to our records, this address hasn't been in use as a paper warehouse for some time."

"I'll tell you what's a crime, mister. I've had a postal inspector trying to blackmail me for a little while now. What do you say to that?"

"One of our boys?"

"That's right."

"Blackmailing you over what?"

"Well, sir, I couldn't tell you. He—he was never specific. Just insinuated he knew about something nefarious going on under our aegis."

"And you weren't doing anything wrong?"

"On my mother's grave, sir!"

"Did this fellow give you a name?"

"No, sir."

"Did you go to the police? Better still, the Inspection Service?"

"No. No sir, I guess I didn't."

"Why not?"

"Oh, I suppose I just didn't want to stir up any trouble."

"And what did he ask from you?"

"Well, sir, nothing specific."

"Didn't say what he thought you were up to and didn't ask for anything specific in return. Doesn't sound like much of a blackmailer to me."

"If you'd seen the notes you'd understand."

"I'll have to see them, of course."

"I—you see, I threw them away."

"You're sure of that?"

"Yes sir."

"That's destruction of evidence in a case involving the

United States mail. I'm going to have to get inside and look around."

"I don't have the key."

"Isn't it one of those on the ring there on the sidewalk?"

"I must have brought the wrong ring."

"Mister, we're going into that building now if I have to get a locksmith."

The man knelt down and picked up the key ring, and when he arose again he hit Melvin in the face with the hand holding the keys, then turned and ran back in the direction whence he came. Face smarting but unscratched, Melvin took after him and wrapped his forearm around the man's throat and sent him crashing to the pavement.

"I'm done messing with you, fellow. Now stand up and give me those keys and you and I are going to have a looksee inside that building there, and you're going to give me a straightforward accounting of whatever monkey business is going on in there, you hear?"

The man stood slowly, nodding, and as they walked toward the warehouse's front door, Melvin had the decency not to look the quietly sobbing smut peddler in the face.

KAPLAN ARRIVED AT City Hall at seven-thirty P.M., well after normal office hours, and was met downstairs by a very tall man—six and a half feet at least, with thick orbital bones, obtruding cheekbones and large ears nearly perpendicular to his skull. "Come with me, the mayor will see you directly." The man's air was diffident but polite, his voice a deep baritone.

Upstairs he found Mayor Woodman seated at a big

desk. He arose and walked around it, grinning and hand extended. "Good to meet you, sir, Fred Woodman at your service."

They shook hands and took their seats. "Do I detect a trace of a Down East accent, your honor?"

Still grinning, the mayor shook his head no. "You're not too far off, though, it's Vermont. Came here eight years ago and here I am mayor already. You?"

"Passaic, New Jersey. Came here pursued by the patent trusts."

"Those trusts. Lost out in the end, didn't they? Well, the east coast's loss is our gain. Now what's this you wanted to see me about, Kaplan?"

"I'd like to hold a war bond rally on the steps of city hall."

"Bond rally? How's that?"

"War bonds aren't selling too quickly and the government's having a hard time convincing people they're a sound investment. Or even explaining to people what they are. My idea is we get some picture stars to give a show, make some speeches. Have all the papers cover it, film the thing and put it into the newsreels."

"I see, I see." He cupped his chin and looked down at the carpet. "Now what does the mayor get out of this?"

"Of course you'd be highly visible in all the proceedings, sort of a master of ceremonies."

"That's grand, Kaplan, and of course I love publicity. But baby needs new shoes."

This took Kaplan aback. "Sorry, your honor?"

"Traditionally, when approval's needed for an occasion such as this, there's a small matter of tribute."

He found his mouth open as though he were making a reply he hadn't composed yet. "Of course." He reached for the check book in his inside jacket pocket. "If I might borrow your pen."

"For God's sake, man, not a check. Have some cash sent over."

"Will two hundred suffice?"

"Make it five."

He stood and extended his hand. "Five hundred it is. You'll have it this afternoon. Is it all right to hand it off to"—he gestured toward the antechamber—"your man out there?"

The mayor stood and, taking Kaplan's hand, nodded. "Of course. Throckmorton's got my absolute trust, honest as the day is long."

As Kaplan left the room, he could have sworn he heard the man muttering, sotto voce, "Lousy Jew."

"YOU'D BETTER BOTH get over here," Clyde said over the phone.

"We're dining," George said. He rolled his eyes and mouthed Clyde's name to Irene, who giggled through a mouthful of fettucine alfredo, a dish she'd just made for the first time. The sauce tasted all right but had the consistency of wallpaper paste and the pasta overboiled.

"I said you'd better get over here. I've got a man locked in the storage closet claims he's a goddamn postal inspector."

George stood up. "I'll call a cab, be there as soon as possible."

"What the hell?"

"Our blackmailer has materialized." He got the operator and arranged for a taxi.

Irene tossed both bowls of fettucine into the trash. "We can get something to eat later."

CLYDE HAD BEEN nervously playing with what remained of his hair and it stood up at various amusing angles from his scalp. His collar was undone and sticking out and his face was such a farcical mask of anguish that at first sight Irene wondered whether maybe the whole thing wasn't a prank. "Jesus Christ, you took a long time. Come on upstairs, he's awake and banging on the door wanting out."

"He wasn't awake before?" George asked.

"Soon as we were both upstairs I grabbed a piece of rebar and bounced it off his skull." Clyde hauled open the screeching metal door of the freight elevator and hustled them inside it. The whole building smelled mustier to Irene than usual, with a hint of mold she hadn't detected there before.

"You could have killed him," Irene said over the clanking of the elevator.

"Far as I know he might have done the same to me."

They got off the freight elevator to the sound of something metal slamming against a heavy wooden door and a muffled voice shouting. "You realize this is a federal offense, unlawful sequestration of a federal officer? Equivalent to kidnapping and therefore a capital offense."

"I think he's threatening you, Clyde." A streetlight outside shone through a window. Otherwise the only other light in the corridor was a single twenty-five watt bulb hanging from the ceiling next to the elevator. The three of them stood together beneath it, their faces hidden in shadow.

"Is that a woman's voice?"

"You claim you're a postal inspector," Irene answered. "Are you the one who's been writing us those funny letters? We've saved them you know, they're in a safety deposit box at the bank. I believe blackmail is illegal as well. Or is it extortion? I get the two confused."

No answer came from the storage closet.

"I don't think you're here on behalf of the postal service, are you? Those letters didn't seem very official."

"Let me out, will you? I'm not here to make trouble. I want to help."

"Help with what?"

"Making dirty pictures."

Clyde stamped his foot on the floor. "He wasn't talking that way outside. He was threatening me."

"Is that true, mister?"

There was a pause before he answered. "I had to make him take me seriously."

"If we open up do you promise to behave?"

George used his hand to guide him along the wall to the main light switch.

"Yes."

The whole second floor was now illuminated, the walls a pale green with a darker but equally sickly green beneath.

"My husband is armed," she said, wishing he had in fact thought to bring his revolver from home.

"I'll be good."

Irene spoke quietly. "He sounds like a little boy pleading with his parents for a puppy."

"I don't want money," said the voice. "I've got plenty. I want to invest."

"We weren't looking for investors," George said. "Anyway, why invest in a business you know nothing about?"

"I know how the postal system works and how to avoid trouble."

"Yes, but what's in it for you? What makes you think our little enterprise is something to invest in?"

There was a silence. Then: "I'd like to meet the girls."

Irene burst out laughing. "I'll bet there are girls in Indiana who'd be nice to you if you tried."

"Yours are special. The one with the dark hair and the funny smile and one tit—bosom—smaller than the other. I'd like to meet her."

Irene exchanged glances with Clyde. He meant Trudy. "She's not with us any more."

"How's that?"

"She's dead," Clyde said.

"That's not so. I happen to know she and that blonde she says is her sister are raising those two little kids who pester Tommy Gill in the movies. Saw their photograph in one of the motion picture magazines."

Irene had to sit down.

The man in the supply closet continued. "By the by, if that really is her sister then those cuntlapping scenes were even filthier than I thought."

Clyde was holding on to the piece of rebar he'd brained the stranger with, and George's fists were clenched. Irene wondered if they were really going to have to kill him, and thinking about Trudy and Victoria and the kiddies she knew she was prepared to help, if necessary.

◆ ◆ ◆

TOMMY WAS FEELING warm and happy. He and his friend Milt were with the girls at the bar at the Hotel Rockford downtown tying one on, with the two men well ahead of their female companions. Cressida was seated next to Milt at the table, and Tommy next to Marceline. The counterman had on his best suit, five years old but hardly ever worn and thus like new.

"What is it you do in life, Milt?" Cressida asked.

Tommy spoke for his pal. "He's a restaurateur."

"Ooh."

"And a chef."

"How nice," Marceline said. "A man who can cook!"

"Will you be going into the armed forces?"

"I was already in the army. That's where I learned to cook. Two years, wasn't the life for me."

"And have you a wife?"

"Well, ladies, I'll tell you the truth. I do for the time being, but she's down in San Diego and shows no signs of returning."

"Poor fellow," Cressida said, placing her hand just above his knee, beneath the tablecloth so no one saw.

"And you ladies, what's it like in show business?"

"I'll tell you honestly," Marceline said, twirling a coil of blond hair between two fingers for Tommy's perverted benefit. "It's awfully rough. Moving from town to town on one circuit or another and having to fend off mashers and stage-door Johnnies at every turn. We think the moving pictures are going to be a lot better way to live."

"Have you made some pictures already?"

"No sir, but Tommy's working on it." She beamed at him, expecting a response. Instead he turned to face the bar and snapped his fingers at the bartender, then made a circular hand gesture for another round.

"Once on the Pantages circuit Mr. Pantages's assistant himself tried to cop a feel off of Cressida and she knocked him down with a right hook right in the snot locker!" Both girls laughed.

"That guy," Cressida said. "He was a skinny little creep who thought the chorus girls were his private harem. He got up with a nosebleed and said he was going to have me fired, but Mr. Pantages kicked him out of his office and called him a nelly for letting a girl coldcock him." Something occurred to her and she put both palms to the sides of her face. "Oh, Marceline, fellows, did you read about Mr. Pantages's little boy? He was playing U-boat with some of his pals up in Seattle."

"U-boat?" Milt said. He'd been ruminating on the course his life had taken of late when the mention of war snapped him back to the present. "Who?"

"Mr. Pantages's little boy was playing U-boat."

"Playing under water?" He'd heard of Pantages but didn't see how you could play U-boats.

"On land, you dope. He was being the U-boat on his bicycle and he was trying to get past his little chums who were the good guy boats, and one of the boys had an air rifle and shot his eye right out!"

On hearing this Tommy leaned back and roared. "Shot his eye out!"

Marceline gave him a playful slap on the knee. "Now that's not funny, Tommy."

This made Tommy laugh that much harder. "The hell it's not. Just picture it: tough as nails, the kraut captain looks through his periscope peddling his bicycle past the deadly Allied armada. Suddenly a shot rings out! Or maybe more like a little *pffft* noise, 'cause it's an air rifle, and now the little bastard's on the ground crying, eye hanging out of the socket!"

Milt was laughing too now. Cressida was visibly sore at Tommy, and Marceline was trying her darndest to keep a straight face. Sensing trouble, Tommy stood up and downed his fresh drink in a single swig.

"You know what I say, let's get ourselves a suite upstairs and have us a party!"

MELVIN SAT IN the storage closet, a single bulb hanging orange from the ceiling, growing dimmer and then brighter as he assessed the situation outside. It seemed unlikely they planned to let him join their little operation, in fact it seemed considerably more likely to him now that the tone of his dispatches had been a tad too threatening, that they viewed him as a menace and not a potential comrade in the cinematic arts. If he were in their position, what would he do?

There was a tool chest in the corner. Not especially well-equipped, but he found a long Phillips-head screwdriver and a sheet of heavy gauge sandpaper. He began to sharpen the business end of the thing.

THE SUITE HAD a vast sitting area and two bedrooms. Tommy had managed to get a Victrola sent up and some loudmouth opera singer was yodeling about something sad in Italian. The guests had started to arrive—two couples were already necking on the davenport—and Marceline sat on the sill in the front room looking at the crowd moving along the Main Street sidewalk below. An actor she thought she recognized had shown up already plastered and was hitting on Cressida, who listened to his supposedly hilarious anecdote with a perfect, hostile disdain that was imperceptible to her interlocutor, who by the look on his face was certain he was going to charm the bloomers right off her.

Milt came over and handed her a gin rickey. "I don't understand why he can't just throw a party at that big old house of his," he said.

"He's keeping clear of it at the moment. Wife's trying to serve him with divorce papers. Staying somewhere different every night. We've been up in Ventura County the last few days, just came back to town because of the bond rally."

Milt took the rickey from her hand and took a small sip, then returned it. "Sorry, just wanted to taste it. Never had one of those."

"Don't be sorry. Where do you live, Milt?"

"Little apartment in South Pasadena. Nothing like what you're used to."

She laughed at that. "You'd be awful surprised at what I'm used to."

"Had a little house in Glendale but when the wife took the kids away it didn't seem so small any more, and what was I paying that kind of rent for, anyway, living by my lonesome?"

"Sorry about the wife and kids."

"My own fault. I worked real hard and when I was done for the day I wanted to relax or carouse, one or the other, and she didn't like me doing either one. Then I didn't come home for a couple nights and she wanted to know where the hell I'd been. I said, 'Running the restaurant' and she said, 'You know damn well I meant at night' and I told her I didn't rightly remember but it involved passing out in Westlake Park and waking up early enough to open the diner on time. That wasn't the only thing but that's a pretty good example of what used to go on."

"Look who just walked in, Murray Stanton."

"Who?" Milt looked over his shoulder in the direction of the door.

"He's a stage actor. He's playing Othello now."

"All right."

"I haven't seen it but I saw his picture in the paper last week and he made quite an excellent Negro. Maybe he's going to be at the bond rally, too."

"He ever been in the movies?"

"No, they've never been able to lure him yet. I bet they will before long."

"In that case I've never seen him and I don't care. Say, Marceline, seems like you like me all right."

"I sure do, Milt. Being with Tommy we mostly meet picture people and they're all the same. You're different."

"So I mentioned my little place down in South Pass. It's small but I keep it neat and clean."

"Uh-huh."

"You know, by the standards of old bachelors."

She laughed. "That's a point in your favor."

"I just thought maybe you'd like to see it. We could get away from here and come back for the rally in the morning. I got my helper opening the restaurant for me."

She touched a finger to his chest. "The problem, you see, is Tommy might not notice if I were gone for a while, but overnight, he'd sure pick up on that. I have another idea. Why don't we go down to the front desk and get another room and charge it to the Gill party. After a while I could go back to the party and you wouldn't have to go all the way back to South Pasadena to sleep."

"You think Tommy'd be all right with that?"

"Tommy's throwing so much money around these days he'll never know. Trying to spend it before that sow of a wife can get to it."

Tommy was over in a corner miming the story of the little Pantages boy getting shot off of his bicycle to some vaudeville people and didn't notice when they slipped out of the room and down the stairs.

"IF THERE'S A good crowd it would be better to have a handheld camera, yes?"

"I haven't learned to operate that gizmo yet. I'll set up the eight-by-ten, take pictures from the vantage point they're setting aside for me and that'll be fine and dandy. Mrs. Buntnagel's husband didn't say anything about paying for two photographers. Studio's got their own men for the smaller formats."

Flavia closed her eyes. Her patience for the old man's stubborn ways was tested to a greater and greater degree the further her pregnancy advanced. "I know how to operate the Speed Graphic. Two of us will be better than one."

"What are we going to do about dinner?"

"If you hadn't chased the old woman away by shooting my fiancé that wouldn't be a problem, now, would it?"

He was sitting in his big wing chair in the study, reading the evening edition of the *Times*. He tapped at an article in the front section. "I tell you what, I don't think this draft business is right or even legal."

"Not even going to try and argue with me, are you?"

"I could try and talk her back."

"I already tried and she likes me more than she does you."

"I don't suppose you'd consider fixing something."

"I'm with child. If you want to make something I'll supervise but I'll be damned if I'll do the cooking."

"How about we go to the Pig and Whistle and tomorrow after the bond rally I'll look into getting a new cook."

"I'll even assist you in the attempt."

IRENE SAT AT the editing table with her chin in her cupped hands, wondering what the hell they'd been thinking, going into this whole crazy venture as a lark. It was illegal; of course it was going to end in disaster. George and Grady were still negotiating with the man through the door, but she'd seen after a few minutes that they weren't going to get a straight answer out of him. He plainly knew all they were up to and he wanted to meet Trudy, and he was either a postal inspector or he wasn't. In either case he knew enough about their little enterprise to put them all behind bars, possibly including Trudy and Victoria.

Their options, as she saw them, were the following:

1. Take him at his word, let him meet Trudy and take part in the production of the dirty pictures;
2. Let him out of the closet and tell him to take a flying leap at the moon, hope he'll just give up after all the effort expended;
3. Kill him.

She liked option three the least. She was at heart a moral person and didn't relish living the rest of her life burdened with the knowledge that she'd killed another human being. But the first meant working with an unstable person, possibly an outright lunatic, and worse, it meant exposing Trudy to an unacceptable level of risk. As for the second, which seemed to be close to what George and Clyde were leaning toward, there wasn't a chance in hell that this person who'd been bold enough to write poison pen letters and brazenly appear at the studio was going to turn around and walk away with a rueful shake of his head and a defeated smile.

MILT SAT ON the edge of the bed, feeling a little low, notwithstanding the fact that he had just lain with a woman for the first time in eight and a half months, and a far more attractive woman than any whose company he had theretofore enjoyed.

"Feeling blue, sugar?"

"Kind of rotten, rubbing bellies with my buddy's girl, and in a room he's paying for to boot."

"I'm not his girl, I'm just . . . part of his circle, you see the difference?"

"However you call it, he wouldn't understand."

"Sure he would. He'd be sore, but he knows how things work in this world. He hasn't got any claim on Cressida or me. As long as he treats us okay we're happy to be at his service, if you like. But he doesn't have any say in who else we screw or don't."

He shook his head and picked at a little hole in his undershirt. "I guess I just don't understand the way you show folk live your lives."

She pulled up behind him, kissed the back of his neck. "Listen, Tommy's a sweetheart in his way, but I'd never be his girl, wouldn't marry him. I'll sleep with him if it gets me a step up in the picture business. But he's off his trolley, and once you get past the fact that he's funny and a big spender and kind of famous there's not much to recommend him."

"If that's how low you hold Tommy, where does that leave me?"

"You're a sweetheart, Milt. If I wasn't trying to get ahead in the picture business I'd be your gal in a second." He looked out at the offices across the street. The people had gone home and the windows were dark.

IRENE WALKED OVER to where George and Clyde stood and put one hand on the one's shoulder and one on the other's neck. When they looked at her she shook her head, jerked a thumb at the closet and drew her finger across her throat.

Clyde looked stricken, and the color drained from George's face.

Clyde pointed his right index finger and mimed firing a

gun. George shook his head and pulled out a match safe, then removed a single match. Clyde looked around the room and whispered, "No insurance." Then he picked up the piece of rebar he'd brained the man with earlier. "With the two of you holding him I can do it."

Irene felt immediately nauseous at the idea of restraining a man while he was being beaten to death with an iron bar, but she nodded. They returned to the door and George called out.

"Listen, mister, we're going to open the door up and let you out so we can talk about this in a civilized manner. All right?"

"Sure."

George and Irene stood ready to grab him and Clyde practiced swinging the rod before unlocking the closet and opening the door. There was a strong bump on the door from the inside and van de Kamp burst out, easily evading Clyde's clumsy swing in his direction. He was holding a long screwdriver and he punctured Clyde's throat with it and took off running. After a half-second's shocked hesitation George took off after him. Van de Kamp stopped by the freight elevator, waving the knife, slid the big iron gate open and entered the cage.

"You oughtn't to have tried to trick me, mister," he said, cranking the chain downwards. George was trying to remember where the staircase was when he finally heard Irene's wailing. She was bent over poor Clyde, who was twitching and gurgling as blood spread across the dusty wooden planks.

"Jesus, he's bleeding to death!"

• ◆ •

"I DON'T SEE how this rally's going to do the war effort any good," Victoria said. "No one cares a fig about any of these people. Get some big stars out there and maybe they'd come, but Tommy Gill? That Magnolia Sweetspire? And the kids?"

Trudy sat with little Ezra, looking at a picture book about a family of kittens. "If Mr. Kaplan says it will help, then we've got to do it, don't we? Heckfire, I don't even know what a war bond is."

"You'd think they could make it a joint effort, get Sennett and Lasky and those places to participate. Fatty and Mabel, maybe Norma Talmadge, you see what I mean? This business of it being just Provident makes me think it's just a stunt for the studio and not for the war effort at all."

"Well, it'll be an exciting and amusing diversion for the kiddies. Getting up in front of a big crowd and kicking Tommy Gill in the seat of his pants! Tommy sure won't like that."

TOMMY HAD ACHIEVED a level of drunkenness that made him more rather than less detail-oriented, and he looked up from Cressida's giant brunette mane bobbing up and down over his crotch and spoke.

"Where the hell'd Marceline go?"

"Sssshhhh," Cressida said, taking her mouth off of him for a second. "What do you care, honey, you got me right now."

"I haven't seen her in an hour, I bet."

Cressida was back at it, but Tommy's erection was beginning to deflate. She thought about sticking a finger up his ass to restore his ardor but he was already pushing her away from him. "Haven't seen Milt, come to that." He yanked his pants back up, buttoned them and pulled his suspenders over his shoulders. "You've got to get up with the chickens to fool Tommy Gill."

Cressida was already arranging her hair back on the top of her head when he opened the door into the suite's parlor, still filled with people. How ever did Tommy know, among all these guests, that those two specifically were missing?

He stood at the door and made a quick inventory, confirming his suspicions. "I'll be goddamned if those two will make a monkey out of me at my own shindig."

The front door opened and Milt came in, and Tommy strode up to him and stuck a finger in his face. It was funny because Tommy was a head shorter than Milt, the former gritting his teeth in anger, the latter unfazed and staring directly downward into the gesticulating index finger, and there was a tittering from the crowd, at least those who'd never watched one of Tommy's tantrums.

"Where the hell's Marceline?"

"How should I know?"

"And where were you?"

"I went out for a breath of air. It was getting stuffy in here while the sun was still up."

"True," said Cressida, who hadn't seen anything but was pretty sure the two had slipped off together. Somebody put a new disc on the Victrola and the attention turned away from Tommy, who stood there looking as though he were ashamed for having accused his friend, though Cressida suspected it was just a loss of dignity and self-control that was abashing him.

"Everybody out," he said. No one paid him any mind, and he scraped the needle across and off of the record. "Party's over, everybody make sure you come to the bond rally tomorrow morning."

The dancing stopped, and the guests regarded one another wondering whether he was serious. "It's only eleven o'clock, Tommy," said an actress he'd been trying to bed for a while. She gave an exaggerated pout. "Can't we keep at it for a while?"

"Everybody out right now or I'll call the front desk and have you thrown out physically."

Milt was headed for the door. Tommy reached out and touched his shoulder. "Say, pal, about what I just said . . ."

"That's all right," Milt said. "You took me for a crumbum. Think I'll take my leave with everyone else."

"Some swell party," said a woman with short, marcelled blond hair as she passed Tommy on her way out and showed him her middle finger. "Piker."

A camera operator and an aspiring actress who'd just met that evening and had already spent the last couple of hours pawing one another seemed grateful for the excuse to leave and find someplace more private.

"Thanks for the hooch, Tommy," the operator said.

"You said it," the actress said, and she stood on tiptoe to give Tommy a brief kiss on the cheek. Other guests left without addressing the host, either sore at him or indifferent to him.

Cressida took Tommy by the hand. "It's all right, sugar pants. I'm going to show you a real good time and you'll be all rested and refreshed for the rally tomorrow."

She kissed him tenderly on the cheek and ran a fingernail across his palm, which made him jump. Oh, she thought, he's going to jump right out of his skin when I stick that finger up his ass.

46

Bill was setting up the Calumet 8 x 10 on a podium cattycorner from City Hall, near the stage but far enough to capture it and show the size of the crowd at the same time, as Flavia and her peglegged fiancé wandered around with the portable 4 x 5 searching for good vantage points and trying to guess where the crowd would be most effectively captured on glass. The first of the crowd had started to arrive, lured in by advertisements in the *Herald*, and in fact only therein. Mr. Dunwoodie, the studio's publicity head, had been certain these would be enough, so he recorded ads as having been placed in several other newspapers several days running and pocketed the difference. The odds of Kaplan bothering to look at the other papers were slim enough; Dunwoodie knew he only paid attention to the *Herald* unless there was a Provident-related story running.

KAPLAN SURVEYED THE grounds set aside for the rally from the stage and felt pleased. This would be a splendid way to raise the studio's profile and assist in the war effort to boot. He watched the old fellow across the street setting up an enormous old camera on a massive tripod and a young woman down on the grounds wandering about with a smaller device, followed by a peglegged man on crutches rather ineffectually assisting her. He noted with pleasure a small number of spectators gathered below, waiting for the show to start. He sat back and thought how glad he was to be out of the haberdashery trade and Kansas City.

INSIDE CITY HALL, where he and the other players were kept before showtime, Tommy was marveling at the fact that he was only barely hung over, after what had been a big night even for him. Cressida had changed his life with a single gesture, and he began thinking about ways to hold on to her. After she'd done what she did they lay there on the bed in silence for a good long while.

"Where'd you learn to do that?" he'd said, gingerly, lest the answer be something indelicate or embarrassing.

"Word gets around. Girls talk to one another."

"You ever done that before? To another fella besides me?"

"Nope. Just heard about it. Hadn't ever tried it before, thought I'd try it on you because you're a special fellow and you were feeling down."

He knew she was lying and he didn't care. Now he was thinking about marriage. Just sign the goddamn divorce papers and make sure Cressida stayed with him until death did them part.

DAISY STOOD WITH Ezra waiting for the show to start, though there was plenty to watch in the assembled crowd. It wasn't as big as some, like outside a circus tent, but there was a great variety of humanity on display, of all ages and classes and situations, and the general mood was one of jollity and good will. She was sure that when those two little movie imps arrived onstage that Ezra would recognize that they weren't his own after all, and that he'd stop worrying that their mother was being kept by that Tommy Gill. The look on his face was placid, as it mostly was these days, and that gave her hope. He was still a reasonably young man after all, with many more opportunities for fatherhood.

A CROWD WAS beginning to gather, but not as many as he would have liked to see by this hour. There was a woman toting a camera. Two camera operators from the studio were on hand with assistants, but where was George Buntnagel? He'd been involved from the very start in the planning and logistics, and here came the morning itself and he was nowhere to be found. Just then the mayor arrived at the podium and stuck his hand out. "Morning, Kaplan."

"Mr. Mayor, pleasure seeing you," he said, trying hard for the sake of the picture business to disguise his contempt.

"I'm running late, just been at the scene of a fire."

"Must have been a bad one to take you away from this."

"Oh, it was. Spectacular, if you like looking at a fire."

ARRIVING AT THE scene George made his way through the mass of unwashed humanity to Sam Jamison, who stood next to his camera waiting for the action to start. "Ready to roll it, Sam?"

"Sure," Sam said, looking him up and down, seemingly appalled. "If you don't mind me saying, Mr. Buntnagel, you look like hell. You feeling all right?"

"I'm well, Sam, old thing. And call me George, will you? No need to stand on formality for a couple of old collaborators like us."

"You sure you're all right?"

"Never better. Now where's Baxter?"

"Up on that balcony with the eight-inch Wollensak, going to try and get the whole act with as few blank spots as he can manage. Meanwhile I'll be shooting the crowd reactions for cutting."

"Excellent, excellent. Carry on, I'm off to find the boss."

"He's up there sitting with the mayor."

"Perfect." He slapped Sam on the back and headed for the reviewing stand.

IRENE HAD JUST vomited for the eighth time, by her count, since Melvin van de Kamp had burst out of the storage closet the night before. This time was behind a rosebush next to a bank building, and there wasn't much left to throw up. Aware that passersby had seen her, she rose to her full height and straightened her suit jacket, then headed once again in the direction of City Hall and the bond rally.

A woman of fifty or so reached out and touched her on the shoulder. "Your first?"

Not knowing what the woman meant, she simply smiled and nodded.

"I could tell, you look so put out by it. Well, don't worry, it goes away after a few weeks."

It was only after the woman had passed out of earshot that Irene realized the woman had understood her to be pregnant, and she laughed for the first time since the phone call from poor Clyde.

MYRNA WATCHED THE scene outside from an office provided by City Hall by arrangement with Mr. Kaplan so she wouldn't be pestered by Tommy Gill. She was thrilled that people were coming to see her in person, along with the others, of course, but the bills posted all over downtown had her name, her stage name anyway, bigger than Tommy's. This was it, what she'd left Tennessee for, what poor Barney Sykes had died for.

The door opened and two women came in, accompanied by those two kids who were always making Tommy Gill's life miserable in those one-reelers. "Mind if we come in?" one of the women asked. "Mr. Gill doesn't much appreciate our presence here today."

"HONOR TO MEET you, Mr. Mayor," George said, and took a seat next to Kaplan.

"His Honor was just describing a disastrous fire," Kaplan said.

"Five alarm, Mr. Buntnagel." He pointed toward the northwest, where a column of black smoke stood against the bright spring sky. "Still burning. Looks like arson, too. One fireman's in the hospital with third degree burns."

Kaplan grabbed his arm and supported his back as he slid to the floor of the platform. "George, you can go home if you're sick."

"No, boss, just a little lightheaded."

"You look deathly ill. I'm not asking you, I'm ordering you to go home."

George nodded without making eye contact and got to his feet.

MELVIN WAS TALKING to a man selling paper cones with roast peanuts inside. "You ever sell roasted chestnuts come wintertime?"

"Doesn't really get cold enough there's any demand," the vendor said. He had a blond brush of a mustache and wore a deerstalker cap with the earflaps pulled up, and Melvin could tell he wanted to be left alone to concentrate on his trade.

"Boy, they're sure good, though, nothing like it on a winter day."

"Uh-huh." He yelled to the crowd. "Peanuts! HOT roasted peaNUTS!"

Melvin walked away with his hands in his pockets, already bored with the peanut man. He had a lot to consider. He'd watched the beginnings of the fire at the warehouse. It started on the second floor where the storage room was, and less than a minute later he watched two of his captors leaving the building without the third. They scurried off away from him, and that was when he understood that he'd killed a man. It was less of a burden on his conscience than he'd imagined such a thing would be. Anyhow the man he'd slashed had been planning to kill him, he was certain of that.

It was about seven or eight minutes from his first sight of flames sparking along the curtains that something exploded inside, and then the flames really got going. His dream of being the king of a little corner of the world of vice was delayed at the very least, all those films gone up in an inferno of celluloid and silver nitrate along with the sets and equipment. Idly he wondered what would happen when the films that were out for rent started getting returned in the mails; the now-defunct Magnificat Educational Distribution Company would be found out for makers and jobbers of filth. If the damned fool had just listened to Melvin he'd be alive and in business, even more successful than before.

As for the man and woman who'd assisted his attacker, he considered various means of learning their identities; articles of incorporation, real estate records, perhaps something he could glean from the local post office. He regretted that he was *persona non grata* at the good old postal service, but he didn't suppose that there'd be much chance of anyone recognizing him if he came in with a pasted-on Vandyke and a pair of drug store spectacles.

And then, idly scanning the throng for attractive ladies, he spotted one he recognized, disheveled and nearly reeling, as though drunk, even as he was certain somehow that she wasn't. It was the very woman from the night before at Magnificat.

THE NUMBERS OUTSIDE weren't what Kaplan had wanted at all. With quarter-page advertisements in all the papers for three days running there should have been a great many more spectators, and he intended to interrogate Dunwoodie about it. It was a quarter past noon and the announced starting time, and he gave the order to start the show.

◆ ◆ ◆

MYRNA WAS ON first, with Mr. Kaplan himself introducing her with the aid of a megaphone, which he handed her and with which she gave a fairly rousing speech about transatlantic bonds and the treacherous Hun who had to be stopped before he could wreak his vicious damage upon our own shores.

DESPITE HIS DISTASTE for the politics of the occasion Bill was happy to see Myrna in her guise as Magnolia Sweetspire, and he thought he might make an enlargement or two of the scene for the studio gallery. He didn't know she'd seen him there but as she finished she gave him a little wink and he waved back.

TRUDY ESCORTED THE kids to the door through which they were to emerge onstage. "Remember your cue, kids. When Mr. Gill takes off his hat and throws it on the ground, you go out and do what you were told."

EZRA WATCHED TOMMY Gill's act without smiling, and Daisy had a notion she shouldn't, either. His cheek muscles were the only part of his face that was moving. They were about fifteen feet from the stage and he didn't seem to be aware of her presence any more at all.

IT WAS THE old drunk-getting-ready-for-bed bit. He hadn't bothered to prepare anything new and he didn't want to perform with anyone else, since the whole goddamned rally had been his idea and now every goddamned contract player at Provident Studios had horned in on his thing. His version of the bit was as good as anyone's, even

Chaplin's, and Chaplin would have said so himself, if he'd ever seen it. He threw in a little bit of his impression of old man Gill, too, just for his own amusement, and to his immense gratification the bit got a laugh from the crowd, which was smaller than he'd envisioned but an audience nonetheless. A wise old showman had told him once, "Don't worry about the people who didn't show, play for them what did."

He became aware of a big palooka standing with his arms crossed, watching the bit and scowling. The girl next to him was watching the man's face and looking worried. There was an anger in that look so intense that it manifested as stillness, and Tommy was damned glad it wasn't really aimed at him. He was just the guy who happened to be onstage when the gorilla was feeling that way.

THEY WERE JUST offstage when Tommy dropped the hat. As he bent down to pick it up, a process slowed by a drunkard's diminished physical coordination, little Ezra zoomed onstage and kicked him in the left buttock. He went down like a pro, uninjured, but he hadn't been expecting it, in fact Kaplan had assured him that those two little bastards weren't to be in the show at all. Pearl hit him with a prop umbrella as he struggled to his feet.

"Goddamn it to Hell, you little cocksuckers better get right off this stage before I beat the shit out of the whole two of youse," he said, rather louder than he'd intended. The kids looked at one another, trying to decide whether he was really mad or just playing, and when they started giggling and running around him it was too much for him, and he reached out and managed to get little Ezra by the throat, squeezing tightly and eliciting a strangled cry from the boy.

It was at this very juncture that he understood that the man who'd been staring at him from below had climbed up onto the stage and was approaching him, knife in hand and an expression of absolute hatred on his face. He released little Ezra's throat.

KAPLAN STOOD UP. First Gill bellowing curses at the tots like a bosun in his cups, and now some lunatic climbing onto the stage.

"What the hell's happening over there?" the mayor asked.

"Not part of the show," Kaplan said. He headed into City Hall, the most direct route to the temporary stage.

IRENE WAS WATCHING the spectacle, enjoying for a few seconds the sight of the kids tormenting Tommy, then horrified at the sight of him grabbing the child by the throat, and now transfixed at the sight of the stranger menacing poor Tommy, who in his confusion at the latest turn looked funnier than he ever had on the screen, absolutely confused and terrified.

FLAVIA WAS LOADING and unloading the Speed Graphic as quickly as she could activate the shutter, with Henry passing her fresh film holders as required. Something was happening that she hadn't prepared for, and she hoped there were going to be enough plates to cover the entire mess.

♦ ♦ ♦

BILL WAS CONFIDENTLY and calmly doing the same thing with the old Calumet 8 x 10, possibly the only one among the various still and motion picture camera operators to be aware that they were recording a murder. If he could have stopped it he would have, but as it was he contented himself with doing what he'd been paid to do: photographing the Provident Studios War Bond Rally.

TOMMY HOWLED AND held his hand to the wound on his stomach. "Jesus Christ, you stabbed me!" Little Ezra had run back into City Hall with his sister on his heels, but she'd stopped just as Ezra *père* stuck the knife into Tommy Gill's abdomen for the second time.

"Papa?" she said, not at all sure whether this man was in fact the dimly remembered head of the family, nor whether Mr. Gill was really bleeding or whether this was part of the show.

Ezra Sr. stopped what he was doing and beamed at her. "It's me all right, sugar." As he stabbed Tommy a third time she ran after her brother into the building.

CRESSIDA WAS WATCHING from the crowd when it happened. She knew immediately that something was badly wrong, because Tommy had gloated about the fact that the kids weren't to be included in the bond show, at least not while he was on. At first she took the big man mounting the stage for another unannounced surprise from the treacherous studio, but Tommy's cries of shock and pain weren't faked. There wasn't any way for her to get onto the stage without getting into City Hall, and that wasn't going to happen. As it was she stood there and watched the latest iteration of her little dream die.

CHARLIE DANVERS WASN'T part of the security detail, which was small and made up of rookie officers, the chief of police being reluctant to waste resources on a motion picture publicity event. He was on foot patrol nearby and thought he'd take a minute to see what the show was like. The crowd was either laughing or muttering about the odd mix of comedy and drama. When the man with the knife stood up Charlie saw that the blood on the knife was real, and he could hear the anguished moaning of the comedian. The attacker yelled after the little girl running back into City Hall.

"Pearlie! It's me!"

He hauled himself up onto the stage and pointed his service revolver. "Stop where you are and drop that knife, mister," Charlie said. The fellow turned to face him and dropped the knife onto the unvarnished pine planks of the temporary scaffolding. Then he gave a mean little crooked smile, pulled a short-barreled revolver from his pants and turned again to follow the child into the building.

IRENE SCREAMED AND, turning, found herself face to face with the perverted postal inspector, who grinned and grabbed her right breast.

"How you doing this morning, toots?"

TRUDY GRABBED PEARL and Victoria little Ezra and they took off running in the direction of the room where they'd waited just a couple of minutes earlier for the show to start.

"Trude!"

She stopped dead for a fraction of a second at the sound of that voice, then ran faster and shoved the girl into the room, followed by Victoria and the boy, and when the latter closed the door behind her and Trudy heard the lock click shut she turned to face him.

He was beaming, as though he hadn't just stabbed a man, a famous man at that, in the presence of his children, as if the last few years hadn't happened at all. His arms were held wide open as though he were expecting a warm embrace for their reunion. "It's sure enough me, babe, come back for you!"

AN AMBULANCE CREW came running through and outside to the stage carrying a stretcher, passing Officer Danvers on his way inside. Kaplan watched as they ran to Tommy Gill's supine form and started taking his vitals.

He was still breathing, but his pulse was running at 150, and the smell alerted the attendants to the severity and nature of the abdominal wounds. Even if they got him to County General for surgery there wasn't any hope. He looked up at them as if to ask what his odds of survival were. His voice came out as a whisper and the attendants leaned in close.

"Goddamn it all to fucking hell anyway, that lousy bitch of a wife is going to get all my money."

FIFTEEN FEET FROM him the officer pointed his gun at Ezra's head. "You best put that gun on the ground, mister."

Ezra turned to face him, still smiling that lopsided grin. He lowered the gun. "This here's my wife, officer," he said, and he started walking toward her.

To everyone's surprise, including her own, Trudy strode in his direction.

"You son of a bitch, you show up here? Now, of all days?"

"Aw, sugar, I got excuses for everything."

"Of course you do, you always do, you got an excuse for skipping town whilst I damn near bled to death?" She pointed toward the door and the stage outside. "And speaking of bleeding, how about that? And in front of your own tykes!"

"That son of a bitch put his hands on little Ez, you saw it," he said, pleading. He gestured with the revolver toward Danvers. "He seen it too. I got a right, don't I?" His expression soured. "And you said in that picture magazine he was just like a papa to the brats, and I suppose he's been taking care of you, too, while I been gone."

Trudy took a swing at his face and missed. He raised the revolver again and waved it.

"You'd better keep back, woman."

KAPLAN WAS STANDING next to the police officer, wondering how long this could go on before someone else died. From outside he could hear the sound of shouting as the crowd came to realize that something had gone badly wrong, that this was no longer part of the show. He reached into his vest pocket for his cigarette case, hefted it a couple of times, and heaved it at Ezra's head. It was a good case, monogramed and sterling silver, nice and heavy, and it hit the man's forehead with a loud clunk of metal on bone. He looked away from Trudy.

"Why don't you threaten a man for a change, you cunt-lapper?" Kaplan said.

Ezra turned to him and pointed the revolver straight at his face. Officer Danvers fired and Ezra went down to the parquet, missing a goodly portion of his braincase and the contents thereof.

As the ambulance attendants brought Tommy Gill back inside on the stretcher, his face covered by the sheet, Trudy stepped up to the other corpse in the building and kicked it in the organs of generation.

"Good riddance, you son of a bitch."

Kaplan picked up his cigarette case, now marked with a scratch he already knew he would never have removed. He took out the last remaining cigarette and lit it. "Am I to understand that this big ape was really the children's father?"

"That is a fact," she said.

"It's a good thing you managed to keep them away from him all this time."

She sniffled and nodded her head, then bent down. Victoria stuck her head out of the room wherein they'd hidden.

"Wait until they've taken him away," Trudy said.

WHEN DAISY SAW the second stretcher being taken out of City Hall she knew it was Ezra. She wasn't puzzled any more over why he'd done it; he'd genuinely believed those two motion picture children were his own. She found it hard to walk, her muscles all stiff, and she didn't know where to go anyway. Should she talk to the police and possibly get herself into trouble, maybe explain the delusion that led him to assassinate a completely harm- less stranger? It seemed crazy to her that she'd ever thought she loved him, or wanted to marry him and have children. She wasn't even sad. Maybe that would come later, when she got home and saw his few things scattered around the room.

BILL, FLAVIA AND Henry had already reconnoi- tered and were collecting their equipment and the exposed plates for the return to the studio and the work in the dark- room that lay ahead for the afternoon. "Got some doozies, I think," Bill said.

"I got one of the galoot climbing onto the stage, and I'm almost certain the knife's in view," Flavia said.

"I've got one of the knife in his belly, if his arm wasn't moving too fast, and I don't think it was. It should be a beauty."

Henry packed the assorted plate holders into the car- rier and prepared to load them onto the truck. He still wasn't speaking to the old man, and maybe he never would, but he had to admit he was anxious to see the photo in question.

"THANK YOU FOR joining me, miss."

"It's Mrs. But call me Irene."

"I'm surprised you agreed to join me. Our initial meeting was marked by such unpleasantness."

She looked at the menu. They were in a tea parlor

unknown to her, a few blocks from City Hall. "What the hell. A lot's happened in the meantime. Say, do you always talk like that?"

"Like what?"

"Like the villain in a play. I thought you were some kind of postal inspector."

His feelings seemed hurt. "I speak like a gentleman."

"So what do you want from me now? You followed me from the warehouse."

"I didn't. I just happened to spot you in the crowd. If you hadn't been so frowsy I might not have noticed you."

"Golly, thanks."

"You had a rough night."

"I'll ask again. What do you want?"

"I don't know. Nothing, I guess. The warehouse is a total loss, is what the morning editions are saying."

The waitress came and she ordered tea with milk and a honey cake, grateful she didn't feel like puking any more. The postal inspector ordered coffee. The waitress, a plump woman with a wispy mustache, offered a sad, sympathetic smile and waddled away.

"What did you stab him for?"

"Was he—were you all not planning to kill me?"

She didn't answer.

"All I wanted was to be part of it."

"So you came all the way from Indiana? Did you quit the post office?"

"I left my position. Also my wife, and I took a good deal of money. I was planning to invest it in the firm."

She shook her head. "I'd say you could have it all

now—the mailing lists, all the business records, but they're all gone now."

"We could still partner up. Clearly there was someone in there who knew how to make pictures. And the women players, they must still be available?"

"My husband directed the good ones. He and I are out for good after last night." The coffee, tea and cake arrived, and Irene poured her cupful. "I never had to get rid of a body before. I suppose arson wasn't the best solution, but we were caught off our guard."

"But the women. You could put me in touch with them, if I were to take up where you left off?"

Irene started laughing. "That's it, isn't it? You're a stage-door Johnny is all."

"I'm particularly interested in the pair I mentioned to you, the ones I saw in the motion picture magazine."

She took in a deep breath and stopped laughing. "Oh, no. Not them. They've left that behind."

"Maybe they could be persuaded to return. If it was known that the mother of those adorable movie children and her so-called sister had been onscreen licking one another's pussies . . ."

"That's rotten. That's worse than stabbing Grady."

"I'd settle for just meeting them. They've been very much on my mind since I saw them for the first time. Perhaps I could meet them at the charming house from the magazine feature?"

"No."

"Then they could come and see me." He wrote down an address and handed it to Irene. "It must be an interesting story, how you and that other fellow came to get into a business like that. Clyde Grady, he was born to do it, I could see that when I stopped him on the street, but you two've got class."

47

FILM STAR GILL SLAIN AT WAR RALLY
Assailant Is in His Turn Slain by Hero Officer

**He Was Jealous of the Comedian's Success—
Provident Studios Chief Had Hand in Disarming Killer**

Yesterday's War Bond Rally at City Hall was disrupted by the arrival of a homicidal maniac who stormed the stage as beloved comedian Tommy Gill was working his funny magic with Provident's Kutup Kids, who thanks to Mr. Gill's physical courage were unharmed by the killer. After stabbing Mr. Gill in the abdomen with a fisherman's fileting knife, the lunatic pursued the tots into City Hall where their terrified mother and auntie awaited. Inside City Hall Mr. George Kaplan, President of Provident Studios, engaged in a courageous struggle with the brute, who in addition to the knife also carried a revolver. Entering the fray was Officer Charlie Danvers, whose cool head in the face of terrible danger allowed him to draw a bead on the struggling pair and finish off the deranged madman. The assassin has been identified by the Los Angeles Police Department as Ezra Crombie, aged 32, of undetermined address and occupation.

The ambulance crew that fought valiantly to save his life report that the funnyman's last words were "Suffering savior, the pain. Please, fellows, tell my dear wife how much I love her."

It went on for some length, damning the dead man with nothing more than his name to go on, lionizing Tommy Gill and the hero copper and Kaplan himself, who read the story with pleasure, despite a bit of sadness about poor Tommy Gill. This was superb publicity for the studio, especially for the three one-reelers with Tommy in the can but as yet unreleased, all of them featuring the kids. Their future was all set, and he'd see that they and their mother were happy at Provident. The cherry on top was the word that since the news about the murder, bond sales in Los Angeles had risen by thirty-two percent compared to the week before.

HENRY HAD BEEN so busy assisting Flavia that he hadn't paid close attention to the goings-on, and so it wasn't until the prints were finished that he recognized his old traveling companion Ezra. He pointed this out to Flavia, who said it was a good thing he was dead. Henry agreed but felt a tiny bit of regret, since the man had saved him from possible murder and almost certain cornholing back in that railyard. Bill was delighted at the quality of the majority of the negatives, especially since he'd decided that although his eight by tens were certainly work made for hire and therefore property of Provident Studios, the four by fives Flavia had made with the Speed Graphic were property of Ogden Photographic Studio and therefore available to the highest bidders. He admitted to Flavia that he'd been wrong about the smaller camera, a rare occurrence, and peace was made in the house.

IT WAS FIFTEEN minutes past the appointed hour, and Melvin waited in his room, increasingly impatient and considering his options. He still didn't know the names of Grady's two confederates and Grady was beyond punishing. But if those two women didn't show up he could certainly expose them as the wicked women they were. Quite possibly the children would be taken away from them, and they'd know then what it meant to break a promise to Melvin van de Kamp.

Then there was a knock at the door. He felt his pecker starting to swell as he crossed the room to answer it, and it retreated instantly when he saw the two men standing in the doorway displaying the all-too-familiar credentials identifying them as United States Postal Inspectors.

"Melvin van de Kamp?" the first one said. He was a big one, and he looked like he was already planning mayhem whether Melvin cooperated or not.

"No sir, my name's Reginald Rostand," he said. "I'm the nephew of the celebrated playwright, if you're wondering."

The second inspector, a smaller and more delicate-seeming man, shoved him hard and the two entered the room.

"Cut the shit, van de Kamp. We got a tip you were at

the Nottingham and we showed the clerk your wanted poster."

"He misidentified me because I haven't given him a gratuity."

Now the big man backhanded him and he fell backward and onto the bed. "You dumb cocksucker, we know what you look like." The little one pulled the wanted poster from inside his jacket and pointed at the photograph, Melvin's official Postal Service portrait. "Your luck's run out, you traitor."

"We don't take kindly to our own kind turning on the United States Postal Service. The Marshals Service were going to arrest you, that's who the lady called."

"The lady."

"Anonymous tip. They were all set to come and get you but one of them said, let's let the postal inspectors do it, he's one of their own."

"Was one," the other one said.

"They thought we might like to take a crack at bringing you in."

"I won't be any trouble, boys. In fact I have some information you can use, I've got the goods on a racket that's sending obscene materials through the mails."

"Murphy, you hear that? Obscene materials."

"In fact, it's my belief that your anonymous tip came from a woman involved in that very operation."

"Fitz, you worried about obscene materials or about traitorous cocksuckers who trifle with the integrity of the United States Postal Service?"

Murphy was the big one, and he walked over to the

window and opened it. Fitz closed the door to the room. Melvin wasn't too worried. He knew this was a scare technique to get him to confess to more than what he'd actually done.

Murphy looked out the open window. "Geez Louise, sixth floor. That's a long ways up, ain't it?"

"All right, fellows, you got me fair and square. You can take me away and I'll cooperate."

HE DIDN'T SCREAM, wasn't even afraid. He had played his hand badly, he knew it, and there just wasn't any angle left. Money gone, marriage gone, his career with the postal service ended in disgrace, not a chance in hell of meeting the women he'd idolized, much less of collaborating with them on masterpieces of onanistic delight. He hadn't ever heard of postal inspectors killing anyone, but then he'd never heard of a postal inspector besides himself going rogue. He hit the sidewalk in front of the hotel with an appalling crack and splattered blood all over a brand-new Chevrolet Series D Touring sedan.

EPILOGUE

1918

"What the devil will you do in a backwater like San Buenaventura?" Feeney asks. It's a warm Wednesday evening and the Flying Scotsman is nearly deserted.

"Same thing I did here, take pictures. My granddaughter and her husband will be doing most of that anyhow. And I can buy a bigger studio there for less than I sold my old one for."

"Granddaughter's still working?"

"Why shouldn't she?"

"Woman with a baby. I never heard of such a thing when it wasn't an absolute necessity. Anyway, won't you miss the excitement of the big city?"

"It's a train ride away." Bill finishes his beer and puts a dime on the bar. "I may be back in here one of these summer evenings, Feeney old chum."

IRENE IS INVOLVED in an affair with a well-known actress of the stage whose fits of rage are beginning to wear her down. She thinks about ending it, leaving New York and going somewhere else for a little while. Trudy and Victoria both report that their corner of Vermont is lovely and would be a good place for her to paint, and their house has not one but two extra bedrooms, in case George wants to take a break and come along as well.

◆ ◆ ◆

TRUDY SITS ON the porch and watches the children play in the yard with some of the neighbor kids. Inside the house Victoria is fixing supper, roast chicken with dumplings and peas from the garden. The sound of the river is soothing and she can smell flowers in the air. She's never known the difference between one flower and another except for the very obvious ones like roses or dandelions, and she thinks about walking down to the Wilkins's store and picking up a copy of a book she'd seen there the week before, *A Guide to the Wildflowers of New England.*

Little Ezra is climbing a tree with the Webster boy from down the road, calling each other funny names, while Pearlie and the Webster's daughter sit on the ground talking about something apparently grave. Neither of the children had questioned the move from California, or asked many questions about why they weren't working in pictures any more. They'd accepted those things as they'd accepted all the other upheavals in their lives, and they seem content here. She has enough money set aside to last a long while—she'd held on to most of the kids' salaries, and the studio paid for a great many of their expenses back then—and she's invested a good-sized chunk of it with the advice of the Buntnagels. Lately she's been thinking she'd like to learn a trade and maybe start a business, but she's not quite sure of what sort yet. That's all right, though, there isn't much missing out of her life just now.

ACKNOWLEDGMENTS

with an apology to Freedy Johnston

Thanks to my agent, Noah Ballard, and to everyone at Verve. Thanks also to my editor Mark Doten and everyone at Soho.

I am grateful to Dr. Derrick Mosley for his assistance in tracking down the typographical error in Bill's Isaiah Thomas New Testament, and to Ace Atkins for his help with the geography of old Los Angeles.

Finally, "The Devil Raises His Own" is the title of a song by Freedy Johnston on his lovely 2010 album *Rain on the City*. Some time after I gave the book its title I realized that the phrase was not in fact a common idiomatic expression but, in fact, an original coinage of Johnston's. Titles aren't subject to copyright, but it felt wrong to use it without his blessing. I made an attempt to contact him through social media and later through the intercession of a mutual friend (thanks Teri!) but both attempts failed. I tried to come up with a suitable alternative but it was for all intents and purpose too late—the title had stuck. All I can offer as recompense to Mr. Johnston is to suggest that you go buy all his records, which, as a fan, I believe you will enjoy . . .